ADVANCE PRAISE FOR *YEARBOOK*

"With *Yearbook*, Johnson does his part to stamp out boring art, one sentence at a time."
—John Baldessari

"Oh man, what a charming and deeply enjoyable novel . . . Lester is the perfect guide back to that bittersweet era known as the senior year of high school—a time shot-through with joy and agony, as life pivots decisively away from adolescence. And what a great motif Johnson's found in the yearbook itself, that nostalgia-packing dispatch from the past."
—Peter Mountford, author of *A Young Man's Guide to Late Capitalism* and *The Dismal Science*

"*Yearbook* takes us on an unforgettable journey into the senior year of high school . . . Compellingly told, brilliant in its ventriloquistic ability to capture their voices, this tale compels the reader to fall in love with these students' raw desire and sheer ecstasy."
—Scott Driscoll, author of *Better You Go Home*

"Jesse Edward Johnson's *Yearbook* is a highly original account of the thorny, hilarious world of high school. Set in 1996 but entirely in sync with contemporary adolescent angst and hijinks, the novel centers on the emotional development of its narrator Lester Smith, a jaded smart-aleck—part Holden Caulfield, part contemporary hipster."
—Paula Marantz Cohen, author of *Beatrice Bunson's Guide to Romeo and Juliet*

A NOVEL BY

Jesse Edward Johnson

PAUL DRY BOOKS
Philadelphia 2017

First Paul Dry Books Edition, 2017

Paul Dry Books, Inc.
Philadelphia, Pennsylvania
www.pauldrybooks.com

Copyright © 2017 Jesse Edward Johnson

Printed in the United States

CIP data available at the Library of Congress

ISBN-13: 978-1-58988-118-1

for Elicia

CONTENTS

They also serve who only stand and wait.

—JOHN MILTON

Hey! Ho! Let's go!

—THE RAMONES

SEPTEMBER 4, 1996

As Johnny Milton likes to say, they also serve who only stand and wait. I stand quite well, and I can wait with the best of them. In this case, I am standing in the library of Victory Memorial High School, and waiting for the start of senior year.

At my side is the one and only Freesia Price. This is a day she's been anticipating much longer than anyone should anticipate anything. She's shopped for new clothes and selected an outfit—pale blue capris, a yellow-and-white striped shirt, and brand-new, bright-white Keds—with another no doubt lying in wait for tomorrow. Her wine-red JanSport backpack is fully stocked, her hair is parted perfectly, and her astonishing green eyes are boring through one of the interior windows that separate the library from the classrooms of the main building.

Let me explain. You see, whoever designed this place had a strong preference for little-used shapes. The main building is a large dodecagon, with classrooms at the edges and our spacious library—also a dodecagon—at the center. As a result of this dubious design, the windows of the library look into the classrooms. Having gotten to campus way too early—at eager Freesia's eager urging—we've taken refuge here in the inner dodecagon, with time enough for an early morning stroll along these improbable interior windows.

"Who is *that*?" Freesia wonders aloud. Her brow has settled into its signature furrow.

1

In the classroom on the other side of the glass, a lanky, thirty-something man with shaggy brown hair is up at the blackboard, chalk in hand. He finishes writing whatever he's writing, then pulls the world map down to cover it up. If he's noticed us, he isn't letting on.

As Freesia continues to take in this impromptu performance, I turn my attention to the shelf under a neighboring window. This is my satellite office: the yearbook shelf. I'm pleased to see that they're just as I left them. These books, these beautiful, bountiful books, so neatly bound, so orderly a set on their shelf, provide a kind of sustenance. I always know that they are here, and that I can come visit them whenever I want. They are, for the most part, always the same, year after year—the photographs, the captions, the fonts—like cave paintings with glossy pages.

I pluck *Going Places* ('96) from the shelf and turn to my junior photo. It isn't the best of portrayals. That's a full-on smirk, folks: I can't deny it. And the black-and-whiteness of the picture isn't doing me any favors. You get the general shape of my face—longish, with a slightly crooked nose and luxuriant eyebrows—but not much more than that. You see the hesitation in my eyes, but not their gray-blue hue. You notice that my hair is parted—much less perfectly than Freesia's—but you miss out on its lackluster blondness.

But this year will be different. Now that we're seniors, we'll get a color photo of our own choosing, and a quote to go along with it.

"The class of 1997," I say, sliding *Going Places* back into place and removing *Badger Prints* ('83) from the shelf. (There are no badgers anywhere nearby. Still, Bernie the Badger is our mascot, and has lent his features to many a classic yearbook title.)

"Can you believe it, Les?" says Freesia, turning from the window.

"Yes," I say, tucking *Badger Prints* into my backpack, "it's all too believable. Tell me something less believable," I say, returning to her side.

Now our lanky, shaggy-haired thirty-something has stepped

onto a chair at the front of the classroom, and appears to be mouthing some words to the students who aren't there.

"Oh come on," says Freesia, with an elbow to my ribs and a sprinkle of a sparkle in her eye, "it's our time to shine." This is calculated to soften me up—not so much the elbow as the reference to *Time to Shine* ('85), one of history's finest achievements in the Yearbook Arts.

"We'll see," I say.

Other than a color photo and a quote, is there really any reason to believe that this year will be better than last year?

"Lester," she says. "That's Room 9. That must be the new AP Humanities teacher!"

So it is: the man chosen to replace Ms. Rasmussen, who has, alas, decided to lighten her teaching load. With her goes my input on the syllabus (plenty of Milton, thank you very much), as well as my Most Favored Student status. Considering that hers was the only class that could rival the marvels of the yearbook shelf, this represents a major changing of the guard.

As if in response to Freesia's sudden outburst, the star of Room 9's one-man show starts doing little turns, up there on his chair, little tiptoed 360s, patting himself on the head, first with the left hand, then with the right. He does several circuits, still mouthing whatever he's mouthing, and it seems like he might go on like that forever, but then, on the fourth or fifth revolution, his eyes catch mine, and he stops, mid-whirl, with one hand in the air, and his eyebrows raised as if they're connected to that hand by the tiniest of strings. With this raised hand he waves a weak, perplexed hello, then hops to the floor.

I catch the door of Room 9 with my foot as it closes behind Freesia, swing it open with a backward leg-sweep, and duck into the room. Some of our classmates have already staked their claims to desks. Pocketing my road copy of *Paradise Lost*, I slink over to a desk at the back, next to the desk where Freesia is setting up camp. (She knows I'd never join her at the front.)

The bell rings as a few stragglers straggle in, and the newest member of the ward—our climber of chairs and writer of things on the blackboard—turns to face us. He's got a mixed-up look about him. He's disheveled, yes, but also trying not to be. He's wearing brown wool slacks, and the bottom of a sky-blue dress shirt peeks out from the hem of his brain-gray sweater. One point of the collar is tucked into the sweater, but the other has been dislodged, and seems to be enjoying its freedom, pointing out and up at the ceiling. His wide brown eyes move back and forth as he surveys us, the denizens of AP Humanities. Behind him, the world map is doing its job admirably, covering up whatever he wrote on the blackboard. A faint buzz from a wayward bulb or vent is the only perceptible sound.

From her next-door desk, Freesia kicks my foot. Already she is beaming.

"Hey there!"—bursts the new guy, finally—"How's it going? I'm Jeff. Jeff Traversal. Or Mr. Traversal, I suppose. But Jeff is fine by me. What do you call your teachers?"

No response.

"Anyway," he soldiers on, with a tactical clearing of the throat, "I have some handouts, but before I pass them around," he says, thrusting a finger into the air, "I want to show you something."

With a dramatic flourish, he pulls the cord on the world map. But the map has little appetite for drama. It shoots upward a foot and then stalls. Our would-be showman, this Traversal, yanks on it again and again it stalls, this time even farther down, mere inches from the blue-gray industrial carpet. He kneels and tries again, and then again, but the map just isn't having it. Even from my vantage at the back, I can see that his sweater has become too literal for comfort. He sleeves away the sweat on his forehead, then springs back to his feet.

"Okay," he sighs. "Well. Technical difficulties. No biggy. On to the handouts!"

He fumbles open a leather satchel and removes a stack of handouts. He takes one for himself, and deposits the rest on the desk of Tina McTovey. Blessed Tina: you always know where to find her, in the front row of the class, notepad and pen at the ready. She's the Freesia of the Juniors—minus Freesia's verve and whimsy.

"Pass those around, will you?" Jeff implores. Poor Tina: she wasn't expecting this. The cap of her pen has gone missing, buried beneath the stack of handouts. "Please?"

Tina rises, smooths her skirt—black, long, wrinkle-free—and begins to make her way around the room. Jeff deposits himself on the collapsible table, and starts tapping his rolled-up copy of the handout on his knee. His socks almost match: one black, one midnight blue.

On the first page of the handout are the words "Course Reader"—penned in what must be the Traversal hand (a hasty, all-block-letter font), and below that, "AP Humanities." I flip it open to the Contents: JOYCE, it reads, and HEMINGWAY and FAULKNER and BARNES and WOOLF. WRIGHT, it urges, in its precarious script, and BALDWIN and PYNCHON and MORRISON and BARTHELME. And other names, and names alone—as if these names alone say everything.

"Here's the deal," he says, planting his palms on the table. "There *is* an official reading list for this class. And those books are great and all, but they're not what I would have chosen. So what you have there is a little supplement. A course reader. Any questions?"

You know, even before the question has been asked, who will be the first to respond. "Are we going to read *all* of this?" says Freesia, flipping through the pages.

"I hope so!" Jeff returns.

"Cool!" she says, pushing her hair behind her ears.

"And you are?"

"Freesia." She straightens as she says this, and punctuates it with a smile. Jeff smiles back, happy, no doubt, to have found this early ally.

"This is a *lot* of reading," counters Tina from her front-row seat. I can't see them, but I know exactly what her eyes are doing: probing Jeff, boring into him. He is the insect, her gaze the searing beam of light from the magnifying glass.

"You don't have to read *everything*," says Jeff. "I sort of see this reader as something to do *instead* of the assigned readings, not *in addition* to them, okay?"

He looks around. We look around, then back at him or at the floor. The silence deepens, then opens to a breach, and into that breach I stream.

"Wait a minute," I demand. "Does this mean we're not doing Milton?" From the pocket of my trusty blue flannel, I retrieve my road copy of the poem. Its spine is held together with packing tape, and the cover is torn in such a way that it reads, *John Milton: Paradise Lo.*

"Well, yeah," says Jeff. "I thought we'd look at some more modern stuff."

If he thinks that this is all I need to hear, he's wrong. "Isn't everything after Milton kind of pointless?" I ask him.

"Oh come on, Lester," says Freesia, fixing me with those deep green eyes.

"Hold on," says Jeff, hopping off the table. "Lester raises an important question. It's Lester, right?"

"Aye," I aye.

"You're getting at some fundamental issues, Lester."

I am?

"He is?" says Freesia.

"Yes," he says, then starts to pace. Some kind of vein has been tapped, it would seem. Where it will lead is anyone's guess. "Yes," he repeats. "Absolutely. You could even say it's *the* problem of modern literature. What do you do when it feels like everything's been done? In the words of Samuel Beckett—who's in the course reader!—'I can't go on, I'll go on.' So in a sense the bigger question is, how *do* you go on?"

Having done two full laps around the collapsible table, he stands off to the side of it, holding his copy of the reader in the air like a conductor's baton.

"I don't know," I say, thumbing through the reader. "Sounds like a waste of time to me."

"Give it a rest, Lester," pleads Freesia.

"Okay," says Jeff, attempting a casual stance, leaning against the collapsible table, arms crossed. "Just for the sake of argument, what would *your* course reader look like?"

Too easy, Jeff: too easy. "Well," I say, "for starters, how about a little Jonathan Charles Milton?" For emphasis, I poke the cover of *Paradise Lo.*

"Okay," he says, twisting the middle button on his sweater. "What else?"

"The Ramones. Six weeks of Milton, and another six weeks of Ramones."

Game, set, match.

"Milton and the Ramones." He's nodding slowly as he says this, staring at an unmapped region of the floor. Careful, Jeff: that button can't be twisted forever.

"But I thought everything after Milton was pointless," broadsides Freesia.

"Good point," says Jeff. "The Ramones weren't touring in the 1600s, were they?"

"That's just it," I inform him. "They are the Milton of music."

"Please," says Freeze.

"The Ramones are the Milton of music," says Jeff.

"Yes," I say. "It all comes down to right numbers. Right numbers, Jeff." For emphasis, I pound my fist on the glob-shaped desk. "Right numbers!"

"Apt numbers," he replies.

Come again?

"You're quoting Milton, right? I'm pretty sure it's 'apt numbers,' not 'right numbers.'"

Now it falls to me to cross *my* arms. "Semantics."

"Anyway," says Jeff, with a confederate glance at Freesia, "this class is going to be a lot of fun, all right?" Again he begins his circuit around the collapsible table, as if he's left something on the other side—but no, all he left there was the need to go back to the side he just came from, traversing the entire southern hemisphere of the map, back and forth, and forth and back. "It'll be a lot of reading," he admits, "but also a lot of fun," he claims.

"And even if you feel a little confused at times, that's part of the experience, okay? Confusion is productive," he asserts. "In fact, when it comes to modern literature, confusion is kind of the point."

As if to emphasize this point, most of my colleagues are giving him looks of unvarnished confusion.

"Okay," I say, ducking back into the ring, "if confusion is the point, then why even bother? Why not just read books in Finnish? Or better yet, why don't we just put your reader in a blender and—"

Shwap! Yes: *shwap.* The world map has come to Jeff's rescue, shooting suddenly upward, and revealing the words that he wrote on the board before school. In flaking, poorly-constructed letters—the font from the Contents of the reader—is the phrase, *I WILL NOT MAKE ANY MORE BORING ART.*

"Ah, our icebreaker! Okay," he says, rubbing his palms together, "this is going to be good. Who here," he wonders aloud, picking up a box of chalk from the lip of the blackboard, "is familiar with John Baldessari?"

No one.

"No? Not really? That's okay. He's an artist," he informs us, now shuttling from desk to desk, breaking pieces of chalk as he goes and placing the nubs on our desktops. "Back in the seventies, he got asked to do an installation, and he did something pretty cool. We're going to re-create that installation."

We've all got our chalk-nubs now, and Jeff is standing at the front of the room, pausing for effect. "Now," he says—having let the pause extend a bit too long—"each of you has a piece of chalk."

"Really, Galileo?"—this I think, but do not say.

"One by one," he says, "or all together—however it happens— I want you to get up, go to the blackboard, and write the same phrase you see here: I will not make any more boring art."

He stands aside to clear the way. For no one.

"Should we, like, do it now?" inquires Tina, who has abided this frivolity with admirable calm.

"Sure. Yeah. However it happens." Jeff's voice falters just a little, betraying his creeping sense, perhaps, that this attempt at openness and whimsy is falling to the floor like a burned waffle.

But my colleagues do as he has asked. One by one, they make their way to the blackboard and chalk their versions of the phrase. Some are small and compact and neat, others large and flowing and all out of proportion with the size of the blackboard. Freesia promptly runs out of room on the board, and hastens back to Jeff's desk for tape, then tapes a piece of paper on the wall beside the blackboard and goes on scribbling her squiggly, looping version of the phrase on that. Everyone is suddenly entwined in a game of improvised Twister, kneeling, leaning, standing up on tip-toes, laughing nervously, swept up in the unexpected thrill of scrawling out this unexpected phrase on the blackboard. Jeff stands off to the side, amused and pleased: his icebreaker is working! Everyone is swarming to the warmth of the nest.

Almost everyone.

Jeff finds me at my post at the back of the room. "Would you care to join us?"

"I don't know," I say. "What if I like boring art?"

"Come on. It won't kill you."

I rise slowly. Slowly, slowly do I rise. And just as I get clear of my desk, the dlong of the bell marks the merciful end of class. I shrug at Jeff, and smirk triumphantly at Freeze.

"Sorry, Jeff," I say, handing him my copy of the reader, then back-pocketing *Paradise Lo*. "Looks like boring art wins this round."

FIFTH PERIOD CAN'T COME soon enough, but soon enough, it comes. It's the last class of the day, the one we've all been waiting for: Yearbook. This will be my second tour of duty on the crew. If a sigh of relief could take the form of a high school course, it would be this most pleasant space of time, which asks us only to reminisce about VMHS yearbooks gone by, and do our best to live up to their shining examples—eventually.

Leading the charge into this delicious swamp of idleness is the man we all call Pancake (mostly because no one really knows how to say "Panczewksi"). He teaches all of the truly useful offerings: Woodcraft (Intro and Advanced), Automotives, Welding, and—by the stroke of some divine grace, if not because of his editorial prowess—Yearbook.

Pancake always wears the same thing: flannel button-up shirt (usually navy blue, sometimes forest green), red suspenders, brown pants. He has thick glasses that make his eyes look like broad saucers. And he is ample. He's a lot of human. Which means that when he's sitting down, he tends to stay that way for quite a while. His hair he keeps buzzed short. I take as many of his classes as I can.

Pancake's domain is the space we call the Vortex—or VOC/REC. TECH., as it is officially, inexplicably known. The Vortex consists of two shops—Wood and Metal—and an automotive garage, with an afterthought of a classroom attached to the wood shop by way of a half-glass door. In Yearbook, the only period on Pancake's instructional schedule that doesn't involve the use of loud machines, the shops lie dormant, and we're reconciled to the classroom.

"Here, Ter-bine," he says, addressing me by the stretch of a nickname that only he uses, "pass these out." He hasn't gotten up. Rather, he's just sort of shoving the small stack of half-sheets into the air. I rise and gather them.

Most of Pancake's Yearbook students—the "Pancake Bloc," as I like to call them—are a delightful assemblage of hammerers and solderers and sanders of planks. They are the stout heroes of Woodcraft (Intro and Advanced), Automotives, and Welding—thick, strong, square-jawed, Carhartt-wearing kids. Like me, they remain loyal to Pancake—and his easy As—wherever he goes. They accept their copies of the syllabus with hands still darkened by the grease of summer projects.

The Pancake Yearbook syllabus is a thing of absolute beauty. A copy should be sent to the Smithsonian. It is unmatched in its directness, its simplicity, its unabashed typos. The entirety of the document fits easily onto its half-sheet, and reads thus:

YEARBOOK
First Trimest: i. Estabilsh Template
second: i. aquire photos; ii. fill in Template
Thrid tri: i. finalize format; ii. profread; iii. send to printer

Once the sheets have all been passed around, Pancake asks if there are any questions. There aren't. The business of the day having thus been concluded, he opens the bottom drawer of his desk and gets out a fresh box of powdered Donettes—a healthy supply is always at hand—and, with plump, expert fingers, slides open the paper tab and peers into the box with keen anticipation. By then, the Pancake Bloc has begun another round of fart jokes; Freesia and Tina are covering textbooks from other classes with brown kraft paper; and I crack open *Badger Prints*, one of the crowning achievements of the Golden Age of the Yearbook Arts, the 1980s.

There's something magical about these yearbooks from the '80s. The hairdos alone are worth your time. (I'm working on an Ode to Ashley Blackwell's senior photo hair, constructed circa March of '81.) And everyone has this great smile, this look of, "Hey, how ya doin'?" Even the ones who were trying to play it cool. I think of the parties they must have had. Sitting on the hoods of Camaros, wearing tight jeans, drinking beer from cans. And their senior quotes: so confident, so optimistic. The quotes from this, the '83 volume, are, I think, the very best. Nelson Dalloway: *No use tryin' what can't be done; I'm outta here—it's been quite fun.* Barbra Stokes: *The future is an open journey.* Mark Mitchell: *Left to my own devices, I'd eat pizza every day.*

There are truths in there.

THE DAY ENDS without much fanfare, and we're disgorged from the main building like water overspilling a drain. This is another feature of the unfortunate layout of our school: the doors of our classrooms open outward, straight into the maw of Mother Nature. So instead of indoor hallways—our genius architect decided—we have outdoor walkways.

From the edge of the student lot—my favorite place to stand and wait—I scan the throng, surging moth-like toward the sunlight, for tidbits of useful intelligence. A new car here, a Lakers parka there. The skaters are skating around in ominous circles. The debaters are moping as a group. A few stray leaves are skimming across the pavement. The nauseating smell of fresh-cut grass pervades the air.

Freesia bounds toward me through the crowd. She is a minor weather system unto herself, moving quickly over featureless terrain. Backpack slung tight over both shoulders, a textbook tucked under her arm.

You wouldn't necessarily expect us to be friends, but somehow we're already going on two years of near-constant bickering. Toward the end of sophomore year, we had World Lit together, a real beauty of a class. Freesia proved to be a worthy opponent, and so, I guess it's fair to say, did I. And at some point, she must have decided—her moments of decision are clear and sharp and decisively acted upon—that we were to be friends, and pounced. I was sitting on a bench outside on a cloudy day. I was probably reading *Paradise Lost* (what else?). She strode right up to me, and stood there, like a column, until I finally looked up. "You can't ignore me forever, you know." "I guess not." "Where do you live? I'm driving you home." "You are?" "Yes. The bus is dumb. Meet me at my car after school." And so began my illustrious career in the passenger seat of her blue Subaru wagon.

"Isn't it great to be back?" she says, arriving at my standing spot, dreamily surveying her peers as they disperse. Her features are sharp: a nose that turns up at the end, and high cheekbones that flare out when she smiles.

"No," I say, "it's not."

In the middle distance, at the far edge of the lot, I make out my younger sister Grace. She is new to this place, but already she has found her crowd. They proceed in formation—strength in numbers is key, especially for unsuspecting freshman—toward the woods, for reasons not entirely clear.

"There goes Grace," I say.

"Who are those other girls she's with?" says Freesia.

"I don't know," I say.

The woods have swallowed Grace entire now.

"Come on," says Freesia, "let's go!"

She leads me over to the Subaru, which is parked as close to class as you can get without driving onto the Common. We get in, and Freesia revs her engine once, slides in a fresh CD—Alanis Morissette—and joins the growling procession of buses as they head out into the bright, wide, late summer air of King's Island.

King's Island: the term has its problems, chief among them the inconvenient fact that it isn't an island. It is, much to the dismay of the handful of hapless tourists we get during the summer, a peninsula. There are many peninsulas in the world, and many of them have interesting shapes. Ours is not an interestingly shaped peninsula. It's a slightly ovoid thing, like a long balloon or the head of a monitor lizard. To get to civilization from this corner of the corner of the world that is the Puget Sound, you have to drive across a narrow isthmus. It's a quick and painless journey, and yet many of my peninsulamates still refer to trips to "the mainland" as if they require extra provisions, or extra reserves of fortitude and bravery—as if all those Fred Meyers and Shell stations and Taco Bells out there, in the great wide world, form some kind of Viking gauntlet. Trial by Fire Sauce.

There is one main highway that runs the length of the peninsula—a highway which we call "the highway"—with other roads snaking here and there. These roads don't lead to much, because there isn't much to lead to. There are many, many trees, mostly evergreens—Doug firs, hemlocks, cedars, madrones—but also lots of disappointing maples. A general dampness pervades, a softness of turf. And the town at the center of it—Kelpton of name, though never called by it—gives us just enough: just enough to not go totally insane, and just enough to never have to leave.

The roads don't lead to much, I should correct myself by saying, until you hit the water. But there there is much indeed: beaches, shoals, spits, reaches. Inlets, baylets, creekflows. The beaches of King's Island save it from an otherwise unremarkable geographical fate. They are many in number, each of them littered with the driftwood that travels all its hundred thousand miles to arrive at our stick-out. It's pretty much a given that we're headed to one of them now.

"Let's go to Spurlock," says Freesia, checking her mirrors yet again.

The choice is a good one. "Make it so," I say.

The scenery along the way is set to Pacific Northwest on auto-repeat: stands of firs; swarms of blackberries; rust-red madrones leaning out over the road. Gardens with their fences raised to keep the deer away from precious kales and chards. Through the sunroof I make out the faint traces of a dissipating jetstream high in the pale blue sky.

Our sharp-featured, green-eyed chauffeur is in high spirits—the first day of school is a major holiday on the Freesian calendar—high enough to get bold with her line of inquiry. "Have you heard anything from your dad?" she asks, turning down the Alanis, as we round a bend near Middling Field. She wants this to sound casual, I can tell, but her hands, holding tight to the wheel, say otherwise.

"Not really," I say.

The Father, as I call him, used to be a writer. He had a hit way back in the '70s—an attempt at setting *Paradise Lost* in 1960s California, so I'm told—and then he went cold, or quiet, or something, and the literary world hasn't heard from him since. Now he only writes postcards. Most of the postcards he sends depict his latest place of occupation: the Metrodome, in Minneapolis, where he's a "Stadium Facilities Coordinator." (That's a fancy word for janitor.) It seems that there are only two good shots you can get of the Metrodome. The first, as you might expect, is from above, where you get the stadium in blimp's-eye perspective. It's an impressive shot if done correctly. The second is from within, where you are positioned as the tiny spectator looking up at the Teflon roof.

But the first postcard he wrote wasn't a shot of the Metrodome. It was a picture of a fluffy orange kitten, left on our kitchen table on a cold March morning, toward the end of sophomore year. The text of it was short, and not particularly sweet:

Family:

There comes a time in a man's life when he must venture forth to find the things he's left behind. And so it is I bid you adieu. Where I fly is hell, it may be true, but I myself refuse to yield to it.

~ E.N.S.

Since then, my mother and Grace and I have clambered forward, unsure as of yet, it seems, just how to fill the silence of the void he left behind.

"Here we are," says Freesia. She bursts from the car and starts marching toward the water.

Spurlock Spit is one of the few beaches on King's Island that is reliably sandy. And in the sun the sand is hot, and the logs are warm, and the water so bright that you can barely look at it.

By the time I've gotten out of the car, Freesia is already halfway to the water. "Are you coming?" she shouts, turning to check my progress from the edge of the sand—the same stretch of sand where The Father used to throw a Frisbee to our dog.

"Not just yet," I say, too low for her to hear.

I'll stand some more, and wait a little longer.

SEPTEMBER (CONT'D)

*I*T'S A LOW-SLUNG, BREEZY Friday afternoon. We've set up camp at our standard after-school outpost: Best Friend James's house, a mid-sized rambler on a pretty little bluff above a harbor—a view which BF James and his dad steadfastly refuse to maintain. The bank is tragically overgrown with maples, which surge into those spaces of air where the view should be.

When BF James first came here, back in seventh grade, he was immediately cast as an idol by the ruro-suburban white kids of King's Island. He wasn't just black: he was black and from New York. He was also very tall. So even though he'd never played organized basketball before, he was put on the varsity squad without a tryout, and even after a series of humiliating on-court miscues the coach wouldn't pull him from the lineup. It wasn't until he drop-kicked the ball into the bleachers during the first quarter of a game against The Marsden Academy that people finally took the hint.

He never did take on the role that had been so eagerly thrust upon him. He didn't like rap music, it turned out, and no, he didn't sag his pants, and he didn't not wear glasses. So a quiet *no thank-you* was his response to the general call to adulation. He'd much prefer to sit on the floor of a back hallway during lunchtime, wearing a Ramones T-shirt and reading *Neuromancer*. The hallway he chose happened to be a favorite haunt of Yours Truly—and the rest, as Joe Ramone likes to say, is hooray for the USA!

BF James is the perfect complement—or antidote, it sometimes seems—to Freesia. He is quiet and content and is, in general, game for the game and along for the ride. Good for a quip, and often quick with an insight, but rarely there to insist on his own insisting. He takes only middle-of-the-road classes—nothing too easy, nothing too hard—and gets a B+ (more or less) in everything. Whereas Freesia is driven to be the best at everything she does, BF James does everything just well enough to show he could do it that much better if he had to. Freeze wants the gold; BF James is just happy to be somewhere on the podium—or, in this case, on the concrete half-wall that runs along the driveway, eyes fixed on his Game Boy, his out-of-season parka draped liberally about his massive frame. It's good to have him back.

"How was New York?" Freesia asks.

BF James just got back from New York this morning. He was visiting his mother, who edits some magazine that no one's ever heard of. It's a pro move, really, missing the first few days of school, one that BF James has been known to execute to perfection.

"Dope," says BF James, looking up from his Game Boy, daylight pooling in his glasses. "I met one of the developers behind Deep Blue."

BF James has been consumed, for the better part of 1996, by the Deep Blue/Kasparov chess match. Man versus machine. He's convinced that Deep Blue will spawn our overlords—any day now.

"That's awesome!" Freesia says.

"So what did I miss at Vehemence?" he asks.

("Vehemence" is BF James's way of pronouncing "VMHS." We're working on getting it more widely adopted.)

"Not much," I say.

"Not true," says Freesia. "There's a new English teacher. Mr. Traversal."

"Oh yeah? What's his story?" wonders BF James.

"He's awesome!" bursts Freesia. "He made his own course reader."

"Course reader?"

"A little pamphlet full of extra reading," I explain.

"Hmm," hmms BF James.

"It's full of really cool stuff," says Freesia. "I've already finished most of *Nightwood*."

Of course she has. Freesia is a textbook completist. Give her a passage, she'll find and read the rest of the book. She can't and won't accept the world in excerpts. It must be swallowed whole.

"I like how laid back Jeff is, don't you, Les?" She isn't finished gushing just yet. "And don't you think he looks kind of like Ethan Hawke?"

"I hadn't noticed," I say. "And for the record," I continue, stealing one of Freesia's favorite phrases, which she likely stole from me, "I don't buy this 'how do you go on' mumbo jumbo. With apt numbers, and fit quantity of syllables, that's how you go on."

"Are you sure it isn't 'right numbers'?" says Freesia.

BF James has returned to his Game Boy. He often chooses to sit out our little spats—the word for that, I think, is "wise."

"Have you even looked at the reader?"

"No," I say, "I've been too busy familiarizing myself with Baldessari. You know, John Baldessari? Are you familiar with him?"

Under other circumstances, Freesia might roll her eyes at this. But during this, the festival period of the Feast of the First Week of School, extra indulgences will be allowed.

"You mean the artist?" BF James says to his Game Boy.

"Yeah," I say. "How do you know who that is?"

"My dad knows him."

BF James's father is a well-known cartoonist. But if you ever have occasion to enter the Taylor Residence, you might not be convinced of his existence. He spends most of his waking hours holed up in his study, drawing things and reading things. If you ever do manage to speak with him—a pleasure which I, not being of the Baldessari set, have had on precious few occasions—it will become clear where BF James got his pithiness and bone-dry sense of humor.

"Wait a minute," says Freesia. "Your dad knows John Baldessari?"

BF James responds with a shrug. Big deals are no big deal to him.

"Come on," I say, retrieving the basketball from the yard. "Let's take some shots."

Despite—or perhaps because of—BF James's adamant refusal to play basketball, I like to consult the hoop that he and his dad inherited from the previous owners of the house. It is a perfect oracle, the Taylor hoop. You can ask it questions and then shoot the ball and if you make the basket the answer is yes.

The ball leaves behind a moist yellow circle in the unmowed grass. I wipe it down with the sleeve of my trusty blue flannel, then bounce-pass it to Freesia. "Heave something up."

She turns to face the hoop, which hangs over the garage. "Will I get into Brown?" she asks, then tosses up a mid-range jumper.

Clank.

"This game is dumb," she decides, leaving the ball to trickle into Neighbor Karl's yard. "I can answer questions for myself."

"That's not how it works," I remind her. "The point is that the hoop knows all, not you."

"Whatever, Les," she says, settling in on the half-wall next to BF James.

"Okay," I say, dribbling the ball between my legs, "you guys ready to hear my new Grand Plan?"

"Yeah," says Freesia, unzipping her backpack, "let's hear your new 'Grand Plan'."

I spin the ball high into the air and let it fall and spin-bounce back to me.

"New York," I say.

"New York?" she says. "What happened to hitchhiking to Antarctica?"

(My last Grand Plan was a little light on logistics.)

"Yeah," says BF James. "Why New York?"

"Two reasons," I say. "First, the Morgan."

"The Morgan?"

"It's a museum"—BF James, by way of the screen of his Game Boy.

"And a library," I add.

"You need to go all the way to New York to go to a library?" Freesia's trademark incredulity is stirring back to life.

"Not just any library, Freeze. They have the only surviving manuscript of *Paradise Lost*."

Here it is, a little late but right on target: the rolling of the eyes.

"Okay. So what's the second thing?"

"CBGB."

"CBGB?"

"It's a club," says BF James, his interest piqued enough that he looks up from the Game Boy. "The Ramones got their start there."

"Okay," says Freesia, "let's say you've actually answered the 'why' part—which, for the record, you haven't. When are you going to go? And how will you get there?"

"I don't know. I'm still working out the details. But first I'm going to write a letter to the Morgan."

"Saying what?" says Freesia.

"I don't know. I'll introduce myself, I guess, and state my intent. Then see where it goes from there."

"Sounds dope," sums up BF James.

New York: yes. It's all very clear to me now, as clear as the view should be from BF James's house on this bright September afternoon on King's Island, a place that is about as far as you can get, in space and spirit, from the only surviving manuscript of *Paradise Lost*.

I dribble a few tight circles to channel the excitement of the visions of the city in my head, then turn to face the hoop. "Okay," I say, "I've got it. Here's my question." Dribble dribble dribble dribble dribble. "Will I make it to the Morgan?"

I toss the ball high into the air, a majestic hook shot that seems almost to attach itself to the sky before landing several feet from the hoop.

I'M LATE TO SCHOOL, but early to Morning Break. The bell dlongs the end of First Period just as I enter the foyer. I'm not sure that most schools have a foyer. But that's another thing about the magical design of VMHS. It isn't just one crumbling dodecagon. There's more: polygons on polygons. For appended to the main dodecagon, by way of this central foyer, are three satellite hexagons: the theater, the lunchroom, and the main offices of the administration.

I proceed to the lunchroom, where I find safe harbor in the form of Mr. Washburn, who is standing in a corner, chewing on his customary clove. Despite his often-wayward diction, it must be said that Mr. Washburn is one of the few true intellectual luminaries on campus. He teaches all of the European History classes, plus some Mickey Mouse American stuff (Medieval France is where he really shines). Washburn graduated from high school in 1948. That ranks him pretty high up on the totem pole as far as seniority goes. Add to that a stint in the Korean War and you have a man who can pretty much wilt with his glance anyone else on staff. When all else fails, you can count on Wash to tell it like it is.

"Smith," he says. (We're on a last-name basis.)

"Wash."

I join him in his standing as my colleagues swarm the room. It's a flurry of blue jeans and high tops and backpacks and Disc Men. The opening and slamming of lockers, which someone decided should line the lunchroom walls. In the middle distance, Grace is flitting from right to left, her head cast down and mostly hidden by the hood of her oversized black sweatshirt, her bag almost dragging behind her.

"Who's that you have your eye on, Smith?" Washburn wonders.

"No one."

"You do have your eye one someone, I imagine," he persists. (Just about every conversation with Washburn comes back to courtship and its discontents.)

"Not necessarily," I counter.

"Come on, Smith. You're a good-looking kid. Underneath that horseshit haircut and that crappy flannel shirt, there's a handsome devil lying in wait. And if you didn't slouch so goddamn much, you'd be pretty tall—taller than me. A tall, blonde, blue-eyed cowboy stud. Time to find yourself a pony and ride."

"I'll take that under advisement," I say.

He looks out over the junk-food-eating students and decides it's time to elaborate on his Golden Rule.

"The problem nowadays is disease," he says. "When I was your age, Smith, the path was more open, if you know what I mean. Fewer obstacles." He squints into the wall of beigeish lockers on the other side of the room, working the clove, the lines carved deep in his face, his bushy white eyebrows growling downward. His mustache is getting slightly out of hand, and a lawn of white stubble is sprouting on his ruddy, veiny cheeks. His eyes are dark and hard and full of life. It occurs to me, quite suddenly, how much he resembles Gene Hackman. Even his voice.

"Now you have these land mines," he continues, "and you don't even know where they are. Now you have to use a condom, for chrissakes, which is like tending a crocus with steel gloves. Damned shame."

"Is this all you think about?" I ask, watching as Grace, now with the hood of her sweatshirt in the Down position, holds up a mirror for a friend, laughing at something the friend has said.

"It really isn't the same nowadays. When I was young—a long time ago, let me tell you—when I was young, all you had to worry about was pregnancy and fathers. Now there's AIDS. You're better off just stroking it. Speaking of which: Where are you applying to college?"

"Nowhere," I say.

"Nowhere?"

"Nowhere."

"You're not going to apply?"

"I'm not going to apply."

Now the friend is holding the mirror for Grace and Grace is applying lip gloss to her lips. She caps the gloss then puckers her lips and checks her work.

"What are you going to do if you don't go to college?"

"I don't know," I say.

"You don't know? That's bullshit. Come on, tell me. What are you going to do?"

"No, you tell me," I say. "What are *your* plans? Or is this pretty much it?" These words come out more sharply than expected.

"Damn," says Wash. "I guess I touched a sore spot."

I don't respond.

"Tell me this at least," he says. "Why not?"

"Why not what?"

"Why aren't you applying to college?"

"I can't."

"What do you mean you can't?"

It's hard to say, I want to say. I can't just up and leave, I'd like to say. I can't just leave a postcard on the kitchen table and be gone.

"I'm needed at home," I say, watching as Grace makes her escape through a side door.

He grunts, or growls, or grunt-growls, scowling, arms folded, working the clove.

The bell tones, and my peers begin to scatter in panic. Washburn doesn't seem to be in any more of a rush to get to Second Period than I am. "The world is replete with shittiness, Smith," he says. "All you can do is minimize your exposure to it. September—for Christ's sake, it's already September. You know what that means?"

"Autumn?"

"I don't either."

I'm sitting on my bed. It's just before midnight. I open The Father's turntable. It's a big, boxy thing, with a clear plastic cover that swings open on two hinges at the back. Along the front is a panel of wood veneer, and a large, scratched, silver volume knob. It is the perfect host to the one and only record that I own: *Ramones*.

I draw it from its sleeve and lay it on the platter as if it might break at the slightest breeze or breath. I cajole the tonearm into service, get out my writing table—a plywood square—and lean back on the bed as those familiar chords, so stark, so elegant, begin to fill the air.

I jot down a few notes on a piece of torn-out notebook paper, then turn to the form of address. After trying out various opening phrases—"Dear Sirs," "Ladies and Gentlemen," "Mssrs."—I go with "Esteemed Colleagues."

Esteemed Colleagues, the letter begins, *I am writing to express my interest in visiting the only surviving manuscript of* Paradise Lost.

I stop and stare at that sentence as "Beat on the Brat" gives way to "Judy Is a Punk," then cross it out. I'm about to start again when a soft knock phlumphs against the door.

I open the door to the sight of my mother, up much later than she tends to be awake (she gets up at 5:00 every morning to go running before leaving for her job at the County Courthouse). She is wearing the faded pink terrycloth bathrobe that she has worn around the house for as long as I can remember. Her hair is pulled back into a pony tail.

"What's up?" I say.

"Oh, nothing," she says. "What are you working on?"

This she asks as if my room is on her standard rounds.

"Oh, nothing," I say. "Just my college application essay."

She nods absently. "Can I talk to you for a second?"

I follow her down the hall to the kitchen, where two cups of herbal tea sit steaming. I sit at one of them and watch the steam go whirling up into the atmosphere. Hers she stirs, and in her stirring stirs a palpable tension.

If The Father is a lost philosopher drawing lines in the sand as the rest of the world goes about its business, my mother is a midsized speedboat running out to sea. She works long hours—hours that have gotten even longer, it seems, in the months since he left—and when she isn't working she's gardening (which is to say that when she isn't working, she's working). When she isn't working or gardening, she's cooking, eating, flossing, sleeping, or—on rare occasions—indulging in a re-run of *Murphy Brown*. You could say that she is like Freesia in being all business ("All Biz Freeze," as BF James once called her), but the comparison doesn't really hold up. Freesia is All Biz in a way that doesn't suck the air out of the room. My mother exudes a stronger sense of being in control, and of not being willing to cede it. In light of this, it seems strange that she and The Father were ever together, and even stranger that they slogged through nineteen years of what must have been a bad thing all along.

"How's school?" she asks.

Even an inquiry as innocent as this sounds wrong when spoken in the Smith household. Such normal, idle chatter has been banished from these parts for years (if not forever), kept at bay by the dark, tight silences of bodies avoiding each other in space.

"Oh, just fine, Mother. All the usual graphs and charts."

I pretend to be reading the Gary Larson comic on the side of my mug.

"What are your plans for the weekend?" she asks.

"They're still in development."

"What about Freesia?"

"What about her?"

"How is she?"

"She is well," I say. "I see her. We speak."

"Any dates coming up?"

She's overdoing it, overplaying her hand. Getting even more awkwardly casual.

"Yes, in fact, the entire month of October is coming up. I believe there are thirty-one discrete dates in the month."

"You know what I mean."

I do know what she means, but don't know why she means it. It's not as if her own attempt at union didn't fail.

She can't quite sit still through this. Picking up her spoon to stir some more. Holding it above the cup to let the tea drip into the swirling vortex. There is something lurking behind the facade of this failed attempt at mother-son small talk.

"I want to talk to you about your sister."

There: there's the buried lead.

"Grace."

"She's sleeping a lot."

"She's growing," I say.

"She's still not handling this well, Lester."

It was Grace who found the postcard of the fluffy orange kitten lying on its back, left on our kitchen table on that cold March morning. There in her Hello Kitty slippers, alone in the soft and woolly light of early morning.

"Well," I say.

"Who does she hang around with at school?"

"Oh, I don't know, the usual gatherings. The usual groups."

"Seriously, Lester, what kind of crowd is she with?"

Kids with wallet chains and smokes behind their ears. Their standard formation is a circle on the grass at the edge of the woods.

"I don't really know, okay?"

"I found this in the bathroom last night." She reaches down, picks up a bottle, and sets it on the table. Jägermeister, empty. "I know it's not yours."

"And I'm guessing not yours, either."

"You need to take this seriously."

Still no one goes into his study. Still the blank sheets of paper sit on his desk in a perfect stack of botched potential. Boxes of things are stacked in the closet, full of what we dare not seek to know. His rug is there. His lamp.

"What do you want me to do?"

"I want you to talk to her."

"Lester the wise, the walking Enlightenment."

"Talk to her."

THE DAYS GO BY. The light grows shorter. Everything else remains the same.

In AP Humanities, Jeff has us sloshing through the brackish waters of his reader, and has proposed a dizzying array of "creative responses" to the reading. In creative response, I continue to slip Milton into our in-class discussions. A full-fledged boycott isn't off the table.

In Yearbook, we have settled into our customary groove. We're already two weeks into the school year, but you wouldn't know it from our progress on the project—or should I say, the glorious lack thereof.

On this particular Friday afternoon, Pancake is in fine form. He's in the navy blue shirt, and the part of his hair seems especially straight and narrow. He's ready for the weekend, folks. Soon after the period begins, he fishes a fresh box of powdered Donettes out of his desk. I watch him appraise its contents, waiting until he's chosen the day's first specimen before making for the front of the room.

With work on the Template proceeding on its snail-paced schedule, Pancake is willing to indulge the occasional guest lecture on the Yearbook Arts. The Pancake Bloc makes for an obliging, if not entirely attentive, audience for these lectures. Today's is the latest in a series which I've been developing for quite some time. The working title of the series—it may never have a final one—is "The Golden Age: VMHS Yearbooks, 1981–1988."

"Today," I begin, "we shall address the question of the senior photo."

The other members of the class—those outside the Pancake Bloc—seem to have little time for these considerations. Freesia and Tina McTovey are bent over textbooks, doing homework for another class, and the younger kids are huddled around a Monopoly board.

"Let us consider," I continue, ignoring my ignorers, "a few case studies."

The first photo is the photo of Vann Downing, from the 1981 volume. Importantly, the VMHS yearbook was still printed in black-and-white at that time—we wouldn't see color for two more years—but many of the stylistic principles that define the Golden Age are already present. Vann's photo is a perfect example: it's a head shot, with some kind of drapery hanging in the background. His hair has been sculpted into a perfect little nest of ringlets. And he's smiling—smiling very, very big. You might say that, with that one smile, he ushered in a whole new era of senior photography. And you'd probably be right.

"The second photo I'd like to draw your attention to," I say, drawing their attention to the second photo, "is that of Maureen Phelps, from '85." I hold up the photo. Oh beautiful Maureen! She's adopted the smilingness of Vann Downing, and the up-ness of his hair. She's even got some drapery behind her. But she's taken it a step further, folks: she's seated, and hugging her knees to her chest. "I have chosen this photo," I inform the Pancake Bloc, "not for its uniqueness. Just the opposite: I have chosen this photo because it has so much to tell us about what a senior photo is all about. It gives us just a hint of personal expression, folded into the draperies of yearbook convention."

Not even I know how much I mean what I say, but I do like saying it. Freesia has joined the party now, leaning back in her chair, arms crossed, feet propped up on a neighboring desk. Pancake, at his desk, has assumed a fairly standard pose: his large arms folded over his chest, his head cocked back, his eyes closed in slumber. (If only we could see inside his dreams!)

"Lastly," I say, opening the third yearbook I have borrowed from the library, "the 1986 edition." There are numerous Maureen Phelpses in *Badgerama*: a lot of hairsprayed hair; a lot of draperies behind the figure in the photo; a lot of hugging knees to chests. But I am interested in something else. "Check this out," I say.

I turn to page 40: Digger Grimes. And yes, you have that right: he's standing in the bed of his pickup, arms raised to the world, as if to embrace the everything of everything. (Oh Digger! You expected so much—I can only hope the world delivered on its promise.)

The appearance of this truck has stirred the Pancake Bloc to vocal approval, which in turn has stirred our blessed Tina from her toils. "Wait a minute," she says, surfacing for air. She's scowling. "You just said headshots were best." Judging by the intensity of those deep brown eyes, and the thorough furrow in her brow, this is no minor inconsistency.

I have to think carefully about my response—you wouldn't want just anything to go down in that notepad. "As is often the case," I rejoin, "the exception proves the rule. Think of the air as the knees he's hugging toward himself. And think of the truck as the drapery."

Tina cocks her head to the side, examines Digger's widespread arms once more, then shakes her head. "That doesn't make sense," she pronounces, then, without further comment, goes back to her math problems.

"Any other questions?"

The Pancake Bloc is silent. But the phone on Pancake's desk is not. It rings quite suddenly, loud and stark and shrill, jolting Pancake awake with a grunt. It rings again. He answers it. And then his face goes white. "She what?" A pause. "I'll be there right away."

He hangs up the phone and shoots out of his chair faster than would previously have seemed possible, then starts waggling into his army-green jacket.

"What's up?" I ask.

"My wife," he heaves. "She's in the hospital."

"Oh dear," says Tina.

"I have to go," says Pancake, waddling toward the door, with one arm still flailing to find the arm of the jacket. He opens the door and turns to us just before leaving, his face awash in worry. "They don't know what it is."

It's a bright, warm Thursday afternoon, but the sun is already fading. You know that there aren't many days like this left in the year, but there isn't much you can do about it. All you can do is head to Spurlock Spit, lie on a log, and begin to draft a postcard to The Father.

In his most recent postcard to me—an exterior shot of the Metrodome—he seems to want to seem to want something:

> Lester:
>
> I am prepared to establish new forms of engagement. To that end, please send a list of recent readings—annotated, if you wish. I will respond with comments and additional suggestions.
>
> ~ E.N.S.

His handwriting is probably the most careful thing about him—even more careful than his syntax. I try to picture him out there, writing this—stroking his mustache, wearing his red-and-black checked jacket, a cigarette smoking in a nearby ashtray—but it's hard to bring the image into focus.

I do, however, have some worthy fodder for a return postcard. I'm lying with an arm across my eyes, speaking into the blindnesses of wind and arm; Freesia is seated on a nearby log, tossing little chips of driftwood into the sand.

"Take dictation," I say.

(A rolling of the eyes)

"You just rolled your eyes. I know that without looking."

"I'm not going to 'take dictation,' Les."

"Then what good are you to me?"

"What are you dictating, anyway?"

"A postcard to The Father."

"How about I just commit it to memory?"

"Even better. *Dear The Father,* it starts."

(A peek through the arm-block; Freesia straining sand through hands)

"Why don't you just call him 'Dad'?"

"*Dear The Father,*" I continue. "*I am in receipt of your postcard dated 7 September 1996. While I do not wish to respond specifically to the query presented therein*—are you getting this?"

"Every word."

"*Therein* is exactly the kind of word we need. Show him I've got some moves of my own."

(Another glimpse through the arm-block; Freesia scratching indecipherable glyphs into the upper quadrant of the log; face in shade and cradled by her chestnut-colored hair)

"*I nonetheless wish to communicate to you my intentions regarding a text that is as familiar to you as it is to me.*"

"Let me guess: *Paradise Lost.*"

"Freesia Price, ladies and gentlemen: master diviner."

"Is this about your new 'Grand Plan'?"

"It so happens that it is."

"What is it with you and that stupid, boring book?"

"*Specifically,*" I dictate, "*I wish to share with you my desire to visit the sole surviving manuscript of* Paradise Lost—"

"Why are you using that voice?"

"*—which is housed at the Morgan Library in New York.*"

"I still don't know how you plan to get there."

"*I shall send you, under separate cover, a draft letter to said institution, requesting permission to visit said manuscript.*"

"*Said,* Lester? *Said?*"

"Yes, *said.* That's what I said. *Said.*"

"You know what I think?" (Scooping her hair out of her eyes)

"What? That he'll be jealous?"

"No. I think you need to think about your future."

"I *am* thinking about my future. A big, bright future that includes the sole surviving manuscript of *Paradise Lost.*"

"I give up."

And with that, she gets up, brushing the sand from the folds of her jeans, and strides off down-spit.

"Hold on," I shout after her. "You need to help me decide how to end this."

She continues toward the Subaru, where she will sit, silently fuming, for several minutes—perhaps even starting the car and pretending she might speed away.

"*I would appreciate*," I dictate to the waves, the wind, the sand, the reeds, "*your candid feedback on the tenor and the content of said letter. Said said said said said.*"

I look up at the sky, where a few clouds are coming on, harbingers of coldnesses to come, then stand, shake the sand from my pants, and move in the direction of Freesia, who is already returning to extract me from the dusk.

THERE'S STILL NO OFFICIAL WORD on Pancake's mysterious sudden departure. His substitute for Yearbook is Joey Cialuzzi, the wrestling coach, a short, wiry man with brillo-pad hair and a Super Mario Bros. mustache. His signature gesture is the double thumbs-up, and his standard get-up is a pair of tight blue jeans and a black T-shirt which features the motto of the wrestling team in large, white block letters: GET LOW. He's right at home in Pancake's chair, chomping on gum and zinging the Pancake Bloc with innocent insults. Like Pancake, he has a pretty lax policy on coming and going, which means he's pretty loose with hall passes. Once you have one of these passes, you can extend its validity for the better part of the period. Today I ride the pass into my personal sanctuary.

The library is just as it's supposed to be: empty, cold, and badly lit. I have a particular task in mind—one inspired by a piece of new intelligence I got from BF James this morning (his sources are sound): Jeff Traversal is himself a former Badger, class of '82.

I head straight for the yearbook shelf and slide out the pertinent volumes—*Good and Badger* ('79), *Badger Traxx* ('80), *Badger Pride* ('81), and *Changing Times* ('82)—and bring them to a nearby table for inspection.

What does the young Jeff look like? Not so unlike the Jeff of present times. In all of his yearbook photos he looks more or less the same. He looks a little flabbergasted, as if he's surprised that his picture is being taken. His hair is a stringy flop of wet-leaf brown which betrays only a baseline attempt at styling. One half of his mouth is turned up in a partial smile; the other remains in a neutral position. It's a wry smirk, a recognition that the world is just the world, so what the heck.

His senior quote is predictably predictable: *Two roads diverged in a yellow wood, and I—I took the one less traveled by.*

I lay the volume on the shelf, still open to that image of an earlier Traversal, and turn to the windows that give onto the classrooms. I'm rewarded with an uncommon sighting: my sister in class. Freshman English, by the looks of it. Back of the room. Head down, hood on. Black T-shirt, black hoody, baggy black jeans. Black gloves with the fingers cut off at the knuckle. This has been the uniform of this year in Grace's life. I watch for several minutes, looking for signs of animation. At last she lifts her head, looks out the window toward the woods, then puts it down again. And in the intervening space I see she isn't doing nothing. There's a pen in her hand, and several sheets of paper on her desk.

I feel I have an angle now, and slink out of the building just before the day's last bell. As Grace emerges from class, I make my move.

"Hey," I say.

"What do you want?"

"Can't I just say hi?"

She is walking fast, head down, wishing there were dust to leave me in. I follow her to the edge of the student lot. There we stand, like half-sunken stumps, our peers flowing around us.

"How's it going?" I ask. This seems harmless enough.

"Who wants to know?"

"I don't know," I say. "Inquiring minds?"

"Did Mom put you up to this?"

"Up to what?"

"Don't be dense."

"What were you drawing?"

At last: her eyes meet mine. Swimming in makeup, piercingly

blue. From the looks of it, she's just applied a fresh coat of black dye to her hair.

"Were you spying on me?"

"And if I was?"

She zips her sweatshirt.

"It so happens," I persist, "that I saw you from the library. I was there on other business."

"It so happens," she says, mockingly, "that what I do is none of your business."

Her hood goes up, and a car pulls up to us: Flynn Ross's souped-up Brat. This is a notable development. Flynn Ross is the captain of our vaunted wrestling team. When he isn't wrestling, he is mostly in or near that car. White paint, red stripes, large spoiler. Foam banana hanging from the mirror.

He gets out and leans against the roof, sneering his perpetual sneer. Dark stains line the seams of his backwards yellow LSU hat. The stereo is blasting speed-metal. He nods at me, then nods at Grace and Grace gets in.

Flynn revs the engine loud enough for everyone to hear, then pulls away, then revs it even louder as he coasts to the road, where he revs once more, and then peels out with animus and urgency, tires squealing, stereo blasting. The roar of the engine is loud in the distance long after the car is out of sight. Somewhere in that maelstrom is my sister.

FROM OUR HOUSE you can walk to the water down a long, straight gravel road. The road ends at a bluff above a small park accessible only on foot and by kayak. It is one of the many forgotten places on King's Island.

The waves this morning are timid, lapping, merely, against the great belly of the earth, until a large freighter passes in the distance, stirring them to great heights of 18 to 24 inches. I am here to behold this, from my perch atop a beached log, in lieu of another installment of AP Hum. This log has all the wisdom you won't find in Jeff's reader, with its straw-man Milton stand-ins.

I get to campus with time to burn before the start of Second Period and set up shop in my satellite office. As I'm thumbing through the yearbooks, a quiet voice calls my name.

"Lester."

I turn to see who has addressed me, though I know already it is Iris Rasmussen. She doesn't so much walk as glide to where I'm standing.

"Can I borrow you for a few minutes?" she says. "I've been meaning to speak with you."

Rasmo (as I call Ms. Rasmussen) is the senior member of the VMHS English faculty. She's been here since the pipes weren't leaking. She is blind, legally speaking, which makes it all the more remarkable that she always seems to know when I enter her airspace.

I escort her to her classroom on the rim of the main dodecagon, though she hardly needs the help. The trail has been worn over decades of coming and going.

"Lester," she says, easing into her chair, a large, plush, old thing, brown and velvety, perfectly rounded to the contours of her thoughts, "how is everything going?"

"Great."

"Your sister has joined us, has she not?"

"Yup."

"How is she doing?"

"She's very fourteen."

"How about you? How do you like Mr. Traversal?" Her eyes are a dull gray, but somehow lustrous. They bore into you without your really noticing.

"He's okay, I guess," I say. "A little loosey-goosey for my taste, but my colleagues seem to like him."

"Tell me this, Lester," she says, folding her papery hands on the marble handle of her cane. "What are your plans for after high school?"

"That's still TBD," I say.

"It's time you started giving the matter some serious thought," she says.

This is the standard refrain around these parts. What are your plans? What are you going to do? What are you planning to be going to do?

"Well," I say, "I do plan to send a letter to the Morgan."

"The Morgan?"

"Yeah. They have the only surviving manuscript of *Paradise Lost*. I'm going to see if I can visit it."

"Okay," she says, massaging one hand with the other. "But what then?"

"What do you mean?"

"Why do you want to visit that manuscript? Where do you go from there?"

"Well," I say, "I don't know. I mean, it'll open other doors, right?"

"I'm not sure it works that way."

"Let's just say I'm keeping my options open."

A kid outside presses his face against the window, then goes on walking.

"What about the SATs?" she wants to know.

"What about them?"

"Have you taken them?"

"I can't say I have," I say.

"You need to, if you want to go to college."

"Maybe I don't want to go to college."

"What about your grades?"

"What about them?"

"Lester," she says, leaning forward ever so slightly. "I spoke with Ms. Ortega. She says you dropped out of summer school."

What can I say? I didn't like the food.

"And now you're skipping AP Hum."

What can I say? I didn't like the mood.

"Lester," she says, "you're not on pace to graduate."

If she's expecting a particular kind of response to this, it doesn't seem I'm apt to give it.

"It's time you started applying yourself again, Lester," she says, gazing into the space above my head.

"I'll take that under advisement," I say, buttoning my sleeves for departure. "I should be going. I have some glue to sand."

I NINJA MY WAY out to the Vortex, where I'm greeted in the classroom adjoining the wood shop by a warm, familiar face—the face of a man who has little to no interest in the state of my test scores.

"Pancake!" I exclaim. "You're back."

He's been gone for over a week, leaving in his wake a trail of yearbook-flavored tears. It's good to see he's back to his morning commute, that perilous trek from the sawdust-covered floors of the shop to his desk for Donettes.

"And you need a haircut," he rejoins, easing himself into his chair.

"You've got some splainin' to do," I point out.

"What?"

"Yearbook."

"What about it?"

(Poking around in the box of Donettes, extracting the day's first specimen, holding it to the light for inspection)

"You've been gone."

"I know." He has this grin he likes to have—this delightful little grin that tells you how tickled he is to know something that you don't know.

"You look like you swallowed a saw-blade," I say.

"Maybe I did."

(Donette)

"Care to explain?"

"I guess I could," he says.

"But why spoil the fun, right?"

(Laugh; cough; grunt; Donette)

"You want to know the truth?"

"Yes," I say, helping myself to a Donette, "I want to know the truth."

"My wife had a baby."

I pause, mid-finger-lick. "Really?"

"Yup."

(Donette; Donette)

"Wow. Congratulations."

"Thanks."

"A name, if you please?"

"Hmm?"

"The child, does it have a name?"

"Yeah. Buck."

"Wonderful."

"He eats like a tank."

(Vivid, if a little hard to picture)

"A baby," I say. "Buck. Buck explains a lot. But couldn't you have planned this a little better?"

"Nope."

(Grunt; Donette)

"Why not?"

"Didn't know Brenda was pregnant till he came." (Sucking the powder from his fingers, one at a time, like tank-like Buck at the breast)

"Oh," I say. "Wow." (Whoa!) "So when can we expect order to be restored?"

"How d'you mean?"

"In Yearbook."

"What about it?"

"When will you be back?"

"Not gonna be back," he says, running a finger along the interior of the box. "Not doing it this year."

"What do you mean?"

"I'm with Buck the afternoons."

"Oh dear," I say—as our dear Tina M. would say. "So Cialuzzi's staying on?"

"Nope. Traversal."

"Traversal?" I can feel my crest falling.

"Yup. Starting next week."

"You can't be serious."

"I'm serious as rust."

"But Pancake—"

"Ahp"—hoisting up a plump, coarse-grained hand—"take it up with Proctor Relaford."

WHO IS PROCTOR RELAFORD? A good question—a very good question indeed. The kind of question that some people may even be capable of answering. For my part, I can only paint a few broad strokes. We'll have to pencil in the rest as we go. Let's start with his title: "Proctor." What exactly *is* a "Proctor," you might ask. To which I would reply, again, "good question." In this case, it appears to be the title he has assigned to himself, in lieu of the more descriptive "interim principal" or "guy on the school board who somehow is our principal for a year even though it doesn't really seem like he knows what he's doing." That title, "Proctor"—whatever it's meant to stand for; whatever it actually does stand for—seems to give him a permanent lease on whatever other title he wants.

You see, our last principal quit quite suddenly late in the summer, for reasons which we here at the bottom of the scrum have yet to be made privy to. Proctor Relaford—who had, apparently, some kind of clout with the school board—has stepped zestfully into the task, elbow-patching his way into our lives with steadfast self-importance and a really keen desire, it seems, to address us whenever he can.

Today he is to address us in the gym at a school-wide assembly: *A Salute to Badger Wrestling*. Is it wrestling season yet? Who knows. Probably not. But no matter. It's never a bad time to salute Badger Wrestling.

The bleachers are full of my rambunctious schoolmates, squirming into place on the rickety wooden benches, hurling insults, tossing things at one another. Freesia and BF James and I ride in at the back of the pack and make our way up to the top row of seats, where Freesia gets out her Calculus homework and BF James starts playing Game Boy on the sly (good call, BF James).

Sometimes the Proctor wears a bow-tie, sometimes a regular tie. Today is a regular tie day, a peachy number that sets off the blotchy pinkness of his skin. His hair is more white than yellow in the terrible light of the gym, and thin enough that, even from the very last row, I can make out the pinkness of his scalp shining through here and there. His coat today is gray and checked, and his horn-rimmed glasses are the perfect capstone to his overall ensemble as he steps to the mic.

"Good day, my children," he begins to intone, but the microphone has other ideas. A harpy-shriek of feedback pierces the air, and bodies cringe and hands go up to ears. The Proctor recedes from the mic, with a look on his face of having been wronged. But he isn't about to be cowed, and soon regains the room with administrative gusto.

As the Proctor wades into his opening remarks, I start to consider the sound of his full name: Archibald Relaford. Archie, Arch. Arcane, archaic, arachnid. The Proctor lives in these permutations, somewhere; somewhere he inhabits the sound of his name, like a silkworm wrapped in silken scarves.

"So without further ado," he utters, waking me from this level-five reverie, "please welcome Ms. Flough to the stage."

A smattering of a smattering of applause goes up as Gloria Flough, the teacher of Current Affairs and World Affairs and Government in Action, bounces up from the front row of the bleachers and scurries toward the mic—to salute something *other* than Badger Wrestling, from the looks of it. A loose gown of a purple sweater billows behind her, and her copious shrub of curly, dark, shoulder-length hair is bouncing pertly. In one hand she is clutching some papers; from the other a Nalgene water bottle dangles down. As she turns to face us, I notice that the frames of her glasses match the purple of her sweater.

Ms. Flough, too, has a name worth pausing to consider. Improbably enough, she pronounces her last name to rhyme with "Louie." But, as I have explained to Freesia on various occasions, the "-ough" ending in English is a particularly vexing arena when it comes to the question of pronunciation. There is "through," but there are also "though" and "bough." And as if these were not enough, you might well be accosted by the occasional "cough," or a rogue "rough." (This last pronunciation is my preferred rhyme for the name of the teacher of Current Affairs and World Affairs and Government in Action.)

"Hello, everyone," she chirps into the mic. The feedback threatens to flare back up, but dies down as quickly as it flared. Flough smooths her sweater-front, then smooths it again. Then lifts the Nalgene bottle and opens the spout, only to lower it again without drinking. "I have an announcement to make," she says, having marshaled some courage for another advance on the mic. "I'm really excited." Now she's getting into it. "I'm really excited. As some of you know"—with this she floats a gaudy, knowing glance toward the Proctor, who is standing just a few paces away, hands crossed at his belt—"I've been preparing an announcement. And that's why I'm here, at this subby."

Freesia elbows me in the ribs. "Subby?" she mouths. I wish I knew what to tell her. BF James has not looked up from his Game Boy.

"And what my announcement is," continues Flough, "is my announcement is about the Issues Initiative." Her hands accentuate her speech, flashing forth in flower-wheels of emphasis. "Which I'm sure that various of you are familiar with what I'm talking about. I'm really excited about it. I'm really excited to let you all know about the Issues Initiative, which we discussed it last spring, at various standpoints. Well—it's going to happen! We're going to get going on the distributions really, really soon."

She beams her fluorescent smile around the gym. And then, without deigning to offer further explanation as to what, exactly, or even generally, she is talking about, she scurries back to her spot in the front row of the bleachers, and the Proctor reclaims his position at the mic.

"Now," he intones, "for the part we've all been waiting for: your Badger wrestling team. Get low!" he bellows, by way of farewell, then jellyfishes back to the shadows.

(*Get Low*: It's a pretty good slogan, really, a sound lesson on the physics of hoisting. You have to get low so as to hoist up your foes from below. If you stay too high, then they'll hoist you.)

The lights dim, and the heroes of the team are unleashed to the roar of "Thunderstruck," led by Coach Cialuzzi in his GET LOW T-shirt. First the freshmen, some of them large, all of them singleted. Then the sophomores, led by Colby Lewis, a corpulent beast of a lowerclassman. Then the juniors, puissant with the promise of the present. And finally the seniors emerge, trailed by Flynn Ross, team captain, two-time state competitor, one-time champ, full-time detriment to the well-being of younger sisters everywhere.

They run in circles, then get low, then do push-ups, then get low, then pound the mats with fists and heads and with their palms. Then—having gotten low again—they chant, with Coach Cialuzzi at the center, driving them on as cattle might be driven on—indoor cattle, cattle bred for grappling in little spandex one-sies.

Freesia looks at me with incredulity. As if to say: *is this really happening?* Yes, dear Freeze, it seems it is.

THREE DAYS LATER—the Monday after the Friday before it—there's a note on Pancake's door, short and sweet: "Yearbook has been moved to Room 9 of the main building." I still find it hard to believe. Has this crucial slice of the Victory Memorial curriculum truly been entrusted to none other than Jeff Traversal?

Yes, it has. For there he is, sitting atop his collapsible table, as we come shuffling into the room. On the blackboard he has scrawled out, in his trademark font, the word *Yearbook*.

Jeff and I have reached a tentative peace in the weeks since our little skirmish over the course reader on day one. According to the terms of this accord, I, for my part, have agreed not to read the things he wants us to read—your JOYCE, your HEMING-WAY, your FAULKNER, your BARNES, your WOOLF—and he, for his part, has agreed, perhaps without knowing it, to let me come to class on an "as-needed" basis. We've had our little flare-ups, sure—I can't just let him declare "The Second Coming" a "signal poem" of the 20th century, can I?—but for the most part the terms of the truce have held. But this: this is something else.

"So," he says, surveying the assembled crew—the gentlemen of the Pancake Bloc, plus Tina, Freesia, and Yours Truly, and those Monopoly-playing underclassmen, about a dozen strong in all. "Does anyone have a copy of the syllabus?"

"I do," trills Freesia, clapping open her binder. She hands Jeff the benevolent half-sheet that is the Pancake Yearbook syllabus. Jeff scans the sheet, flips it over to see if there's more—there isn't—then looks around the room. Perplexity must have its consolations.

"Can someone fill me in on this first task?" he asks the collective. "Estabilsh Template." He pronounces this phrase as Pancake has spelled it.

"That's already done," says Freesia.

"Really?"

"Yes," says Tina. "It only takes us like two days to do everything on the syllabus for the whole tri."

"We don't really get going until January," I inform him. "That's the Pancake Way."

"Wait," says Jeff, still baffled. "What do you guys do in class, then?"

"We brush up on the classics," I say, brandishing *Onward, Badgers* ('84). "Kind of beautiful, don't you think?"

"I don't know," says Jeff, now rapidly patting his thigh. "I think we can do better."

Come again?

"What do you mean?" My grin has self-suppressed.

"Well," he says, rubbing his hands together in the way that he does, "how about a little group activity?"

"Oh no," I say. "Not Baldessari."

"Not this time," says Jeff, with a hint of a laugh. "Who here has heard of the Surrealists?"

"I *think* I have?" says Freesia, turning to me for confirmation—which I do not grant—then turning back to Jeff. "Isn't that, like, Salvador Dalí and dripping clocks and all of that?"

"Yeah," says Jeff. "Dalí's a great example."

"An example of what?" Tina wants to know.

"Of the Surrealist movement," Jeff clatters forward, now pacing back and forth across the world map, "which was basically just a group of artists who took a more, well, *surreal* approach to their art."

"You don't say," I say.

"Anyway," he says, casting a warning shot of a glance in my direction, "the reason I mention them is that they had this game they liked to play. Exquisite Corpse."

"Exquisite what?" says Jimmy Blatt, breaking the silence of the Pancake Bloc.

"Exquisite Corpse," Jeff clarifies by failing to clarify.

"Like a dead guy?" This from Bobby Blatt, Jimmy's younger brother. The Bloc has been stirred to life, at least for the moment.

"Yeah," says Jeff, "like a dead guy. Here's how it works. Each of you will write one word on a piece of paper. Then we make a poem out of all the words!"

"That sounds cool!" bursts Freesia.

It does?

"Okay, let's see," says Jeff, tapping his lower lip, "how about this? If you're in these rows," he says, wandering into the space between the southernmost rows of desks, "write a verb. If you're in these rows"—Freesia's and mine—"write an adjective. And you guys over there," he says, shoving some air in the direction of the rest of the class, "you write a noun. Any questions?"

Cam Drinker, Jr. raises his hand. This in itself is a noteworthy development. Cam, a squat sophomore with short blond hair and bright blue eyes, is the quietest member of the Pancake Bloc. He's a steadfast, square-jawed pillar of silence. In fact, I only know his name because the Brothers Blatt like to razz him unceasingly in unceasingly unimaginative ways (he takes it admirably well, does Cam).

"Yes, Cam?" says Jeff, hopping back onto the collapsible table.

"Is this for the Issue Initiative?" Cam wants to know.

Jeff squints into the question, clutching the edge of the table with both hands. He may or may not know what Cam is talking about. "No, not exactly," he says, in a tone mixing doubt with diplomacy. He looks around the room for help that isn't coming. "Anyway," he says, sliding off the table, "on to the fun part!"

Not so fast, Traversal. There's a Tina in the room. "Wait a minute," she says.

"Yes?" says Jeff, his hands still on the table.

"What does this have to do with the yearbook?"

Jeff pauses to consider the question—perhaps for the first time. He looks around the room, then stands up straight. "I'll let you be the judge of that."

This response clearly fails to satisfy poor wondrous, inquisitive Tina, but she nonetheless gets out a sheet of crisp, white notebook paper. The rest of my colleagues follow suit, and I follow their following suit, and within a few minutes our disheveled yearbookmeister is collecting the disparate pieces of what he seems bent on calling a poem.

"Now," he says, "on to the fun part!" One by one, he sifts through the sheets of paper, writing out three lines on the blackboard as he goes. The final product, I think it's safe to say, isn't likely to be the subject of a Norton Critical Edition any time soon:

> Dumb trucks scream.
> Luminous tractors push big yearbooks.
> Pointless whistles circumambulate bridges.

(I'll let you guess which adjective is mine.)

"So," says Jeff, eventually, "you're probably wondering why we just did that."

"Yup," I say.

"My point," he rejoins, looking out over the dubious faces of the Pancake Bloc, the yet more dubious faces beyond them, "is that the yearbook could be—*more*, couldn't it? It could be fun, and surprising, and a little crazy, like this poem. I guess the question I'm trying to ask is this: Do we want to do the same old thing that's always been done, or something new and different?"

"Easy there, Che Guevara." It's time I intervened in earnest. "We don't need another course reader, okay? The Template will do just fine, thank you very much."

"But isn't it kind of boring?"

He's prodding me. I'll happily prod back. "Boring, Mr. Traversal?"

"Yeah, boring," says Freesia. "I think Jeff is right. Let's spice things up a little."

"Let's not," I say. "That which is perfectly cooked needs no further seasoning. And the Pancake yearbook is perfectly cooked."

"The Pancake yearbook is *boring*!"

"And let me guess," I say. "You won't make any more boring art?"

"Ha ha, Lester," Freesia says.

"Let's take a vote," says Jeff. "All in favor of doing it the Pancake way, raise your hand."

To my utmost satisfaction, and to Freesia's visible exacerbation, most of the hands in the class go up.

"Okay, that seems pretty telling," Jeff concedes. "All in favor of doing something else?"

Freesia's is the only hand that goes up along with Jeff's. She dares not look my way.

"I guess that settles that," sighs Jeff, with a conciliatory raising of his eyebrows and palms. "Boring art it is."

THE AIR OUTSIDE is alive with aliveness, the waning warmth of the earlier-setting sun, as the paved Price driveway opens wide its asphalt arms to us. Freesia throws the car into park and leaps into the loving paws of her golden retriever, given name Hiram. BF James and I sit there for an extra moment, watching her toss him a Frisbee, before venturing within range of his dangerous enthusiasm.

"Hi, Hi," I say, evading his tongue-first lunge.

"Pet him," urges Freesia. "He loves it! Don't you, Hi?" She is a flurry of affection in his face.

"What up, Hi?" says BF James, hands in the pockets of his parka, swiveling out of the way of the dog.

Freesia tosses Hi a ball and bounds up to the front door. "Come on, let's make some chai!"

The Price residence is an exceedingly tasteful Craftsman, built in the '30s and then gutted by Freesia's parents in the earlier part of these rollicking '90s. It's painted olive green, with dark green trim, and little hints of persimmon orange on the window sills. There's a small but perfect yard in front—in which a Clinton/Gore sign is currently planted—and out back there's a Northwest special of a garden, part Japanese sanctuary, part California orchard, all immaculate and fun to stroll through contemplatively. A white fence separates the yard from the driveway, and an arched trellis, bulging with wisteria, hangs over the opening to the flagstone path that leads up to the house. There is a friendly, creaking swing on the porch, where Hiram likes to set up camp—and where Freesia and I have been known to while the summer evenings away, lemonades and arguments in hand.

The inside of the house is no less impressive. Hardwood floors, Persian rugs, a network of expensive speakers emitting classical music and xylophone jazz. The walls are covered with art from all over the world, mostly acquired on family trips.

Freesia's parents complete the picture. He, David, paterfamilias, is an affable, earnest, intelligent small business consultant; she, Marian, is the stately, friendly, sophisticated Executive Director of a community arts nonprofit. They often cutely carpool to Olympia, and they tend to wear the same expression, an expression of genuine warmth and welcome. They are, on the whole, unusually tolerable people. More importantly, they know what they're up to in the kitchen.

We say hello to David—aproned, poring over a cookbook, hard at work on dinner—then make our chai and head upstairs to do the things we do on weekday evenings. I lie on the floor of Freesia's bedroom, tossing a fuzzless tennis ball into the air, over and over, trying to get it as close to the ceiling as I can without hitting the ceiling. BF James flips through Freesia's stack of college brochures. And Freesia fires up her Toshiba and gets cracking on the eightieth draft of her college application essay. Within moments, she has entered Power Mode, a state of total concentration from which nothing can dislodge her.

About forty minutes into our stay, the front door of the house opens with an audible *shoosh*. Marian is home. She makes her way upstairs and comes into the bedroom.

"Hi Lester!" she says. "Hey James!"

"Hey," I say.

"Good evening," BF James salutes, from the low end of his baritone.

She gives Freesia a kiss on the top of the head. "I want to hear about your day. Then," she says, turning to BF James, "I'm going to destroy you."

"Okay," says BF James, cracking his knuckles. "I see how it is."

Several years ago, David gifted Freesia a Super Nintendo, in which her interest lasted about half a day. Fortunately—or, perhaps, unfortunately—Marian stepped in to fill the void, and for the last two years she and BF James have spent numberless hours together in the living room, ripping each other apart in *Mortal Kombat*.

After a trip to the garden with Marian—where we harvest some herbs at David's behest, and Marian harvests the details of Freesia's day—Freesia and I join David in the kitchen, while Marian and BF James retire to their ritual dismemberments.

The Price family kitchen is a space that abounds in opulent surfaces: the stainless steel of the refrigerator; the silver-charcoal-black of the granite countertops; the mahogany cupboards; the rich red of the Kitchen Aid mixer; the pattern of light and dark wood on the surface of the island, where we sit to an array of sumptuous appetizers. The olives: Lucques. The crackers: sesame. The hummus: homemade. A salad of beets swimming in seven types of lettuce. As we talk, the smell of what's to come pervades the air, and it is promising. In the background, Marian and BF James are already yelling at the screen.

"Dad, tell Lester he's being dumb," says Freesia, helping herself to a mountain of salad with the giraffe-shaped wooden tongs they got in Tanzania.

He pours himself a glass of Merlot. "And why would I do that, Peanut?"

"Okay, do you remember that new English teacher I told you about? Well, he's doing Yearbook now. And Lester totally shot him down today."

"Is that so?" Looking to me, one eyebrow raised, one elbow planted on the table.

"I felt I had to take a stand," I say.

"Please," says Freesia. "Jeff is trying to do something very subtle."

"Do tell," I say.

"He's creating an *atmosphere*. Just like in AP Hum."

"Please, no film theory today."

"I mean it. We're having fun in that class. Well, *most* of us are," she adds, with a glance that says enough about who isn't. "We're loose. We're open-minded. He's just trying to bring that over to Yearbook."

"Sounds like newfangled hogwash to me," I say.

"'Newfangled hogwash?'" Her last slice of beet, having been halved as many times as possible by the tip of her knife, is now being fashioned into a mosaic. "What century do you think this is, Lester?"

"That's just it," I say. "This *is* a century. And it's had other decades—other wonderful, wonderful decades. Decades where beautiful yearbooks were produced. But your beloved Jeff acts like this perfectly rounded wheel needs re-inventing. Newfangled hogwash—newfangled hogwash, I say!" I pound my fist.

"You're overreacting."

"You're darn right I am," I say, turning to David, who is clearly amused, then back to Freesia. "Me and John Baldessari. I'm going full Baldessari here—you know, in terms of my overreaction?"

"Who's John Baldessari?" says David.

"An artist," says Marian, entering the frame with authority, and heading toward the fridge. (The throes of combat require frequent hydration.) "Who's Jeff?"

"He's the new guy," offers David.

"And he's teaching Yearbook now," adds Freesia.

"So Lester," says Marian, turning toward the fridge, taking the thrust of the conversation with her, "how are your folks?"

I glance at Freesia, who is glancing at Marian, who had the gall to ask this (to Freesia) embarrassing question.

"Well, still separated, for one thing."

"Is it—how's your sister?" David, ever pragmatic, churns the conversation forward.

"She's hanging in there."

"And your father?" says Marian, donning oven mitts. "Where is he these days?"

"Mom!" (Freesia, swooping in to try to keep the awkwardness at bay. I wave her off.)

"He got a new job."

"Oh yeah?" paves David. "What's he up to?"

"He's working at the Metrodome."

"The Metrodome?" says Marian. "Ow!" (Even through the mitt you can get burned.)

"Yeah. In Minneapolis."

"He's not writing?" (Salting the dishes)

"Mom—"

"Must be hard to be a writer. I can't imagine."

"I don't think he can either," I say.

You can't build up much of a body of work out of postcards.

"You can run," says BF James, coming into the kitchen to see what's become of his foe, "but you can't hide."

Marian laughs, lifting the main course from the oven. "Time to eat!"

The roasted pork loin, shallots, and seasonal squashes, arrayed on a black clay platter, come to rest at center table, and the conversation mercifully bubbles over into other, non–The Father topics: the weather, the Mariners, other tidbits from our first month back at Vehemence. Freesia muses on her latest Top 5 list of colleges (Brown is still atop the list; Dartmouth has just debuted at number five, supplanting Smith). BF James regales us with two-sentence tales of Senior English and Business Mathematics.

After dinner, Freesia goes upstairs to terrorize her college applications; BF James pleads homework, parkas up, and heads for home on foot; and Marian retreats to the study. This leaves me alone with David. Ours is the evening to discuss the important topics of the age, while so many others are wasting their hours on math problems and lab write-ups and personal essays.

"Coffee?" he asks.

"Decaf, please."

He grinds the beans and starts the machine, then pours himself a Scotch (one cube of ice).

"So let me ask you something, Lester."

The amber honey in his glass roils with upward-streaming rivulets as he rolls the ice around with the tip of his finger.

"Shoot."

"Do you have designs on my daughter?"

"Designs?"

The blurby blocky boiling of the coffee in the background. *Blurb-blob-bloddy-block-blurb.*

"You trying to date her?"

"Not especially."

"It's okay if you are—I'm not trying to be the imposing father here."

"Of course not, David. Of course you aren't."

I'm playing with the sugar in the bowl—natural, brown—removing lumpy cubes with the small silver tongs and placing them in a circle around the edge of my saucer.

"Marian and I like you. You're—interesting."

"Interesting."

"I just want to make sure you know how special she is."

"Trust me, she won't let me forget."

"So long as you remember."

"I will. I cannot not."

The coffee is delicious—especially so for the addition, after each sip, of yet another cube of raw brown sugar. You don't want the cup to have a bottom, for you know that the bottom of the cup will announce your departure, but it does. It always does.

I pause outside in the light of the porch on the way out to the road. No sign of the dog. Plenty of signs of the onset of fall. The trees are going orange. The air is crisp. And your breath is a presence on the air.

WHEN I GET HOME, there's a postcard waiting for me. This one is an exterior shot of the Metrodome from street level. Nothing special, just the facts.

Postcard 1 of 3

Lester:

You are many fathoms out of your depth. Your letter to the Morgan is intellectual garbage masquerading as genuine scholarship. You need to revise your approach completely. In the postcards that follow, I shall sketch out a more appropriate course.

PS: You don't even mention All Our Woe.

There is no postcard 2 of 3, and no postcard 3 of 3.

OCTOBER

*J*EFF BREEZES INTO YEARBOOK a few minutes late—one can only assume, based on his routine tardiness, that there's a flexible relation to the schedule on Planet Baldessari—and seems surprised to see, sitting tight-lipped and pensive in his (Jeff's) chair, none other than Proctor Archibald Relaford.

The Proctor likes to drift into classrooms unannounced. He'll drift into this or that classroom, sit for a while at the back, with his fingers at his chin, and then—when we're lucky—step to the front of the room to say a few words. Then he'll drift back out again, headed, one can only surmise, for his next drift-in. We've gotten used to having him around. He's like a bad fluorescent light. At first the flickering distracts you, but after a while you don't even notice it. Today, for some reason, he has decided to grace us with his presence in Yearbook.

"Proctor, what a pleasant surprise!" Jeff manages to exclaim.

The Proctor seems to have a way of carrying with him—in the way that he walks, in his little gasps and breaths and *humphs*—a kind of *atmosphere*, a debris-like extra-ness of space surrounding his body. So as he makes his way now to the front of the room, for reasons not yet clear, he is more, somehow, than just one person. The entire weight of this august institution is resting on his narrow, padded shoulders. When, at last, he arrives at the front of the room he draws, from the inside pocket of his blazer, a small stack of notecards.

"Hello everyone," he says, then clears his throat. Jimmy Blatt looks up, SweeTart in hand. "I have come today," continues the

Proctor, "to share some ideas with you, ideas about literature and letters and the wondrous task before you."

The rest of the Pancake Bloc is clearly caught off guard. Freesia casts an inquisitive look at Jeff, who can only shrug.

The Proctor begins to read aloud: "I would like to begin with a short discussion of one of the greatest poems in the English language."

Over the next several minutes, he delves, delightfully enough, into a lecture on the poem "If," by Rudyard Kipling. Does he think this is an English class? Apparently not, for he ends his lecture with a notecard that begins, "the yearbook is just such a document, is it not?"

Once, at last, he has finished, he slides the notecards back into his jacket, then dabs his forehead with a peach-colored handkerchief. "Are there any questions?"

I can't resist.

"Yes, Mr. Smith."

"So Proctor, tell me something," I say. "What's your stance on Surrealism?"

"I beg your pardon?"

"You know, Dalí? Exquisite Corpse?"

"What Lester is referring to," says Jeff, ungluing himself from the wall, "is a little exercise we did on my first day here in Yearbook. You know, a little warm-up?"

"A warm-up?" says the Proctor, dabbing.

"Yeah," stammers Jeff. "A—a little exercise." (How he must long for a dab of that handkerchief!)

"Go on," says the Proctor.

"Exquisite Corpse," says Jeff, as if this phrase alone explains everything, then steals a glance at me. I wink.

"Who or what," says the Proctor, "is that?"

"Well," says Jeff, "it's a Surrealist game. You know, kind of a way of unlocking the unconscious? Really fun stuff. I have a book of them. But," he continues, finding the groove he sometimes finds when, after long searching, he has a point to make, and no amount of sentences will serve to make it, "the book doesn't really do the movement justice. I mean, what book could? And that's kind of the problem here. We're trying to create this book—this yearbook—but can it really do justice to the complexity of our experience? You know what I mean?"

The Proctor stares coldly at—or *into*, maybe even *through*—poor Jeff, a distorted bar of fluorescent light on each lens of his glasses.

"No," he says, his voice gone dry as desert sand. "I don't."

"Well—" says Jeff, casting his glance around the room.

"It was about opening our minds," says Freesia. "And getting everyone involved." This last phrase is directed at Yours Truly.

"Yes," says Jeff, turning from Freesia to the Proctor, "that's right. That's exactly what I had in mind. A little group activity. To open our minds, and get us working together. Many voices, coming together as one!"

"Hm," hms the Proctor, in a way that suggests that these explanations fall short of the mark, his mark, the mark notched by R. Kipling. "Perhaps we should discuss the matter further at another time. Now, if you'll all excuse me, I am late for an appointment."

And with that, he pockets his kerchief and wafts from the room.

MELKY'S—ANOTHER OF OUR FAVORITE after-school outposts—used to be a bowling alley. Then it was a video store, and then an auto parts store, and then a carpet outlet. Now it's a burger joint. A few of the unmaintained bowling lanes still extend into darkness, their hard, flat surfaces disappearing into the wall of abandoned pin-setting mechanisms. As children Grace and I used to imagine the jobs of those men at the end of the lanes. Where were they, how were they doing what they were doing? How did they get the pins set up so quickly and so perfectly? We would try to knock down as many pins as we could, not to get a better score, but so that we could watch them in action, half-hidden by the machinery of their vocation. "How do they do it, Lester?"

she would ask, beady-eyed, awestruck, marveling at what surely must have been a sign that the world had been made whole and correctly. "I don't know," I would say, sipping a root beer made cold by coarse chunks of crushed ice. "I don't either," she'd reply.

On this October afternoon, Melky's is just how we like it: empty and dark. We collect our beverages—a strawberry shake for me, a Diet Coke (as usual) for Freesia—and make for our booth by the window. We're down our BF James, who is sickly by nature and out for the day with a bout of grippe or ague. The booth is emptier without him—emptier and more contentious.

"You're not going to be hungry for dinner."

"Don't doubt me," I say, hoisting a generous glop of the shake on the end of my straw.

"So, how's your new 'Grand Plan' coming along? Have you heard back from the Morgan?"

"It's a no go."

"Really?"

"Yeah. Those things are so political."

"Political, Les? How could they possibly have rejected you for political reasons?"

"Ask them. I've moved on."

"You didn't send it, did you?"

I stir the shake, working against and around the chunks of frozen strawberry.

"You're so annoying."

I say nothing.

"So what's your next 'Grand Plan'?"

"I don't know. I don't really have one."

"You need to get your shit together," she says, pointing the back of her spoon at me. "I'm serious. You're going to really regret it if you don't."

Like everyone else this side of BF James, it seems, Freesia is concerned about my future. The subject is a permanent fixture in the revolving carousel that is our conversation, a battered figurine with chipping paint. *What are your plans? What are you going to do? What are you planning to be going to do?*

"I don't know," I say. "Maybe I'll paint houses. You work during the summer, save up some cash, and then sleep away the winter."

"You're going to feel different when everyone leaves."

My response: the sucking sound the straw makes at the bottom of a shake. *Hleoeoop.*

"And Jeff," she says. "I still don't get why you have such a stick up your butt about him."

"I don't think I'd put it that way."

"News flash, Les: he's really cool. And smart. And unlike just about everyone else at our stupid school, he actually wants it to mean something to us."

This isn't the first time she has tried to justify the ways of Jeff to me—and isn't likely to be the last.

"Do tell," I say.

"I mean, don't you think it's kind of neat that we have some input on the reading list? And I like that we can write something creative."

Freesia is hopelessly devoted to the fallacy of personal expression. She writes poems constantly. They're quite good, actually, despite the lack of identifiable meter, and the rampant lighthouse imagery.

"Ah yes," I say, "the myth of adolescent creativity. I've heard it before, Freeze."

"Not to mention that he puts up with *your* B.S."

Hleoeoop.

"I think he's going to make the yearbook really cool," she says.

"We'll see," I say. "I think he's out of his depth."

"You're just being difficult."

"You know what's difficult? All this new familiarity I have. You know, Baldessari, Exquisite Corpse, luminous tractors—are you familiar with those?"

"I am now. And you know what? I'm *glad* I am. But not Lester. No, Lester just wants to plug a bunch of boring crap into the Template."

"Yup."

"It's a waste. Jeff has some real experience. A *Ph.D.*, Lester. And you expect him to be just like Pancake."

"The public has spoken on that question, has it not?"

"You know what I think, Lester?" She is depressing the drink-identifying dimples on the lid of her Diet Coke. Her drink is now, apparently, every kind of drink.

Yes, I do. "No," I say. "What *do* you think?"

"You're afraid of success."

"Is that right, Dr. Price?"

"*You* could get a Ph.D.—*could* being the operative word."

"I've thought about it," I say. "But I don't know. Too much bureaucracy."

"Like you even know what you're talking about." She likes to wrap the wrapper of the straw around her finger, then tie it in a bow. "Why do you think he came back?" she wonders aloud.

"Who? Melky?" (As far as we can tell, there isn't an actual Melky behind Melky's—none that we've seen, anyway.)

"No—Jeff."

"I don't know," I say. "Why don't you ask him?"

Freesia can only roll her eyes far enough—about a quarter turn of the wheel—to notice that I'm speaking in earnest, for once. For there he is, in flesh and bone and ratty sweater.

"Jeff!" she exclaims.

"Freesia," he says, then turns to me. "And my very own Brutus." I bow my head. "Mind if I sit with you?" he says, hoisting a chair from an adjacent table.

"Make yourself comfortable," I say. "This is the finest booth that Melky has to offer."

Jeff disjackets himself and sits. We're a triangle now, with Freesia and me emboothed, and Jeff in his chair at the end of the table.

"So," he says, looking around at the walls of the place—the ancient movie posters, some of them shriveling, the small shelf of random trophies on the opposite wall—"is this where the cool kids hang out these days?"

"Obviously," says Freesia.

"I remember when this place was a bowling alley."

"Did you grow up here," asks Freesia, "or just go to high school?"

"Just high school," says Jeff. "We moved around a lot."

"Military?" Freesia guesses.

"Nah. Restless Father Syndrome."

"It gets around, doesn't it?" I say.

"Indeed it does. So," he says, passing his hand over an ancient mustard stain. "Tell me. How are you liking AP Humanities?"

"It's great," says Freesia. "I really, really like the class."

"Good," says Jeff. "I'm glad to hear it."

"And the reader—it's awesome! I"—she turns to me for support before saying the rest (Freesia gets embarrassed when pressed to announce the extent of her overachievement)—"I read all of *Nightwood*. And then all of *To the Lighthouse*."

"Wow!" Jeff is duly impressed—impressed enough to roll up one of the sleeves of his sweater.

"She's a completist," I inform him.

He turns to me, still with only one sleeve up. "I trust your opinion of the readings is a little different, Lester?"

"I think that's fair to say," I say.

"You miss your Milton." Now the other sleeve gets rolled, but it's too little, too late: the first one is starting to slide back wristward.

"Not true," I say, brandishing *Paradise Lo*. "He's with me everywhere I go."

"Let me ask you this," he says. "Why Milton?"

I surprise myself by laughing, then lean back in the booth. My cheeks feel warm. I look at Freeze, who bores her copper-mines of eyes into mine.

"Well," I say, absently fingering the discarded wrapper of my straw, "that's a rather long and winding story."

Jeff looks around the cavernous interior of Melky's, and the lack of other customers. "I've got time," he says, then plants his forearms on the table. Now both sleeves are at half-mast.

"Maybe we can get into it some other time," I say.

"Come on, Les," says Freesia. "Tell Jeff about your new Grand Plan."

"Grand Plan?" says Jeff. "Sounds intriguing."

"I'm afraid it isn't," I say. "In fact, I have no such thing. I prefer to leave the planning to others."

"Come *on*, Lester," Freesia presses on, "don't be annoying."

Jeff waves her off, then leans back in his chair and starts tapping a finger on the surface of the table, then starts wagging it at me. "I have an idea," he says, then—he can't help himself—rubs his hands together in the way he does. "Why don't you do a defense?"

"A defense?"

Isn't everything I do already a defense?

"Of Milton," says Jeff, leaning into the idea. "Think of it as make-up work. You'll write a paper, and present your research to your peers."

As if he's this action figure you can just tote out of the closet for Show & Tell. John Milton: 1608–1674. Special powers: blank verse; long sentences; classical allusion. Weaknesses: blindness; sanctimony; classical allusion.

"I don't know," I say.

"Come on," he says. "I bet you have a lot to say about him. It'll be like a Ph.D. defense in miniature. Show us why he belongs on the syllabus."

Freesia's eyes are alive to the idea. The poster for *Deliverance* is silent on the question.

"Okay," I say. This causes Freesia's hands to clap together. I raise a finger to stem the tide of her enthusiasm. "I'll think about it."

I'M AT THE INTERIOR windows of the library, looking in on Spanish—having just checked up on Sophomore English—when a presence wafts into my presence, a presence with a voice like a gelatinous cello.

"Mr. Smith."

Spying, I have been espied. Today is a bow-tie day for our fair Proctor, a pale blue one to match the icy waters of his eyes.

"Proctor." I do my best to match the solemnity of his voice.

"May I speak with you for a moment, in my office?"

"After you, good sir."

As I follow the Proctor through the foyer and into the main office, I note again the peculiar, particular qualities of his gait— or is it a lope? (A saunter? A general drifting?) It is hard to determine when, exactly, he has taken a step. He sort of just gestures his body in the direction of his destination, and before you realize he is actually moving, he is halfway there. Somehow he always looks like he is simultaneously in a hurry and taking his sweet, Proctorian time. He is ever reaching into pockets, checking his watch, adjusting his lapel, twisting his neck, smoothing out a pant leg.

I wave a cheerful hello to the lead secretary, Carcherry Mitchell ("my dad liked cars, my mom liked cherries"), and then follow the Proctor down the hall and into his office.

One thing is immediately clear: the Proctor takes his stewardship of the Principal's Office seriously. It's as if all his uncertainty about the office, in the abstract sense, has been transferred to the literal thing. Every little surface is shiny and clean. Not a single mote of dust will be tolerated—not on Proctor Relaford's watch.

"Please," he says, leading me to the corner of the room, where two leather chairs sit facing each other across a glass coffee table, "sit down."

I sit. He sits.

"Mr. Smith."

"Mr. Proctor."

"Where are you in your studies now," he says, twisting one of his cufflinks, "third year?"

"Fourth."

"Ah—a senior," he muses, scooping a handful of macadamia nuts out of a little pewter urn that sits at the center of the table.

"Yes."

"How's the vista, from the top of Snowdon?"

This he selects from what I gather is his basket of standard references.

"It's a little cloudy, sir."

He tents his fingers, leans back, gazes out the window at the Datsuns and Fieros in the faculty lot.

"Mr. Smith, you seem to have a certain—how shall I put it—*literary* sensibility."

"Do I?"

"Indeed," he says. "Indeed you do."

"Good to know," I say.

"I wonder if you can tell me, Mr. Smith." Now he leans forward a little, as if someone's listening. As if anyone would want to. "What are your impressions of Mr. Traversal?"

Ah ha: he's come to the meat of the matter. "Well," I say, buying time to think of some words that will sound good without making too much sense, "he's kind of like a knight without a sword, isn't he?"

He laughs a buttery, villainous laugh. "Quite so, Mr. Smith. Quite so. You see, it has just come to my attention that Mr. Traversal has presented a list of supplementary readings in AP Humanities. Tell me, what is your impression of that?"

"You know what I think, Proctor?" He leans in a little closer. "There is really only one word for Traversal and his reader." The Proctor's hands are clasped, his knuckles white. "And that word," I say—unable to resist the pun—"is travesty."

I lean back, crossing my hands on my belly in a way the Proctor might. He nods slowly, and slowly leans back into a lean whose angle mirrors my own. He's looking into me, absorbing me, assessing me. "And is it true, Mr. Smith, that there's some sort of—how shall I put this—*lesbian* treatise on that list?"

I have no idea. But I nod my head solemnly, and solemnly does he nod his.

"Mr. Smith, you strike me as being a keen and kindred intellect. Why don't you join us this Thursday for the quarterly meeting of the Humanities Council?"

He says this as if I know—as if anyone would know—what he's talking about. His damp left temple is pulsing.

"I'd love to," I say, keenly, kindredly.

"Splendid. The meeting will begin at 6 PM."

"6 PM?"

It appears that I've agreed to do something that results in zero hours of missed class.

"Yes. At my home."

At his *home*?!

"Carcherry will give you the address. Splendid." He holds the little urn out to me. "Macadamia?"

TODAY IS NOT A Melky's day. No, today we proceed directly to BF James's house. Our taciturn host is happily back in action after spending two days cooped up in the house, consulting the finest medical mind on this peninsula—the one and only Dr. Mario—and drinking Mr. Pibb. He sets up camp on his half-wall. But today is an off day for his Game Boy. Instead, he has a little pocket chessboard, which means he means to play out game 6 of Deep Blue/Kasparov for the forty-fourth time. Freesia pirouettes along the far edge of the blacktop, all the way to where the basketball is lying.

"Do you want to hear what I got on my ACTs?" she asks, spinning the ball in her hands.

Freesia prides herself on her prodigious performance on standardized tests. If only there were more of them for her to take. Surely there must be other combinations of letters that can be scrambled together in the name of denoting yet another form of assessment.

She turns to the hoop and prepares to let fly. "Should I submit my ACT scores to all the schools I'm applying to, even the ones that don't ask for them?"

Swish.

She does a little touchdown dance, then gathers the ball and tosses it to me. The ball is inflated just enough to bounce, if pretty unwillingly. It's a brownish gray to match the brownish gray of the leaves in the small and unmowed lawn.

"Have you given any more thought to Jeff's idea?" asks Freesia, pirouetting back in my direction.

"What's Jeff's idea?" says BF James, bringing out a pawn.

"He wants to trot me out for show in AP Hum."

"He doesn't want to 'trot you out,' Lester." She cancels her session of blacktop ballet abruptly and turns to BF James. "He wants Lester to do a defense—like you would to get a Ph.D., like Jeff."

BF James casts a stony glance at Freeze, and then at me. "Could be dope," he says, then turns back to the chess board. "But sounds like too much work."

"Exactly. And for what?" I say, bounce-passing the ball to Freesia.

"For your enrichment," she says, bounce-passing it back. "And for me."

"For you?"

"Yeah," she says. "For me. If you don't do it for yourself, do it for me."

"I'm still thinking it over," I say.

I dribble in a circle. I size up a jumper, then back down.

"Let's let the hoop decide," she says. The gauntlet's on the ground. "Or are you afraid of what your 'oracle' will say?"

I gaze into her gaze. "Okay," I say. I don't have much of a choice, now do I?

"Hook shot," offers BF James. "From just inside the free-throw line."

(There is no free-throw line on the Taylor family blacktop; it must be inferred.)

I size it up, toeing the invisible free-throw line. "Okay," I say. "Looks good to me."

"No," says Freesia. "Let me do it."

"Even better." I toss her the ball, then lean against the half-wall and cross my arms.

"But not a hook shot," she says. "Granny style."

This is a difficult concession to make: Freesia's granny shots are uncannily accurate. But I accede. "Okay."

She sizes up the shot, then spins the ball in her hands, then bounces it once, spins it again, and lets fly.

Rim right, rim left, net.

Freesia does this little fist-pump that she does—a gesture she picked up watching Sonics games with her dad, I'm pretty sure. "Yesssssss."

"The hoop has spoken," pronounces BF James.

"Yes it has," says Freesia.

"But I have terms," I say.

A Freesian rolling of the eyes. "Terms?"

"Yup. In the first place, I want Zdenik's bag."

"The exchange student?" wonders BF James.

"Yeah. He has this plastic shopping bag he uses for his school bag. It's unprecedented."

The bag is white with red handles, which can be used to cinch it closed. On the side of the bag, there's a picture of a beautiful, scantily clad woman. Over her bare midriff, it reads: *JILT*. (What does *JILT* refer to? I have no idea.)

"I'm not going to ask him for his bag, Lester," says Freesia.

"See what you can do. Second, I get music-choosing rights for the rest of the year."

She stares into me for several seconds, then counters.

"The trimester."

"Fine."

"Will that be all, Professor Smith?"

"For now."

She wants to be annoyed—and is—but still she knows she's won this round.

As Johnny Milton likes to say, October on King's Island is a weltering mess. It will rain in the morning, and then get sunny, and then decide to rain again. It will rain for days on end. It will do nothing—whatever "it" is—but spread grayness all around. Today the day is spreading grayness all around. Gray the pavements, gray the sky. Gray the hulking wreck that is the main dodecagon of VMHS, and gray the concrete pillars propping up the awning that surrounds it. Gray my peers, and gray their graying backpacks and sweatshirts. And yet, the day seems bright to me, quite bright indeed, as it offers the first opportunity to deploy my newly acquired music-choosing rights.

As it happens, I have just acquired another in a string of reckless Ramones bootleg CDs, this one wonderfully, tantalizingly German. It provided the soundtrack to this morning's ride to school, and you better believe it'll be blasting again as we flee the grayness of the campus for the grayness of town. As I slide it into the player—aftermarket, Aiwa; Christmas '95—I give Freesia what can only be described as a maniacal grin.

"What can this Ramones CD possibly have that your seventeen other Ramones CDs don't?"

My collection of Ramones CDs—which rambles carelessly all over the landscape of bootlegs, compilations, re-issues, studio sessions, etc.—is importantly distinct from my one crucial record, which is the analog mother to all these scattered digital orphans.

"Nothing."

"Nothing?"

"Nope."

"Let me get this straight," says Freesia, thrusting the car into fourth for emphasis. "You just paid thirty bucks for a CD that gets you exactly zero new songs?"

"Correct."

"I'm speechless." (This is doubtful.)

"I'm not," I say. "In fact, I have a lot to say about it. In the first place, there's the order of the songs. The songs are in a completely different order on this one. And then you have the liner notes. And don't even get me started on the cover."

The cover features a border of Ramones album covers surrounding the drop-shadowed title of the album: *Ramones-Festspielkonzertmusik.*

If Freesia could roll her whole body, and not just her eyes, she would. Instead, she rolls her Subaru into the expansive, empty parking lot of the King's Island Public Library.

The King's Island Public Library is housed in an old brick building on the north side of town. It's no Morgan. Indeed, there is very little to distinguish it from other public libraries. It does, however, differ from the VMHS library in two important ways: 1) it's non-dodecagonal; and 2) it does, in fact, serve useful purposes other than the housing of yearbooks.

I follow Freesia through the main doors and into the drafty confines of the building. She selects a table for us and plaps her backpack on it, then makes for the Information Desk. Within minutes, she has brought several volumes to the table, and informs me that she's ordered several others from other libraries. She slides one of the books over to me—an anthology of 17th-century poetry—and digs into another one, with her pen and notepad at the ready. She has entered Power Mode. This is my chance to escape, and I seize on it, departing the table for a self-guided tour of the library—the drinking fountain, the children's section, the cart way in back with a single volume (Darwin) lying on it, long forgotten. Out the window, in the neighboring park, kids are running down a grassy hill (the sun has returned, at least for now).

When I get back to Freesia at her table, she looks up. The book in her hands is already littered with torn-out Post-It bookmarks. "Where have you been?"

"Perambulating."

"You're not taking this seriously."

"What's the big rush? We've got time. Come on, let's go look at World Books. I call D."

"Listen to this, Lester." She consults one of the Post-It-bookmarked pages of the book. "Did you know that *Paradise Lost* couldn't get published for two years after it was finished? There was a paper shortage, a plague, and this massive fire that destroyed most of London."

"Let me see that." There's a portrait of Milton on the facing page. I'm struck, again, by how little he looks like you think he would. He's slighter, somehow, somehow less imposing.

"Well look at that," she says, "there's something Lester *doesn't* know about Milton."

Know to know no more.

"Can you imagine that, Les? A paper shortage, a plague, and a fire, all at the same time."

I put the book back on the table. "Maybe BF James is right."

"What do you mean?"

"This is too much work."

"No," she says, "it's not."

"Come on," I say, "those World Books aren't going to look at themselves."

THE PROCTOR'S HOUSE is a brick-encrusted Tudor on the side of a hill, almost overlooking the Sound. Beige the triangle of stucco over the doorway, brown the half-timber framing. The curtains are drawn, but lit from behind by a warm orangeness.

Freesia leads the way up the narrow concrete steps, which end at a small front porch. Just as we're about to knock, a voice calls up the hill. It's Jeff, bounding up the steps, toting a bottle of Scotch.

"Hey!" says Freesia.

"Hey," says Jeff. "What are you guys doing here?"

Good question, Jeff! Freesia is here, of course, because of Freesia's Law, which states that anything that *can* be put on a college application *must* be put on a college application. And I'm here, I suppose, because of my keenly kindred intellect. I mean, with an intellect this kindredly keen, how could I *not* be on the porch of the Proctor's house at 6 PM on a school night?

"We're here to offer student input," Freesia says.

Jeff eyes the door and exhales bigly, with both cheeks blown full. "This should be fun. Ms. Flough told me I'm an item on the agenda."

"What is that supposed to mean?" says Freesia.

"Who knows," says Jeff. "Some kind of ritual abuse. But Mrs. Rasmussen gave me some very good advice."

"She always does," I say. She almost always does.

"What's that?" asks Freesia.

"*Occupy your hands with some small task*, she said"—his impression isn't half bad—"*so as not to make the mistake of raising one of them to speak.*"

He raises one of them to knock, but it's too late: the door swings open inward, revealing the Proctor's stately grin.

"Mr. Traversal! And Ms. Price, and Mr. Smith. We were starting to worry you'd gotten lost." His grin makes for the hills when he sees the Scotch, which Jeff holds out in cordial offering. "I think," says the Proctor, taking the bottle and holding it out at arm's length, "that we can leave *that* here." He sets it on a little antique table just inside the door.

"Oh, sure," stammers Jeff, "I just thought—well, I don't know what I thought, really." He laughs a nervous laugh. He's already oh-for-one on the night.

"Please," recovers the Proctor, "come in."

We step into the entryway, which is adorned by a wine-red rug, and lit by little stained-glass lamps on dainty tables. The walls are painted billiard green. Straight ahead: a short hallway that ends at a closed door. And to the right: a small sitting room crammed with shelves which are in turn crammed with things in frames: photos, diplomas, certificates, awards, as well as a few odd trinkets and tchotchkes. It's hard not to go in there and start poking around. Instead, we follow the Proctor into the room on the opposite side of the entryway, a parlor decked out with yet more stained glass lamps, plush chairs, a floor-to-ceiling bookshelf, and, off in the corner, a harpsichord (!).

A handful of teachers and students sit waiting, scattered in armchairs around an oval wooden coffee table. On the bench of the harpsichord, Gloria Flough sits loudly silent in a bright magenta sweater, her nest of hair sprayed out and up and in and out and up. Next to her, in a frown-brown leather armchair, lurks Robert Fleniston, a fossil of an English teacher whose classes you must do your best to avoid. He has gained a certain notoriety, among the student body, for never once cracking a smile, and it looks like he aims to keep his streak intact tonight. Susan Ortega, the Spanish teacher, who also does some Freshman English on the side, stands to make room for Jeff as he slinks over to an ottoman in the far corner of the room, with Freesia and me in tow. He sits on the ottoman. We sit on the window sill. On the other side of Jeff sits Iris Rasmussen, my cherished Rasmo, absorbed in the knitting that will allow her to heed her own advice. As we sit, she turns to us and smiles.

The only other students in the room are blessed, earnest Tina McTovey—she sits in a folding chair next to the softer chair of Ms. Ortega, pen and notepad at the ready—and a slender, ghostly, silent type who goes by the name of George Blinge.

"Welcome," says the Proctor, settling into a burgundy leather chair at the far nose of the table, "to the first meeting of the Victory Memorial Humanities Council. Let's turn to the first item on the agenda, shall we?" (There is, apparently, an agenda guiding this meeting, and there may even be people other than the Proctor who have access to it. Somehow I doubt that Jeff is one of those people. And we certainly aren't either.) "The budget."

As the Proctor wends his way through some remarks on the Humanities budget, I cough softly every time he says the word "beauty"—he pronounces the "t" like a "t," and not like a "d"—and Freesia kicks me every time I cough. For his part, Jeff seems to be successfully hewing to Rasmo's advice, occupying his hands by massaging the one with the other, then the other with the one.

"Very well," says the Proctor, at the conclusion of his fiery, inspiring remarks on the budget. "On to the next item on the agenda. As I think most of you know, the main reason we are here is to review and reinforce the Guidelines of the Department of Humanities." (Guidelines?) "To remember the core principles which guide our efforts, so that we might more effectively abide by them." (Core principles?) "In short, we must remind ourselves about the purpose of literature."

With this, the Proctor absorbs the silence around him with a grandfatherly smirk. Freesia's arms are crossed. Tina's pen is whirling away. Fleniston is firmly entrenched in his scowl.

"But does literature really *have* a purpose?" With what he likely means as a good-natured rejoinder, Jeff has as good as tossed Rasmo's advice out the window, and with it some of the air in the room. The orange-red lamplight feels just slightly dimmer. "I mean," he continues, shoveling a little more dirt onto himself, "with all due respect, isn't it kind of pointless? And isn't that pointlessness kind of the point?"

He looks around the room, searching for a beacon of intellectual sympathy. But only Freesia is nodding to the music of his words.

"No," says the Proctor. "Pointlessness is *not* the point. Recall," he says, piercing the air with a short, pink index finger, "the words of Sir Philip Sidney: poetry must teach and delight." His eyebrows are raised. His temples are shiny.

"But what about the part," says Jeff, "where it affirmeth nothing?" For some reason, he's looking at me.

The Proctor does not appear to appreciate the cleverness of Jeff's parry. "I think that's just the problem here, Mr. Traversal. What is it that *you* affirm?"

"What do you mean?"

"I mean," says the Proctor, "that we have a specific set of guidelines regarding the readings in this department. And it is of utmost importance that everyone adhere to those guidelines. I mention this because of recent divagations, shall we say, from the established path."

"Are you talking about my course reader?" Jeff demands.

The Proctor clears his throat, gazes down at a manicured hand. The room is as silent as a wine-red rug.

"Seriously, is that what we're talking about here?"

"Yes," says the Proctor, "that is one of our concerns."

"By 'one of,' I assume you mean the only one?"

"I don't think I like your tone, Mr. Traversal."

"Why don't you just come out and say it?" Jeff demands, liking his own tone. "Why all the 'divagations'?"

Whatever air that remained has drained out of the room. Gloria Flough is biting a nail from each hand simultaneously. George Blinge is staring blankly at something on the wall or the drapes. Tina is getting it all down for posterity.

"Very well," says the Proctor, glaring into Jeff. "It boils down to this. If you wish to supplement the established readings, you must go through proper channels."

"Which are what?" says Jeff.

"I beg your pardon?"

"These 'proper channels'"—Freesia has busted loose from her own crossed arms and entered the fray—"what are they?"

The Proctor looks at her—a little caught off guard, and certainly perturbed—and then he turns to Flough, then to Fleniston. Tina's pen is a fury of jotting. Blinge is all and only Blinge.

"Well," the Proctor says to Jeff, "in the first place, you must make a formal submission."

"Yes," confirms Flough. "Within parameters."

"Okay," says Jeff. "To whom do I make this 'formal submission'?"

"To the Humanities Committee," say the Proctor.

"Isn't that us, the people in this room?" says Jeff, looking around at the people in this room.

"Well, yes," the Proctor must concede.

"So can we just put it to a vote right now?" says Jeff, right now.

"Well, no," says the Proctor.

"Why not?" Freesia is indignant.

A silence, then a Flough: "It's not on the agenda."

"Okay, okay," says Jeff, flashing a palm at Freesia. "How about this. I'll give everyone here a copy of the reader, and you all can decide whether to approve it."

"For next trimester?" says Flough.

"No," snaps Jeff. "This one. This trimester."

"I'm afraid," says the Proctor, "that you're too late for this go-round."

"You can't be serious," says Jeff.

The Proctor glares at him. "Oh, but I am."

Jeff shoots out of his seat. "I don't see the big deal here. It's just a course reader. There aren't any curse words in it. No heroin addicts or—or back-alley hand jobs. So what's the problem?"

There's no immediate answer to this question. Everyone must still be considering the image just painted by Jeff.

The Proctor fills the void: "It is not the job of this department, Mr. Traversal," he says, "to advertise alternative lifestyles."

"What—" sputters Jeff. "Wait a minute. Are you talking about *Nightwood*?"

"It's a lesbian treatise!" bursts Flough.

"You called this meeting because you're afraid of a *novel*? In an *English* department?"

"Mr. Traversal—"

"And what do you have against lesbians, anyway?"

"I don't have anything against—"

"Lesbian," says Jeff. "There: I said it."

"Mr. Traversal—"

The Proctor's hands are raised, but that won't be nearly enough to keep Jeff from starting to spin, in a frenzied circle, and shouting: "Lesbian lesbian lesbian lesbian lesbian!"

Spent, he falls back onto the ottoman and crosses his arms. The Proctor looks like a puppy that's been left in a car too long for comfort. Eyebrows raised. Mouth slightly open. The room falls silent.

At last Jeff speaks again, this time in a tone of partial resignation. "Okay. I'll retract the reader." He blows up his cheeks and sighs out the air.

"You do know we love it, right?" says Freesia, her eyes burning into the Proctor.

"That's not my understanding," says the Proctor, looking at Tina, who keeps her head down, scrawling, then at me. "Right, Mr. Smith?"

Now I see why I've been summoned to this keen and kindred gathering. "Well—" I say. I wasn't expecting to have to pick a side. I don't like sides. I much prefer to stand outside the sides.

"Well it *is* my understanding," says Freesia. "Let the record state," she announces, addressing herself to the top of Tina's head, "that Jeff's Reader has been a rousing success, at least as far as I'm concerned. *Especially Nightwood.*"

"Doesn't that count for something?" Jeff pleads, palms raised.

"Don't play coy, Traversal," says Mr. Fleniston—having saved this lone remark for the moment when it might seem most dramatic—then retreats to his scowl.

"Any disappointment suffered by your students, Mr. Traversal," says the Proctor, savoring the words, "is due to your lack of appropriate administrative foresight. Let's not lose sight of that."

"Let's not," says Jeff, getting up. The meeting is over, as far as he's concerned. He storms from the room, and then the house, reclaiming his Scotch on the way out.

"There's more on the agenda," Flough pleads. (How can Jeff have parted mid-agenda?)

But there isn't more on the agenda. The Proctor calls a prompt end to the meeting, and that is that. Freesia wraps herself up in her sweater and gets outside as quickly as she can. I hang back to escort Rasmo to street level, where her husband's Oldsmobile is rattling at the ready. She turns to me before she gets in.

"Thank you, Lester. That got the blood pumping, didn't it?"

"It was a little heated for my taste," I say.

"A little heat is good sometimes," she says, then gets into the car.

Down the shoulder, the Subaru is already running. Freesia is fierce at the wheel when I get in, clutching it with both hands, melting the windshield with her scowl.

"I hate this school," she says.

"No, you don't," I say.

"Did you see the way he talked to Jeff?"

"I did," I say. I also saw the way he shoved me out two squares, right into the middle of the board.

"You didn't exactly leap to his defense, did you?"

"I think you know where I stand on the reader," I say.

"You and the Proctor both. The two of you should go build a school out of dead British poets."

"Are you done berating me?" I say.

"I can't *wait* to leave this place," she sighs.

And with that, she leaves this place, urging the Subaru back onto the pavement, uprooting many innocent stalks of grass along the way.

JEFF GETS TO CLASS a little later than usual, plaps his satchel on his chair, and heads straight for the front of the room. He stands there for a moment, as if trying to figure out how to say what he's going to say. He looks like he slept in his car, if at all. Hair even more unruly than usual. Dark circles under his eyes.

"All right everyone," he says, at last. "I have some bad news. The course reader has been shot down. I need to take it back. The censor has spoken."

"Welcome back, Johnny Milton!"—this I think, but do not say.

"This can't be right," says Freesia. "It just doesn't seem fair."

Jeff shrugs. "What can you do?"

"What about next tri?" says Tina.

"Yeah!" says Freesia.

"Maybe," says Jeff. The idea has clearly got him thinking—which, as we already know, is a dangerous, dangerous thing.

"Do it!" says a kid at the front, one of those ambitious under-classmen who may or may not have a name. As far as I know, these are the first words he has spoken all trimester.

"Okay," says Jeff. "How about we put it to a vote?" This is a bold move, really, after the democratic approach backfired on him so badly on his first day of Yearbook. "How many of you support the creation of a new course reader for next trimester?"

Most of the hands in the room go up. Mine is not among them.

"Okay. All opposed?"

No hands go up. I've successfully abstained.

"That settles that," says Jeff, rubbing his hands together in the way that he does. "I'll get to work!"

He stands there a moment longer, then rambles back to his desk and sits down and starts scrawling some notes on a yellow legal pad. This seems to mean we are left to our own devices—you know, Hemingway, Faulkner, Woolf, Yahtzee!

When the bell rings, I amble over to Jeff at his desk.

"Hey." This wakes him from his ecstasy of reader fabrication.

"Hey Lester. What's up?"

"That was good fun last night, wasn't it?"

He shrugs. "I come from academia. That had nothing on the stuff I've seen."

"Actually," I say, "that's what I want to ask you about."

"Academic squabbles? I'm your man!"

I laugh. "No. I mean, about my defense."

"Cool, you're going to do it!"

"I promised Freesia I would. But—"

Where to start?

"Are you thinking just *Paradise Lost*?" he asks. "Or maybe a little *Areopagitica* too?"

Areopa-*what*?

"Probably just *Paradise Lost*," I say.

"You think there's enough in there to talk about?" he quips.

I laugh.

"Listen," he says, picking up the baseball on his desk and passing it from hand to hand, "don't overthink it, okay? Just tell us what you like about the poem. Okay?"

I nod, and drift back to my desk and pull out *Paradise Lo* and flip through it for the umpteenth time. But it seems, on this damp morning, like a dead piece of wood, with nothing to say, and nothing new to have said about it.

FREESIA IS AT THE meeting of some club or other—it's hard to keep track of all the different things she does to burnish her college applications—so it falls to BF James and me to patrol the pavements of the Taylor Family Basketball Court & Gardens. It's a breezy day, chilly, unpredictable. Difficult conditions for taking shots with basketballs. But shoot we must. There is a course to chart, and strawberry wafers—an entire package of them, a big one—for BF James to consume. He is Game Boy-less again, but today it's not Deep Blue-related. A paperback, instead, is curled in his hand: *Mona Lisa Overdrive*. (Why must you treat your books so badly, my affable James!)

My hope, today, is that the ball and hoop can help me find a wedge into my upcoming defense, which is, I must admit, beginning to loom menacingly on the horizon, even with Freesia's ongoing encouragement, and regular trips to the Public Library. Yes, I need a wedge, in the form of a passage, a place in *Paradise Lost* where I can moor myself.

"Here's the thing," I say, dribbling. "Book 1 is the obvious choice. You could do a whole trimester on the first 26 lines alone."

"Huh," says BF James. He doesn't sound convinced.

"And if you expand to the whole thing—you know, Satan's passage into hell, and the construction of Pandaemonium—Book 1 will easily win over the horror movie crowd. I mean, who doesn't love a burning lake and a band of hellish beasts?"

This time he doesn't even bother to answer. So I have no choice but to kneel before him and offer a quote: "The mind is its own place, BF James," I speak into the front of his hood, which rises to reveal his quizzical, spectacled face, "and in itself," I intone, rising, and jabbing a finger at the heavens, "can make a heaven of hell, a hell of heaven!"

"That's deeeeeeep," he baritones, dusting his hand on his pants before venturing again into the sleeve of wafers.

"Book 9 is obvious too." I resume my dribbling. The rain is getting slightly harder, pocking the pavement with spots of darker gray. "Eve finally eats the fruit. And the 'finally' is the key part here, isn't it, JT? The poem has been rambling about, winding its mazy way for book after book, and sentence after sentence, and phrase after glorious phrase, and it isn't until we're almost done with it, that it finally delivers its climax!" (Which is all the *less* climactic, I think it's fair to say, because we know it's coming, and have from page one!)

Now I've got the ball tucked under my arm, and I'm pacing back and forth across the court, delivering a version of the lecture in my head, quoting some passages, defending the findings I still haven't found. The scene is easy to envision: Jeff leaning against the wall, the sleeves of his sweater rolled up in earnest; Tina taking notes from her front row perch; Freesia smiling a smile of satisfaction; a few others in the room paying mild attention.

"But Book 6," I go on, dribbling thrice then picking up the ball, "Book 6 is a hidden gem." I have a real fondness for Book 6, for whatever reason. The futility of weaponry. The uselessness of cannon-making, friends.

"Do all of them," is BF James's delayed response. (I have seen this before: he'll hear you, and will register your question, but will delay his answer till he's closed the file on the thing he's doing.)

"Yes"—I drop the ball and clap my hands—"all of them!"

BF James leans back, holding a strawberry wafer aloft in contemplation. "And throw in some Ramones for good measure."

Sometimes you want to plant a big, fat kiss right on the hood of that parka.

As it happens, I have a nice head start. You see, for some amount of months or years, I've been working on a little side project. Is it a book? Perhaps it is—or the making of one. A study of the Ramones. A study that includes a wide diversity of offerings: an Introduction, which introduces things; a Bootleg Catalog, which catalogues the known universe of available bootlegs; an "Interview," which recounts an imagined conversation between Yours Truly and the members of the band, aboard the decks of a 19th-century steamship; a hypothetical VMHS senior quote for each member of the band, with a discussion of why each quote befits the member it's attached to; and lastly, in a nod to you never know what, a section titled "Notes to the Filmmaker."

I settle into The Father's old, fraying swivel chair—the one that squeaks in protest every time it's asked to do its job—and open a bag of Tim's Cascades (Jalapeño) and fire up the family computer. The screen halos to life with a dull gray light that gives way to the opening screen.

Don't overthink it, Jeff said. *Just tell us what you like about the poem.* What do I like about *Paradise Lost*? Everything! The one rule, therefore, I decide, is that I won't delete a thing. I'll just keep adding words and sentences and paragraphs and pages, whatever comes to mind, and nothing that goes in will come out. Everything will stay.

I open WordPerfect and find the document (its working title is "Document1"). I scroll through what I already have, then scroll back to the beginning, then begin again. After every section of what's already there, I decide, I'll add another. For every chapter on the Ramones, there will be a companion chapter on Johnny-boy Milton. Book 1 headbanging to "Suzy Is a Headbanger." Book 9 charming the pants off Joey Ramone's apocryphal senior quote. Things quickly get exciting, as this two-headed beast of a document starts to breath fire, in a way that even Johnny Baldessari might enjoy.

"You'll like this, Mr. Traversal," I find myself saying to the drooping house plant on the desk by the computer. "It affirmeth nothing." (Maybe he'll include an excerpt of it in the next course reader?)

About forty minutes into the fray—I'm really in a groove now, adding sections willy-nilly, changing typeface here and there, plastering lyrics from songs and lines from the poem all over the place—my mother enters the room, unbidden, wrapped in her frayed pink robe.

"Working on your college application essay?" she asks. (Asking this question is also occasion, it seems, to check that the belt on her robe is tightened all the way; it is.)

"Uh, yeah," I say. "What are you doing up at this hour?"

"I don't know. Can't sleep, I guess."

"Try some tea with honey." (That's what she would say to me.)

"I don't know," she says. "Maybe." Then she is silent for a space. Then she speaks again: "Your father called me today. At work."

"Is that so?" I'm absently pressing the arrow keys on the keyboard—up, right, down, left—which sends the cursor in a little dancing square in the center of the screen, over a chunk of text from Book 6.

"Yes," she says. "He says—he says he wants to see you and Grace."

I laugh.

She sighs. "He says he has 'rights,' whatever that's supposed to mean."

I shrug, then turn back to the screen, and append that same phrase to the sentence I most recently typed: *whatever that's supposed to mean.*

"You should call him, Lester."

"Should I, now?"

"It's—you have to think about what it's like for him."

"Do I, now?"

Now I'm just typing whatever letters come to the tips of my fingers: *asdfpoaihdf;lakisdfj;laqsdfhiasoldhijfapoifasd;lfkjas;dlfjkasdf.*

"Anyway, I'm going to bed."

"Nighty night," I bid her.

She turns to leave, then turns back. With her left hand she is clutching the door-frame. "About Grace," she says.

"Yes?"

"Did you talk to her?"

"Well, sort of. Not exactly. But—"

She nods absently. "It's okay, Lester," she sighs. "She's not your responsibility."

And with that, she leaves the frame, and I return to the blinkering cursor on the screen. And it occurs to me that I don't even know if Grace is home. And it occurs to me that this chair that

I'm sitting in, which is worn through to the foam at the center of the seat, was worn through by him, through years and years and years of sitting where I'm sitting now. And it occurs to me, also, that even if I wanted to call him, I wouldn't know what number to dial.

ON THE WAY TO Freesia's house—for a victory lap, really: there isn't much more to accomplish at this point, with my defense scheduled for the morrow, and the essay portion already handed in to Jeff—she's in bubbly spirits. She puts on *Festspielkonzertmusik* voluntarily. And she even turns it up when it gets to "I Want to Be Sedated" (Munich, 1981). And she even turns it down again almost immediately, so that she can say the thing that's on her mind.

"I'm really glad you're doing this, Lester," she says.

I nod. So am I, I think.

"So," she says. "Can you give me a sneak preview?"

"Sorry," I say. "Top secret. You'll have to wait for the main event."

I turn the music back up. She turns it back down.

"Hey, do you want to go to Tolo?"

"Tolo?"

"Yeah, Tolo. It's a dance. You know, the one where girls ask boys?"

She laughs—a nervous laugh? Something courses through me. What, exactly, if anything, is she intimating? I try to think of what I mean to say, but all I seem to be able to do is stare at her. *Do you have designs on my daughter?* She looks at me, then back at the road, then back at me. I'm still staring at her.

"Never mind," she says. "Forget I asked."

The music goes back up, and up it remains until we pull into the paved Price driveway.

"I have something for you," says Freesia, throwing the car into park.

"Oh?"

I follow her into the house—no sign of David or Marian today; nothing cooking in the kitchen—and upstairs. From under her bed she slides the thing she wants to show me. It's a large poster, and it is beautiful.

"I made this for you," says Freesia, oddly bashful, kind of beaming. "Look: this is a timeline of his life. And these are different portraits of him. And here is a list of his works. And I thought this was kind of cool—these are different images that have gone on the cover of *Paradise Lost* over time."

"I'm speechless, Freeze." I really am.

I hold it to the light for further inspection—this clearly took a lot of thought, and many hours of work—then turn to Freesia. "Thanks."

She lays a hand softly on my shoulder. "You're going to be awesome tomorrow, Les." Her hand stays on my shoulder for a space of breathless silence that is broken, at last, by a laugh, or a cough, or the chiming of the clock downstairs.

THE CORD ON THE PHONE on the wall in the hall—our main household phone—is capable of being stretched for many, many meters, far enough to find its way under the door to Grace's room, as it is tonight. (This stretching of the cord under her door is pretty much the only way to know she's home.) The music in her room—Nine Inch Nails, I'm pretty sure—is loud enough to drown out whatever she's saying. It's all a blast of noise to me in the hallway, where I'm sitting against the wall and looking at my notes one last time. Freesia's poster—really a fine, fine specimen of poster—is propped against the wall beside me. With the ghost of the warmth of her hand still on my shoulder, I'm running through the outline in my head yet again, hitting all the key points on the agenda—the importance of the blank verse; the importance of the sentence length; the importance of Joey Ramone's sunglasses—when Grace erupts suddenly from her room. She is holding the phone by the cord, as if the receiver is a fish she's just killed, a fish she doesn't like the smell of. This is how she holds the phone when she answers a call from The Father.

When The Father calls, which isn't very often—only a handful of times in the months since he left—he calls from a pay phone. You hear his deep, methodical breathing before you hear his voice, and when you hear that breathing, you know you're in for a lot of long pauses, with blips and flits of speech thrown in begrudgingly. You can already feel yourself coiling and then uncoiling the cord of the phone.

"Hello?" I say, hauling the phone down the hall, with the cord getting longer and tighter as I go, then sitting back down at a healthy remove from Grace's bedroom door.

"How's school?" he asks, eventually. (This is always his opening salvo.)

"Fine."

I pick at my toenails, the skin on my heel, my toenails. His breathing is a little hoarse today.

"What are you reading?" he asks.

"Mostly *Paradise Lost*. In my English class I'm doing a sort of Ph.D. defense on it. It's tomorrow, actually."

"No."

That is his response. That and more breathing.

"No?"

"No."

More breathing. Then: "Have you considered my remarks on your proposal to the Morgan?"

In his most recent postcard—labeled "Postcard 1 of 3," as you may recall—he had promised to "sketch out a more appropriate course" for my proposal to the Morgan (as he calls it) in subsequent postcards. But postcards 2 of 3 and 3 of 3 never made it into my in-box.

"Yes," I say. "You raise some valid points."

"What it comes down to, Lester, is a *framework*. And that's what you still lack. You're nowhere near a *framework*. You're just casting about for answers, when you haven't lived enough to *feel* the text." A pause to breathe and let his words sink in. "It is, above all, a poem of *loss*, Lester. And until you have experienced true loss—true suffering—you will continue to cast about. You will have no purchase on the poem, Lester—no *framework*."

Another pause for yet more breathing. My wrist is now mummified in phone-cord.

"What I suggest, Lester, now that I give it further thought, is that you hold off. You simply do not have the tools at your disposal. You aren't up to the task. Not now, and maybe never."

Milton's ghostly eyes stare out at me from the upper-right corner of the poster.

"Someday I may be able to explain this to you. But probably not."

And with that, he hangs up. When he hangs up he takes particular care not to let the handset make a noise as he places it on the receiver. I can see him doing this, all these thousands of miles away. He wants to fade away, and not go out clackingly. He wants the space between his voice and all the space that is not his voice to become indefinite. He uses his finger, I imagine, or lays the handset softly, directly onto the tongue of the pay phone. So that you can't be entirely sure that he's no longer on the line.

I WAKE TO THE honking of a horn—the Subaru—then turn over, bury my head under a pillow, and close my eyes again. It's no use: the horn honks again, and then again, and then I hear the slamming of a car door, then a loud knocking on the front door of the house. I lie still. If I don't move, I may be able to cease to exist. Still, still do I lie. No use: Freesia opens the front door for herself, then yells my name from the entryway. I do not answer. It's no use: she trudges down the hall and raps on the door of my bedroom. I lie still and quiet. It's no use: she opens the door and comes in.

"Lester, what are you doing? We're going to be late. Come on!"

"I'm not coming," I mumble into the pillow. She lifts the pillow.

"Come on, get up!"

I roll over, with a forearm up to block the brightness of the morning light, the light of Freesia's importunity.

"You're unbelievable," she groans.

I turn back over.

"Lester, what is going on?"

"I'm not coming," I say, this time to the wall.

"What do you mean you're not coming?"

"I'm under the weather."

"Bullshit. Get up. Get dressed. You're doing this."

Still, still do I lie. Still do I lie still.

"Lester, come on. Get. Up. *Now.*"

It's no use: I don't get up. And do not say a thing.

"Lester," she says. Her voice, I think, is quavering. "If you don't get up *right now—*"

I pull the covers over my head.

She stands there, hovering above me in silence, for the better part of a minute, then turns to leave and slams my bedroom door behind her.

For the next expanse of hours, the only sound is the sound of her Subaru squealing out onto the road in distress, over and over and over again.

NOVEMBER

THE WAVES AT OUR beach this morning are barely there at
all. In that much, at least, they're like the sun. It's gone too,
obscured by the clouds, which are low and dark and mostly
shapeless. I quickly get bored with the log I've chosen and aban-
don it for the water's edge, where I skip a few rocks and then
walk down the shore. The tide is low, and streaks of stenchy
kelp blanket the sand. In the not-too-distant distance, a freighter
crawls up-Sound. If I leave right now, I should get to campus just
as First Period is emptying its contents onto the walkways of
the school.

I leave right now, and get to campus just as First Period is ending. From my perch at the edge of the student lot, I can see my
colleagues streaming out of AP Hum. Among them is Freesia,
head pitched forward, JanSport hugging tight to her shoulders.
There is something about the white of her shoes—I don't know.
What is it? Optimism? Yes: you have to be so confident about the
world to wear shoes that are that white. I wait until she's disap-
peared around the corner before I make my move. By the time
I get to Room 9, all of the students are gone, and the Maestro
himself is lurching for the door, one arm ensweatered, the other
reaching back to find the other sleeve.

"Lester," he says.

"Hey," I say.

"What's going on? Everything okay?"

I shrug, nod absently. For the first time, I notice you can hear
the ticking of the classroom clock, in the right kind of silence.

"We missed you last week." By now both his arms are securely in the sweater. It looks like he doesn't plan to bother with the buttons.

"I wasn't feeling well," I say.

"Well," he says, with a glance at his watchless wrist, "things are sort of planned out for this week"—more "sort of" than "planned," I would wager—"but how about we put your defense back on the calendar for next week? I'm still eager to hear what you have to say."

I shrug again, then shake my head. I look at him. His interest is genuine. His stubble seems to confirm the fact.

"I don't think so," I say, softly. "I think that ship has sailed."

He furrows his brow, then starts to nod. "Okay," he says. "I understand—I think. Let me know if you change your mind. In the meantime," he says, going back to his desk for his satchel, then removing some papers, "you can have this back." He hands me my essay—the written portion of my ill-fated defense, the handing in of which I wish I could take back. It has been rolled into a cylinder and unrolled multiple times. It's peeled up at the corners, and worn at the edges. It looks painfully thick, and painfully thin. "I enjoyed reading this," he says. "I really did. It was"—he searches for the right word—"well, quite a piece of work. I made some comments at the end. See what you think."

I pocket the cylinder—it forms an almost unbearable bulge in the back pocket of my trusty corduroys—and head for the lunchroom to see what I think.

I sit at a table near the trophy case, safely outside Freesia's standard rounds, and turn to the comments at the back. Here they are, in all their barely legible glory:

> Lester—wow!
>
> First of all, let me say that you're a very talented writer. There are some <u>very</u> interesting insights and turns of phrase here. And you clearly have a commanding knowledge of your subject (or should I say, "subjects"). That said, I'm not quite sure how this piece responds to the assignment. In the future, it would

behoove you to hone in on a few specific issues, and put that brain to work in a more focused way. (And ditch the thesaurus!)
Grade: B/B−.

PS: I'm no expert on filmmaking, but I'm pretty sure that an author doesn't have a lot of input regarding the choices that a director makes when adapting his book. Not to burst your bubble—just FYI.

It's clear, without much further inspection, that the "B" and the "/" after "Grade" were shoehorned in after the fact. I roll the thing back up, as tightly as I can, then dagger it down into the top of the table, and then again, and then again and again and again, until the nose of the cylinder is battered beyond recognition.

It's GETTING TO BE that time of year: the cloudy portion of the docket. Those months when the clouds settle in and snuggle up to make nice. I say, *Welcome back, clouds. Come on back in. We've missed you.* We have persisted in this delusion of sunniness for long enough. It's time for a dose of cold amorphous cumulonimbus fact. It's time again for heavy gray—gray outside and gray inside, my friends. But even a cloudy day can be dry, which makes for optimal conditions for portentously heaving a basketball: dry court, no sun, no wind.

BF James, as usual, is sitting on the half-wall that abuts the Taylor Family Basketball Court, working on a bag of pretzels and those crunchy, over-seasoned snacks that come in little bread-shaped pieces ("Spicy Toast," we call them, with no small measure of affection).

"What's on your mind today?" he asks.

"Not much," I say, underhanding the ball up through the net from under the hoop.

"What's going on with you and Freeze?"

"Not much," I say.

It's hard to say who's been avoiding whom. Is she avoiding me because I'm avoiding her? Am I avoiding her because she's avoiding me? I suppose it doesn't matter. Avoidance is avoidance. And until the stove cools down a little more, I don't plan to put my hand on it.

"She seems really mad at you," he says.

"Is that so?"

"Yeah," he says, looking up from his Game Boy, the gray light on his glasses. The damp hem of his black slacks grazing the ground by the soles of his Converse. His parka sagging below his shoulders. "You should apologize."

I hoist up a three. It misses badly.

"Silence is his response"—this from the King of the Silent Response.

"I'm not here to talk about Freesia," I say.

"I'm not the one you need to talk to."

"I have other fish to fry."

"Like what?"

"Like this," I say. "Here it is, the question of the day. And here is the appropriate shot." I'm standing just beyond the elbow— mid-range, a reasonable angle. "Should I boycott AP Hum?"

"Say what?" he says. "I thought you were over your whole anti-Jeff thing."

"Let's just say," I say, "that he needs to put his brain to work in a more focused way."

"What's that supposed to mean?"

"Yes," I say, ignoring his question. "This shot will answer that question: Should Lester boycott AP Hum?"

The shot looks iffy at first. Arcing miserably hoopward, it looks like it will do what I don't want it to do. But then, as if blown by a northerly bent on disruption, the ball bounces off the center of the backboard and drops through the net.

"That settles that. No more AP Hum for Les."

"Damn," says BF James.

"Better to reign in hell than serve in heaven," I quote. "Let's go make some sandwiches."

We go inside just as a drizzle begins its hopeless assault.

Keep your friends close, as Washburn says, *but your apathy even closer.*

It's a blustery Friday, with a three-day weekend coming up (Veterans Day). This is good: it's time I took a little time off from taking so much time off from AP Hum.

I hop the bus home, finding a seat about midway back, across from a sleepy underclassman, a spot where I can easily hide my seniority. We rumble all over the byways of central King's Island, depositing kids in the vicinity of their homes. My stop is almost the last, a circumstance which has given Freesia plenty of time to catch up. The Subaru is parked at the end of our drive-way, with both of the front doors open, as if it's a town car on a tarmac awaiting heads of state. Freesia is leaning against the hood, arms crossed.

"How long are you planning to avoid me?" she wants to know.

"I'm not avoiding you," I say. "I like the bus."

The bus—the bus I claim to like—rumbles off, leaving behind a cloud of murky soot and a jangling of the eardrums.

"Shut up. No you don't. Come on, get in. Let's go for a drive."

"Let's not," I say, heading for the porch.

"James told me about your boycott," she says, not following.

"Good," I say.

"Can you at least look at me, Lester?"

I look at her.

"What are you, five years old?"

"I wish," I say.

She sighs. "Call me when you're ready to stop being such a dumbass."

When she's mad, Freesia can slam doors with the best of them. The Subaru, on this occasion, must bear the forceful brunt of her fury.

SUSPENSION SUITS ME WELL—it is, after all, a condition I've been practicing for weeks.

Here is what happened. I was getting lunch with BF James. He secured his veggie burger, and I my corn dogs, and we began to make our way to our accustomed spot on the floor of the foyer. We were about to exit the lunchroom when Flynn Ross, Grace's wrestler-captain beau, strutted up, playing a character that he's seen more times on film than he may know. The smoke on his breath; the angry yellow of his eyes; a scraggly, days-old beard. But worst of all, the shirt: Ramones.

Something inspired him to characteristic action.

"What you got there, Jimmy James?"

Flynn grabbed the veggie burger off of BF James's tray and took a bite. And then a look of betrayed disgust set up camp on his face.

"What the fuh is that?" he said through the paste of soy protein, enriched wheat flour, pickles, and ketchup, then spit the half-chewed bite of sandwich onto BF James's tray. "You a vegetarian or something?"

Off he stormed, aghast that the world had done this omnivorous thing to him. BF James was remarkably serene. In fact, he looked almost amused. But I was not.

"Hey!" I yelled.

Flynn turned around. "Hey what?"

"You can't do that."

He got closer. "Hey, you're the dipshit brother, aren't—"

My entire tray went flying at his face—and at that shirt he had no business wearing. He had to raise his arms to block the projectiles. And then he was on top of me, raining blows with a force matched only by their imprecision, until Washburn came over to remove the assailant.

So here I am, suspended in suspension (for "fighting")—and out, no doubt, of the Proctor's keenest and most kindred inner circle—walking down the shoulder of the cold and listless highway. But what is this? It appears that I am not the only one who's not at school, as Grace and a friend scurry out of the bushes and onto the shoulder up ahead. I break into a jog to catch up.

"Hey there. Doing a little amateur forestry?"

"Get lost, Les." Head down, picking up speed. Backpack sagging behind, smothered in coded graffiti. A scent of cigarettes on the air.

"Nice to see you too."

"Go away." Crossing the street, leaving us behind, and picking up more speed.

The friend, a short, plump girl with purple pigtails and a nose ring, is more affable: "She's just being weird."

"That's fine," I say, falling into step with her. "We Smiths are experts at the arts of avoidance." Grace has not turned back. "So I guess you guys decided you've learned all there is to learn?"

"Well you're not exactly in class either, are you?" counters Grace's friend.

"Touché."

"I heard about what happened," she says.

"Something happened?"

"With Flynn."

"Oh yes," I say. "A dustup in the lunchroom."

"He won't talk to us about it. Says it was dumb."

"Sounds about right."

"I bet he regrets it," she says.

"Maybe he does." And maybe he doesn't.

"He isn't really like that, you know?"

"Like what?"

"He's different," she insists. "He isn't what everyone says he is."

The Father used to say that the external perception of a man is a refraction of other external perceptions, such that a person's core identity becomes unknowable to anyone other than himself. Pancake, for his part, says that you can't cut a piece of wood that you don't have. We are all, in a sense, searching for the appropriate metaphor. I almost say this to her. Instead I say, "you may be right."

Grace is well ahead of us by now, freight-training northward toward nowhere in particular.

"What's the deal with him and Grace?" I ask.

"I don't know," says Grace's friend. "They're hanging out. He's good for her."

Or maybe not.

"If you say so," I say. "I just need him to stop wearing that shirt."

"Which one?"

"Ramones. You know the one."

"Oh yeah, he just got that. Aren't they cool?"

"No," I chide her.

"They aren't?"

"No, they are. But no, you don't get to say that. And no, he doesn't get to wear that shirt. Because no, you don't know what you're talking about. And no, neither does he."

"Oh yeah," she says. "Grace said you're weird about them."

"She did?" This counts as a minor revelation: that Grace has even thought, let alone said, anything about her rooting aardvark of a brother.

"Yeah, she said you're always listening to them."

"That is correct."

"She hates the Ramones."

One record: one record is all you need. And all you have to do is spin and spin and spin it, and then flip to spin again. You let it spin, then flip it over, then let it spin and spin and spin again.

"Denise, are you coming?" shouts our Grace from up ahead.

"I'll be right there," I shout back.

She shares what I choose to interpret as an affectionate gesture and then turns to keep walking. I stop to allow Denise to catch up to her, without also threatening to catch up myself.

She gets to Grace just as Flynn's Brat pulls up, speakers blasting. I watch from a distance as they pull away.

As PART OF MY plea deal with the Proctor after my little lunch-room joust with Flynn, I agreed to return to AP Humanities. But the Proctor didn't say anything about Yearbook. I have slid deftly through this loophole and transferred Boycott Ops to Fifth Period. But I have returned, in body at least, to AP Hum. During my absence, Freesia emigrated to another desk at the far side of the room. (This should make it easy to maintain the gulf of silence that has opened up between us.)

For our latest assignment, Jeff has asked us to compose a letter to ourselves from the future. My contribution to this burgeoning field of American Letters will require the assistance of BF James.

By the time that we get back to his place, the afternoon is not long for this world, and a light rain has quietly announced itself, the kind that speckles everything while failing utterly to drench. He sets up camp on his half-wall with his Game Boy, and I make for the ball, which is lying against the teetering wooden fence that divides the court from Neighbor Karl's yard.

"I need your help with something," I say.

I'm dribbling contemplatively, you might say, cautiously bouncing the ball, not trying to do too much with it.

"Do tell," says BF James.

"I need your lightning fingertips."

I hurl the ball at the hoop. It clanks off the rim and goes dlubbing into Neighbor Karl's yard.

"For what?" he wants to know.

"You'll see. But first, let's go inside and consult Wichie."

Wichie is a small miracle of technical apparatus, a little electric sandwich maker that someone in the Taylor family—probably James Sr.—picked up at a second-hand store—probably Grampa's Basement—at some recent point in time. It has brought about a revolution in the way that BF James and I approach our post-school snack. In its little clamping, cheese-melting jaws lie a range of experimental possibilities: of bread, of meat, of cheese, of spread. We've been known to go through entire loaves of bread in single afternoons. No week goes by without multiple forays into the realm of Advanced Sandwichmaking (a Pancake elective in the making, if there ever was one).

Wichie has been well loved in its short years upon this earth. Its olive-yellow paint is faded and chipping. It's teeming with scratches, and there's a significant dent in the northwest quadrant of its lid. Today's projects—a Havarti and ham, a brie and tomato, a blackberry jam and sunflower seed—are to be followed by another kind of project.

"Okay," I say, wiping the last little bit of jam from my thumb, "are you ready to take some serious dictation?"

"Step into my office," says BF James, cracking his knuckles, and rising to his feet.

This is a score: BF James, an avid player of games on his vintage IIc, and author of various other adventures in the realm of personal computing, has the fastest typing fingers, I would wager, on our fair peninsula.

We head up to the Command Center, where James the Elder keeps his array of computers old and new. But we're not there for those. It's the Smith Corona we're after.

"Load a sheet," I say.

"It's already loaded."

"Of course it is. Set the margins to Wide."

He sets the margins to Wide, and then we kick into gear, with Lester dictating—and pacing back and forth across the room, and gazing out at the maples blocking the view—and BF James giving a virtuoso performance on the typewriter. The final text reads thus:

Dear Lester: A Letter to Lester from Lester

Dear Lester:

   Welcome to the future! Actually, hold on a sec. I need to turn off my magbodon. What's a magbodon? You couldn't possibly understand. Why couldn't you possibly understand? Because you don't exist here. (I don't either!) Have you ever wondered what it would be like to have a time machine? Me neither. Why do you wear that crappy sweatshirt all the time? Here on Planet Forgbedorby, we don't wear sweatshirts. All we wear are plakes. And we don't eat your crappy burgers and your soggy lunchroom french fries. We eat shpoodledawb and dynx. We still say "crappy" though. We like that word. Here's the interesting thing about the future: future blootcher dootcher zootcher lootcher. And oh yeah, John Baldessari is our overlord. But his name is Baldessari-Mussolini. He's half Baldessari and half Mussolini. The trains all run on time, and the art is never boring. And sometimes we decide to start a world war with the Nazis. (The Nazis haven't gone away -- sorry about that.) We kill lots of people and then we marvel about how great it is to have such great art about all the people we killed. Oh, and also, we play Exquisite Corpse like all the time. But with real corpses.

New paragraph. Anyway, I should probably be going. I need to put a new crabbadabba on my flizzlenoinkeldurmp. And you, my friend -- Lester of November, 1996 -- you need to focus on doing all that nothing. You're good at that. It suits you. Keep it up, kid. You're going nowhere, fast. And sometimes nowhere's where it's at, you know what I mean? (Of course you don't. You've never seen a bazzerary pling!)

Yours Sincerely,

Lester

BF James scrolls out this second page and lays it on the first, then slides them both to me and slips into BF Serious.

"What *are* you going to do?" he asks.

(Et tu, BF James?!)

I shrug. "To tell the truth," I say, "I haven't given it a whole lot of thought."

"You know what that smells like?" he says, sniffing the air theatrically. "That right there smells like some bullshit. You think too much about *everything*. No way you haven't thought about next year."

I'm not saying he's *right*, exactly, but he's actually pretty right. "I already told you, I—"

Up goes a hand. "No," he says. "No more Milton."

Stonewalled. "What about you?" I say. "You got it all figured out or something?"

He leans back in his father's office chair, hands meeting at the back of his head, smiling that big-ass smile that he smiles. BF Serious has exited stage left. This is BF Cheshire, here to drive us all insane until we make him play the ace up his sleeve.

"Do I need to say the secret word or something?"

He opens a drawer and takes out a thick booklet. On the cover it says, *The Evergreen State College*. He slides it to me.

"Evergreen?" I say.

"That's what it says," he says.

"You're going to Evergreen?" I flip idly through the pages of engaging photos: students under trees on campus; students on the steps of the buildings on campus; bodies of water that may or may not flow through the campus.

"Hell yeah I'm going to Evergreen," he says. "You can create your own major! I'm going to study A.I. and gaming. Deep Blue, baby!"

"Did you already get in?"

He shrugs. "I will."

Evergreen. He's going to Evergreen. He's going to create his own major. He's going to major in A.I. and gaming. At Evergreen.

I set the booklet down beside my letter from Lester to Lester. The letter is short and stale and lifeless in comparison. I snatch it up and fold the pages—hastily, unevenly—and stuff them into the pocket of my sweatshirt.

"Hey," I say, "Easy Street is having a sale this Saturday. What do you say?"

"That's it?" he says.

"That's what?"

"Like three sentences about your plans and you're done?"

What are your plans? What are you going to do? What are you planning to be going to do?

"Let's not wear the topic out."

"You should come with me," he says. "To Evergreen."

"I should?" I say.

"Yeah," he says. "You could major in Milton and the Ramones."

I crack half a smile, then send in a scowl SWAT team to suppress it. "I'll take it under advisement."

"Whatever," he says.

"So what do you say—Easy Street on Saturday?"

"Sounds dope," he says, "but no can do. I'm going to Tolo."

"Really?"

"Really," he says, leaning back in the chair.

"Who's the lucky lady?"

He crosses his arms, then grins that Cheshire grin. "I think you know."

"She asked *you*?"

"That's how it works."

"Huh. Tolo."

"You're jealous."

"Uh—no."

"Yes you are."

Maybe just a little.

"So, are you going to buy a suit or something?"

"Nope," he says. "I'm borrowing my dad's. You want to see it?"

Maybe more than a little.

"She's doing this to get back at me," I say.

"Say what?"

"She's still mad. She thinks this will make me jealous."

"Which you are. And no, that isn't why she asked. She asked

because she wants a fly-ass gentleman escort." He dusts his sleeves for emphasis.

There are so many things I want to ask: are they going out to dinner beforehand? Is she buying a dress? Has he secured a corsage? But I just nod and extend my hand. "Thank you for your time."

He follows me to the front door. The rain is coming harder now.

"Don't be mad at me," says BF James from the doorway, by way of farewell. "You had your chance."

IT'S A STORMY SATURDAY evening, with persistent gusts of wind and diagonal rain. This is no night for walking. Still, I'm walking. I start by heading for the beach. There's almost no one on the road. By the time I get there, my hair is wet and my sweatshirt is damp and heavy. No one is down there. Not a soul. And there aren't any boats on the water. The tide is high, and the surf choppy. The winds are lashing against the trees and the rocks and my insufficient sweatshirt. And Freesia's voice is whirling in the wind. *You're going to feel different when everyone leaves.*

It's another 27 minutes to town, a cold and windy 27 minutes. Melky's is empty. A song from the '80s—coming from the radio in the kitchen, not the jukebox—is banging against the walls. I order some fries and sit in our booth by myself. But I don't last long. The fries are bad tonight—they've probably been sitting for hours—and the place is too quiet, too vast, too tinnily eighties. I head back outside, straight into the heart of the rain. *You're going to feel different when everyone leaves.*

By the time I get to campus, my sweatshirt is soaked through. My hair is plastered to my forehead. The dull echoings of "Jump Around" come thudding from the gym. Some fairly well-dressed kids are trickling into the entrance. Some of them have flowers pinned to their clothing. Boys are holding umbrellas for girls. Girls are ducking under them, holding their purses and clutches out of the rain. From the high windows just below the eaves of the building you can see the flashing of blue and red and green and yellow lights. I stop to observe, then go around to the back, where a circle of smokers are huddled up against the wall. I recognize one of them from earlier in the week—Denise, I think she's called. She recognizes me as well.

"Hey, you're Grace's brother."

"Where's she tonight?"

She shrugs. "Who knows. Probably at Flynn's. What are you doing here?"

"Just out for an evening stroll," I say. My back is against the bricks of the gym. Just in front of me, in the dim amber light of a lamp-post, a steady stream of raindrops is dripping from the roof into a puddle in the gravel.

"Do you want to go in?" she asks. It's almost a dare, the way she says this. As in: I dare you to go in there, where the lights are flashing and the music is terrible. As in: I dare you, Lester Smith, a senior, to go in there with me, Denise Something, a freshman, and a friend of your sister.

"No thanks."

"Yeah. Right. I bet it's pretty lame."

I start to walk away, then stop and turn back. "On second thought," I say. "I'm freezing." (This is true: my teeth are chattering.) "I bet it's warm in there. Come on. I'll buy."

Tina McTovey is taking tickets, it turns out. "Hi Lester." Her hair, tonight—in honor of the occasion, one can only presume—is up in a bun, and not pinned back. It's a good look for her.

"No date?" I try to say this in a way that sounds incredulous. She shakes her head. "I find that hard to believe," I add.

She smiles slightly, looks into the cash drawer. "Maybe next time," she tells the stacks of five-dollar bills.

"Are there any tickets left?" I ask her.

"Yes," she says. She's looking me up and down. "They're five dollars."

I hand her two well-worn five-dollar bills, drawn from the pouch of my sweatshirt.

"Is that what you're wearing?" she asks, smoothing the bills on the side of the cash-box before clamping them down in their slot.

"Indeed it is. Is that a problem?"

She shrugs. "It's not what I would wear."

"I bet not."

On we advance, past Tina and her ticket-taking table and into the building. Proctor Relaford is guarding the threshold of the dance, decked out in a blue blazer and pressed khakis. His tie tonight is striped. He smiles at us as we go in. "Mr. Smith. Welcome." He seems prepared to let bygones be bygones (or has had enough sherry to feel chummy with all comers?).

"Proctor," I say, with a bit of a bow, then escort Denise into the strobe-lit gym.

The gym is full of kids I know and do not know, most of them standing against the wall. Toward the far wall, under the basketball hoop, a DJ has set up his implements. Hooded sweatshirt. Headphones around his neck.

We set up camp just inside the door. Denise's arms are crossed. My hands are starting to defrost. I scan the flashing faces that surround us. A group of underclassmen—all boys, and possibly dateless?—is trying out some break dancing moves in a corner. Down the court from them, Ms. Flough is working the punch table, chatting with Ms. Ortega. In the far corner of the room, against the wall of folded-up bleachers, I see BF James. He does indeed look sharp in his dad's old leisure suit. He's laughing, bent slightly forward. He's just created another new major, a major he'll pursue at Evergreen State College. Next to him is Freesia, in an elegant, ankle-length gown. She is laughing too. Her hand on his shoulder.

"Come on," says Denise, seizing my hand, and starting to shake into the rhythms of C+C Music Factory. "Let's dance!"

"No thanks," I say, retracting my hand. "I'm going to go."

"What? Already?" She puts on a dramatic frown. "Come on. Just for a minute."

"Sorry, no can do," I mumble, drowned out by the music, shuffling backwards toward the door. *You're going to feel different when everyone leaves.*

I've gotten warm enough in there to last me the first of the three stretches of the walk home. The second stretch I get through by blowing on my hands and making up majors. For the third my head is just down, and the rain is very hard, and my feet are wet, and my sweatshirt and T-shirt are wet and cold. The house seems forever away, but it does, at last, come into sight, dark against the darker dark of night.

THE THIRD MONDAY in November: you know what that means (or you find out, as some of us do, when you get off the bus in the morning). The start of the Issues Initiative. Signs have sprung up all over the school, like mushrooms after rain. Certain members of the student body are holding them up as we head to the building, instructing us not to go into our classrooms, but into the lunchroom. There we find glorious Gloria Flough, standing at a makeshift dais. She almost manages to wait until the crowd is quiet before she starts to speak.

"Good morning everyone, and welcome to the Issues Initiative!" (Apparently, this is what she was talking about at that assembly, back in September.) "I can't tell you how excited I am about this," she insists. A few distinguished pupils are even looking in her direction.

She goes on to explain the exciting parameters of this exciting endeavor. We, as a school community, are to engage in a series of "student-inclusive" discussions regarding the fiscal priorities of the school. It is, according to Ms. Flough, there on her dais, the first time in District History that the student body will have a direct say in where the money goes. "Therefore"—she inserts— "today we're beginning the initial round of Town Hall Meetings. So come up here to find your groups. I have them on these flip charts."

We flock to the flip charts and find our groups—twenty groups of roughly twenty-five students each, a motley mix of pupils from all four classes, herded together according to some obscure alphabetical logic. Group Tiger, my group, is to meet in a science classroom, a room which normally belongs to Mr. Sundquist, but which will be attended today by—you guessed it—Jeff Traversal.

The science building is a square brick edifice—i.e., *not* a polygon—way off in the corner of the campus. I make my way out there along with a smattering of my peers, through a smattering of rain, across smatterings of rocks and little sticks on the pavement. Upon arrival, I see that Jeff has made himself at home. He's got one of Mr. Sundquist's skulls in one hand. In the other there's an empty mason jar with a soppy, floppy teabag at the bottom.

The room smells vaguely of ammonia and reptiles. My peers and I find seats at the rows of tables and sit in them. Some of the faces I recognize; most I do not.

"Hi," says Jeff, returning the skull to the desk at the front of the room. "How's it going?"

Silence.

"So," he continues, "we're here to talk about some stuff. And what that stuff is can really be up to you. So what do you guys want to talk about?"

Silence Number 2.

"Don't all chime in at once," he says, with a nervous flutter of a laugh.

"Isn't this kind of dumb?" says a young man wearing a Portland Trailblazers hat and a Seattle SuperSonics jersey (a sophomore, if I'm not mistaken, with a name that starts with S).

Jeff writes that phrase, verbatim, on the whiteboard, in his infamous script: *Isn't this kind of dumb?*

"Well, what do the rest of you think?" he asks. "Raise your hand if you think this is kind of dumb."

Several hands go up.

"Now, raise your hand if you don't think it's dumb."

Several other hands go up, one of them belonging to blessed, purposeful Tina McTovey. She's back in Business Mode: her hair pulled back and clipped with a big brown clip.

"All right, good," says Jeff, with visible relief. "Tina, let's hear the other side. What makes this—what should we call it?—this *activity*, what makes it not dumb? Why are we doing this? What's good about it?"

"Well," says Tina, "I think it's really important. I mean, it's our chance to talk about the issues that matter to us."

"Okay. Great. So what are those issues?"

Silence Number 3.

"Seriously," says Jeff, leaning on the desk. "No judgment here. What's important to you guys? What kind of changes would you like to see at the school?"

After another long pause, the hand of a young man in a bright green shirt goes up (his face is unfamiliar, but I bet he'll look back on that shirt with fondness someday).

"Yes?" says Jeff.

"Pop," says the kid in the bright green shirt.

"Pop?"

"Yeah, pop. I think we should get pop with school lunch."

"Great," says Jeff, writing the word *Pop* on the board. "Pop."

"And not just in the machines," clarifies the kid in the bright green shirt.

This, it seems, has broken the ice. A few more hands go up, and a few more things are written on the board. Then more hands go up, and more things are written on the board. And then the raising of hands is abandoned, and we start shouting things pell-mell, and all the while Jeff is scurrying back and forth from one side of the whiteboard to the other, doing his best to faithfully transcribe the words that we are shouting. This manic brainstorm continues until, after close to half an hour of nonstop shouting and transcribing, the board is a mess of words and phrases—a kind of Rosetta Stone, you might say, whose code holds the key to every little wish contained within the walls of

Victory Memorial. It's pretty impressive, really—and even legible, for the most part. Here, for the record, is what's been recorded:

Pop
Trees
Longer break
Student input on readings
Fencing
Karate
Judo
Tae Kwon Do
Embroidery
Blacksmithing (shields & such)
Crowd amulets
More Tolos
Fresh fruit
All you can eat French fries
A herd of cattle
A herd of sheep
A herd of wild dogs
Limo service (one student/day, selected by lottery)
A helicopter pad (helipad)
Bigger desks
More course readers
Cockfighting
A campaign to end cockfighting
A berry patch
A giant tower
Anarchy day
Slip 'n slides
More mashed potatoes
Dungeness crab
A school boat (fishing class)
No more killing bugs for bio
Twizzlers
Sizzler

Skittles
Sour Patch Kids
Watermelons
A raffle for a car
Smashing up a car (for charity)
Dreamsharing
Creamsicles
Camaros
A class on gas engines
A class on guns
A class on peace
A class on how to read the Bible
Porn

"Great," says Jeff, examining the list from his seat atop the desk. "That was fun!"

(It was—it actually was.)

"Here's what I'm going to do," he says, rubbing his hands together in the way that he does. "I'm going to type up this list and submit it to the proper authorities. Then we'll see what happens next. Hopefully something cool, right?"

(Don't get your hopes up, little Jeffy T.)

"So for now you can go, I guess." He says this looking at the board, as if trying to figure out whether he should find a way to bring a typing apparatus out here, to the science building, or find a way to bring those whiteboards somewhere where there's already a typing apparatus.

As my colleagues file out, Jeff is approached by Cam Drinker, Jr. Cam has something to get off his chest. Any time that this squat, blond pillar of silence decides to speak, I take notice. I ease my way over to a spot by the wall where I can hear what Cam says while pretending to be looking at euthanized insects.

"Hi Cam," says Jeff. "What's up?"

"Well," says Cam. He's clenching his fists, starting to rock a little bit from foot to foot. "It's for Yearbook."

"Okay."

"I had this idea." Cracking the knuckles on both hands, one by one, with his index fingers.

"Oh yeah? What's the idea?"

"Metal covers."

My glance veers from the dead bugs to Cam. "Metal covers?"

He turns to me. "Yeah."

"Like Dokken?" says Jeff.

"Huh?" says Cam.

"What do you mean by 'metal covers'?" Jeff wants to know.

"Well, it could be kind of cool," says Cam, clenching his fists again as he explains. "It could be kind of cool if like, the year-book was made out of metal. You know?"

"A metal yearbook?" says Jeff.

"Yeah. All made out of metal. For the Issue Initiative."

A metal yearbook? It's hard to picture—even harder to endorse.

"Like the Madonna book," elaborates Cam. "I saw that once. And metal lasts a long time."

This, it seems, is all that Cam has been waiting to say. For his part, Jeff seems unsure what it will take to get Cam to release himself from his self-induced paralysis. Then he picks up a marker, finds an unmarred sliver of whiteboard, and scrawls out *Metal Covers*.

"Cool," says Cam. "Maybe they'll include that."

Maybe not, young Cam.

His fists are still clenched as he makes his way out of the room.

BY THE FOLLOWING WEEK, the Issues Initiative is a distant dream of issue initiation, and we can return to business as usual—or almost usual, I should say (my boycott of Yearbook now going into its second week).

"Hey everyone!" exclaims Jeff, gliding into the week's last session of AP Humanities. "I've got some good news," he says, plapping his satchel on the collapsible table. "I read your letters from the future. And let me tell you, they are *terrific*. Seriously. Really good stuff. So"—he continues, gliding now from desk to desk to distribute the letters we wrote to ourselves from the place where we're not—"I'd like to spend at least the first part of class reading some of them out loud. Any volunteers?"

Mine is the last letter to arrive on the desk of its author-recipient. He places it face down, but the ink on the last page has bled through legibly enough: a purple F, encircled by a purple circle. I crack open *Paradise Lo* as a girl named Lucy Lin—a junior, and a potential challenger in Tina McTovey's quest for Class of '98 valedictorian—raises her hand. In a strong, assertive voice, she begins her epistle, an account of her journey from the hallowed halls of Victory Memorial to the hallowed halls of Stanford University, and from those hallowed halls to halls more hallowed still. It unfolds in bold, quick strokes, and I have to concede that it's a strong piece, clear in its intentions, occasionally vivid in its imagery. It ends with a question—which is bold in itself—a question that seems to get the others in a sharing mood. Tina reads from her letter—a tale of listening to Willie Nelson aboard the decks of a cruise ship in the Indian Ocean, amazingly enough— and then several others read from theirs. For the most part, they make up in earnestness what they're lacking in imagery and grammar. Then it's Freesia's turn. She's in her new seat, at the far side of the room. We still haven't spoken in an increasingly disarming number of days. I'm shielded by *Paradise Lo*, but I am listening intently. Hers is a dreamlike stream-of-consciousness narrative of the time that has passed as told through the eyes of a dog she'll own someday. The dog's name is Lemon (Lemon?). He's kind of a sad dog, in some ways, but he's friendly and wise, and he's a hell of a writer. The piece is a tour-de-force. Freesia has outdone herself. I'm still considering its closing image, in which an airplane passing overhead turns out to be a butterfly, when Jeff does something rather unexpected. From the inside pocket of his velvety brown blazer, he pulls out a sheet of notebook paper, folded into eighths. The sheet is worn and old and he must unfold it carefully so as not to rupture it along its fold-lines.

"All right," he says. "My turn. This," he says, holding up the sheet for all to see, "is a letter I wrote to myself when I was your age."

He clears his throat and starts to read. "Hello," the letter begins, "and welcome to your life!" This meets with nervous laughter, which seems to spur Jeff on. The letter goes into all the things he did (or was going to have done). He went to college (Carleton, in Minnesota), then traveled the world (Petra first, then the Andes, then the Dardanelles). He learned ten languages. And then he came back to King's Island. But only to give a speech at graduation. He didn't come back to live—not in the version of his life imagined in the letter. And not to teach at Vehemence. And certainly not, one can only presume, to read this letter to a roomful of dazed, uncertain kids.

When he finishes reading it, he looks around the room. "Now," he says. "Why did I read that? And why did I have you write yours? I'll answer the first question first." (Jeff is a fan of the Socratic method—but tends to forget to let his students answer the questions he asks.) "I read mine," he continues, "to show you that—well, to show you that you just don't know, I guess."

He looks like he wants to say more, but he doesn't—not in response to Question #1, anyway. And if he planned to answer Question #2—i.e., why he had *us* write *ours*—his plans have changed. Instead his eyes alight on me—almost, I might wager, by design.

"Lester," he says, "would you like to read from yours?"

"I—" I say. "I don't think so. Not today."

"Come on, Les," says Tina. "I read mine. Freesia read hers."

I steal a glance at Freesia, then return to the safety of *Paradise Lo*. "Maybe next time."

The ensuing silence is cut short by the dlonging of our merciful friend the bell.

"All right, then," Jeff proclaims. "Great stuff today, you guys. See you tomorrow."

I make a beeline for the door. Jeff blocks my way. "Lester, can I talk to you?"

(Why am I always the one who gets detained for further questioning?)

He waits until my peers have left before launching his assault. "Listen, Tommy Ramone. I called your bluff today."

"I noticed," I say.

"This crap that you turned in? It's offensive. I gave it an F."

His eyes are pretty fierce when he wants them to be.

"I noticed that too."

"Is this because I gave you a B on your defense?"

"You mean B slash B minus?"

"You know why this is so shitty?" he says, pointing at my F of a two-pager.

"Because it makes light of terror?" I offer.

"Yes, that's the obvious part. But there's also the lack of engagement. Listen, Lester, there's a reason you like Milton. There's a reason you've even *heard* of Milton. And that's because he *engaged*. He had real courage. He took on a lot more than rhymed poetry."

He pauses to let this sink in.

"At this rate, Lester, you aren't going to graduate. Is that what you want?"

"No," I say.

"Good. I'm going to give you a do-over, okay? I want you to write me an essay in response to one of these." He takes two books from his desktop and holds them out to me. "Pound and Stevens."

I eye the proffered books.

"I'm not trying to get you to agree with me, or love my class, okay? Hell, you don't even have to *like* it. But you do have to *engage* with it. You can't just reject it out of hand. Read these, do a re-write, and I'll call it even. Deal?"

"Okay," I say, taking the books.

"You'll like Pound," he deadpans. "He was a Fascist."

THE WALK FROM SCHOOL to Freesia's house is under-appreciated. You pass through almost all of the known kinds of King's Island landscape: pasture, forest, lumber yard. You go down one big hill, then up another, and then the rest is flat flat flat. There's a field with an old airplane in it, gathering mildew. There's a pond that plays host to some ducks in the summer. And then you take a left on Crescent Lane, and then you're there.

The Clinton/Gore sign has been plucked from the yard, but otherwise things look the same at the Price residence. It's a house that manages to hang on to its class even through the dreariest parts of the winter.

David Price opens the door, bedecked in his apron. Something delicious is being prepared.

"Lester! Good to see you. It's been a while."

"It has, David. Good to see you too."

"Come on in."

I enter the entryway.

"Can I get you something to drink?"

"No thanks," I say. "Is Freesia here?"

"Upstairs."

I go upstairs and knock on her door. She answers with a cold stare.

"What are you doing here?"

"I don't know. I thought you might want to go to a beach or something."

"I have homework."

I stand there. She stands there.

"Come on," I say. "You can pick the place."

She looks over her shoulder—as if to check that her homework will be safe where she left it—then back at me.

"Brogdon," she announces, soberly.

"Perfect."

I sit quietly as she zooms broodingly across the peninsula toward Brogdon Beach. Brogdon is one of many beaches on our circuit—one that we readily admit should be visited more often.

As beaches go, it is extraordinarily generous of log: somehow the currents of the southwest Sound are such that many of the errant logs of the region end up there. You can walk from one end of the beach to the other without touching anything other than driftwood. Grace and I, as young children, would ride our bikes there to do just that. Or, on rare occasion, The Father would drive us in his Gremlin, in which he would sit, reading a paperback, as we scampered among the logs. Now we go there not to traipse but to sit and contemplate the currents and the forests and, beyond and slightly to the north, the tips of the Olympics.

The day is cold and cloudy, but it hasn't rained. We settle on a lunker of a log near the point. I've got a pile of sticks at my feet, and begin to throw them, one by one, at larger nearby sticks. Freesia is picking something out of her shoe.

"How was Tolo?"

"Fun," she says.

"I was there," I say.

"I know."

"I didn't last very long."

"I know."

A bar of darker clouds seems to be coming our way. The wind carries the rich smells of rotting shore-plants.

"Your letter to yourself was really good," I say.

She scoops her hair away from her face. "Do you really think so?"

"Yes," I say, "I really do. Also," I say. "You know, about—well."

I jettison one stick for another, one with a compelling five-point prong.

"It's not that hard, Lester."

"What's not that hard?"

"Just say you're sorry."

Even in this, it seems, she's a step ahead of me. "I'm sorry."

"Apology acknowledged," she says, looking out at the water. "We'll see about acceptance."

A light rain starts falling, swept toward us by the wind off the water.

"What was yours about?" she asks. "Your letter from the future."

"I didn't do one."

She has this way of looking *into* me that is at once highly distressing (to the Lester involved) and highly effective (to the Freesia), this way of ferreting out even the whitest of lies.

"I saw it on your desk. Come on, what did you write?"

"I'd rather not say."

"You piss me off." She throws a rock high into the air and watches as it lodges in the sand mid-way through my next sentence.

"Because I won't tell you what I wrote about?"

"No, because you did something stupid—again. And because—"

She shakes her head, drops the stick she's holding on the pile of sticks under her feet, and starts to walk off down the beach. I watch her, then get up and break into a jog, and even then I only barely catch her at the door of the Subaru, which sits alone in the small gravel lot, its windshield dotted with raindrops.

I stand between her and the door, and take her gently by the shoulders. "I'm sorry."

Her cheeks are bright red. Her hair is stringy with raindrops, some of it plastered to her forehead. It is strange to me that I am only just now noticing the very faint freckles that dapple the bridge of her nose.

"I put a lot into that defense, Lester. And you did too. I actually started to *like* Milton. And then you just—" She shakes her head. "I don't know. I just thought—"

"I'm sorry, Freesia." There's a pause, and the rain starts getting heavier. "Come on, let's get out of this rain."

We sit in the car in silence for a minute or two, watching the rain patter down on the windshield.

"Why did you change your mind?" she says.

"I don't know. It doesn't matter."

"It matters to me."

"I just—I don't know. My heart wasn't in it."

"What *is* your heart in?"

I stare at the rain sliding down the windshield. The sky beyond is a blur of gray.

"I don't know," I say.

"Les," she says, "I know it's been hard, but you need to talk about it."

Maybe she's right. But what would I say?

Mercifully, she lets it go, and seizes on the chance to take the upper hand. "You owe me now," she says, staring into that watery sky.

"I do?"

Resistance is futile—this much I already know.

"Yes."

In certain instances—in most instances, in fact, it occurs to me—there is little you can do to refute Freesia once she has made a proclamation such as this. She knows that she's in the right, and that you're in the wrong, and she also knows that you know that she's in the right, and that you're in the wrong.

"Okay. What do I owe you?"

"You're coming back to Yearbook."

"No," I say. "Not possible. I'm working on some greaves." (I've spent most of the fifth periods of the Boycott Era in the wood shop.)

"Bullshit. Woodcraft will have to wait. You're coming back. Effective next tri."

"Is that right?"

"Yeah. James will be there too."

She's been doing some recruiting.

"I have terms," I say.

"No," says Freesia.

"No?"

"This time I'm the one with terms."

What little ground I had to stand on has crumbled away. I regard her silently, awaiting her terms.

"First, no more Ramones."

"Not even *Festspielkonzertmusik*?"

"*Especially* not that."

I nod in defeat. "Okay. What else?"

"No more of your usual bullcrap."

"Do I dare ask you to explain what you mean by that?"

"I mean that if you don't have anything constructive to say, then keep it to yourself."

I nod in silent assent. "Is that all?"

"No," she says. Now her eyes are lighting up. "One more thing. I want Zdenik's bag."

She smiles. I smile. She's back. I'm back. We're back.

I think.

THANKSGIVING AT THE SMITHS': never a scene of warmth and mirth, but this year it is even worse. We go through the motions, as we always do. My mother makes the turkey and the gravy. I mash the potatoes. Grace squeezes the log of gelatinous, can-riven cranberry sauce into a too-big plastic mixing bowl. All that's missing is The Father's conspicuous absence. (His absence is much less conspicuous now that he's actually gone; when he wasn't really absent, and merely holed up in his study or his separate bedroom, reading or doing nothing at all, you *felt* that he wasn't a part of the business of the house. His absence was a presence in the room.)

We put everything out on the table and sit to the usual, reliable mealtime silence. The dim lamp. The gravy.

"The gravy is delicious," I say.

"Thank you, Lester."

No input from Grace.

We clean our plates and scrape the bones into the trash, and then retreat to our quarters: my mother to the living room to knit and watch the end of the football game; Grace to her room to do the things she does in there in silence; and I to mine. After finding an inoffensive place to stow Jeff's Pound and Stevens, I wander down the hall to Grace's room on a whim. The cord of the phone is taut under the door. I knock. No answer. I knock again, then push the door open and go in.

This is the first time I've been in her room in a long time. It is a space whose autonomy I try, perhaps too successfully, to respect. There are clothes littered all over the floor. Her Hello Kitty slippers—the ones she was wearing on that cold March morning, the morning she discovered the postcard of the fluffy orange kitten—are lined up neatly at the base of her dresser. Her purple lava lamp (a carnival victory from a previous summer) bubbles lazily on her night stand. The phone is on her bed, its cord weighed down by the large volume of Epictetus that The Father gave her for her seventh birthday.

Her window, I discover upon further inspection, has been left cracked for easy return.

I sit on her bed, in the purple dusk of the lava lamp, trying to conjure a memory which that space evokes—a pillow fight or a game of hide-and-seek, a confidential brother-sister conversation—but nothing comes to mind.

When I go back out to the hallway, I almost ask my mother if she saw Grace leave. But the sight of her, so calm there, so content, in her way, to be knitting in the lamplight of a largely nonconfrontational Thanksgiving, answers the question before it is asked. She didn't see Grace leave. She doesn't need to know that Grace is gone.

DECEMBER

*J*EFF PASSES OUT the copies of *Sir Gawain and the Green Knight*—most of them tattered, with peeling spines and pages aged to umber at the edges—and stands at the front of the room, looking blankly past us.

"There will be no course reader this trimester," he says, at last.

"What?" says Freesia. "Why?"

"Apparently," he says, "it's not in keeping with the values of the department."

"What is that supposed to mean?" She still isn't satisfied.

"The Humanities Council has voted it down."

"Wait a minute," says Tina. "I thought we were *on* the Humanities Council."

Good point, Tina: I don't recall having been called to quorum.

"I guess not," says Jeff.

"That's B.S.," says Freesia. "What about what *we* think?"

Jeff shrugs, then consults the top of the collapsible table, then the world map. Then decides he has something to say.

"Here's the deal," he sighs. "I love literature. I'm here because I love literature, and I love sharing it with you. But—how shall I put this? There's only so much you can do within 'proper channels.' It's probably best just to leave it at that. Anyhow," he says, collapsing onto the collapsible table, "turn to the Introduction. Let's read it out loud."

"The pages are falling out of mine," says a stray underclassman.

Jeff tosses him the tape dispenser. It falls short and clatters to the floor.

"Who wants to go first?"

So begins the next round of AP Humanities. In Yearbook things aren't much different.

"Welcome back," Jeff says to me as I enter the room. His tone is matter-of-fact. (I'm almost offended, I must admit, that he seems to be so little affected by my grand re-entry on the scene.) "To what do we owe the honor?"

I nod in Freesia's direction. "Not to worry," I assure him. "I'm contractually obligated to stop my—what did you call it, Freeze? My production of large mammal feces?"

A smirk from Jeff. A rolling of the eyes from Freesia.

Attrition has set in in a significant way. Most of our fellow yearbookers—most of the Pancake bloc, in particular—are gone. Either they decided that the endeavor wasn't worth their time, or they've played enough Trivial Pursuit to last them the year. Left in that room are but four of us from the fall: Freesia, Tina, Cam Drinker, Jr.—he of "metal covers" fame, and the lone remaining member of the Pancake Bloc—and Yours Truly. But we've added one important member to our ranks, who will no doubt increase the parka and Game Boy quotient of the class.

"What's your name?" says Jeff, as BF James loafs in and slumps into his chair.

"James," says BF James. "James Taylor."

"James Taylor?"

"No relation."

A hint of a smile creases Jeff's expression. "James Taylor. Welcome."

BF James peers up skeptically at Jeff through his thick, black glasses-frames, then looks at me. Has Freesia led him astray?

"Okay then," Jeff exhales. "As you were, I guess."

And without further ado we have returned, somewhat morosely, to the nothing we've been doing all along.

In December on King's Island, light is truly at a premium. We arrive at school just as the darkness is lifting, and get out just as it's descending again. Somehow, sitting in cramped desks in the cramped confines of VMHS just doesn't seem like the right way to spend the little available daylight that we have. But what else would we do?

On this cold and dusky Monday afternoon, Fiona Apple serenades us through the soppy fields and stands of listless trees to Freesia's house. Hiram, having resigned himself to the drear of the season, it would seem, pokes a curious head out of his cedar-plank house but doesn't emerge to jump on or lick us.

David welcomes us with cheerful high-fives and we proceed to our outpost on Kitchen Island. Freesia pours herself some lemonade on ice. David pours himself a glass of cabernet, offering me the bottle in a "hey, look how progressively European I am" kind of gesture. I wave him off.

"Where's Marian?" I ask.

"She's running late," says David, swirling the wine around the glass. "She'll be here in a minute." He takes a sip, and seems to approve. "It's good to see you, Les. How's life as a senior treating you?"

"Milk and honey, David. Milk and honey."

"How's your sister doing?"

"I saw her in Flynn's car behind Maximus," says Freesia, chomping on a cucumber circle which she has plucked prematurely from the salad.

"What's Maximus?" says David.

Maximus Pizza is an establishment of less than sterling repute.

"You can't just ignore it," says Freesia.

"Ignore what?" says David.

"What else *can* I do?" I say. "Just go up to her and tell her to stop doing everything she already knows she shouldn't be doing but is doing anyway?"

"Nonsense," she says, now reaching for a carrot. "Hanging around with Flynn is not something she *has* to do."

"Why don't you invite her over for dinner some time?" David submits, donning oven mitts.

"No," I say. "No way."

"Why not?" says Freesia. "She could use a change of scenery."

"Think about it," says David, leaning down to open the oven. "Our door is always open."

Indeed it is: Marian opens the door just in time to join us at the dinner table. Tonight the fare is broiled portabellas stuffed with gorgonzola, accompanied by warm and pleasant conversation, followed by a digestif of fatherly enthusiasm from David. After dinner, he and I stand sentinel around the kitchen island while, in the living room, Marian settles into a recliner with the *New Yorker*. Freesia sits on the adjacent couch, her legs folded under her, getting a head start on next month's homework. She's entered Power Mode. Soft jazz plays in the background.

"I'm glad to hear you're back in action, Les," says David.

(Freesia has just recounted our recent encounters with Jeff.)

"We'll see," I say. "I'm not making any more promises."

"Freesia says this Traversal guy is the real deal."

"He's some kind of deal. But to be honest with you, David," I say, sifting through the bowl of nuts in search of a salted almond, "I think it's still a little TBD as to whether 'real' is the right word."

He pours himself a little more wine. "Tell me, Les. What are your plans for the future?"

"I don't know," I say. "I leave that kind of thing to Freesia."

"Where are you applying to college?"

"I haven't decided yet."

"You don't know where you're going to apply?"

"Not really. I'll figure it out over break, I guess."

"If you want to go to college," says Freesia, entering our sphere for a package of biscotti, with Power Mode on pause, "I'm pretty sure you have to finish high school first."

"Is that how it goes?"

A rolling of the eyes, by way of farewell, as she absconds with the biscotti.

"Listen Les," says David. "I'm not trying to put the screws to you, okay?"

"You're not the one putting the screws, David. Trust me."

He laughs. "I know there are lots of different ways to realize your potential."

"Is that so?"

"Yeah. I mean, we like to beat the drum about college, and that's the direction Freesia's going in, but it's not for everyone. I mean hell, I dropped out of college after three semesters! But Freesia *is* right about one thing."

"Just one?"

He laughs again. "You probably should finish high school."

MOST OF THE WEEK passes painlessly enough. We show up. Jeff shows up. We do nothing. Jeff does nothing. Everything is grand. At the end of the week, we get a reprieve from this demanding regimen of idleness, when the school day is cut short by the heavens.

We don't often get snow. And when snow does fall it usually doesn't stick. Everyone is suddenly ecstatic. Something is happening. This time, we all sense, the snow might stick.

Freesia and I hustle to the Subaru, driven by the driving snow. Now it *is* sticking, and sticking quickly. She eases slowly onto the highway, both hands on the wheel. As we round a bend, we're greeted by a figure staggering toward us through the blur of snowflakes. Freesia slows the Subaru to a crawl.

"What. Is. That?"

Whatever it is, it lurches itself into the road. Freesia slows, then stops. Now we can see what we're dealing with: our humble Jeff Traversal, shivering under a plastic-and-carpet floor mat which has been wrapped, in a manner of speaking, around his torso. He ditches the mat and opens the back door and slides in.

"Hi Jeff," says Freesia.

"Hey," says Jeff. "It's you guys. Thanks for stopping."

"What up?" I inquire, tipping my head toward the ceiling.

"What happened to you?" asks Freesia.

"My car went in the ditch," says Jeff. "There was a squirrel in the road."

He tells Freesia where he lives, and she continues cautiously into the jaws of the storm. He's a courteous passenger, keeping to himself, staring out the window at the snow coming down, trying to wring the blood back into his hands.

After a while I turn to address him.

"Nice jacket."

"I don't have a jacket."

"Hey, let me ask you something."

He appears to have stopped shivering, and full movement has returned to his fingers, which he's flexing repeatedly, just to be sure.

"Shoot."

"That letter you wrote to yourself. How much of that stuff did you actually end up doing?"

He laughs a sighing laugh. "Not much," he says, shaking his head. "Not much." He leans forward between our seats. "This is the driveway."

It's a long, straight thing that goes down a hill and then up another on the far side of a little valley. A wooden sign nailed to a fencepost reads "Hambecker Farm." On the far side of the valley, at the end of the driveway, a big brick block of a house watches over the fields and fences.

I turn back to him again. "Hambecker Farm?"

"That's my mother's maiden name," he explains. "You don't have to go all the way up to the house."

But Freesia's already driving down the hill, over the layer of snow on the driveway.

When we get up to the house, a gray-haired but hale-looking woman is outside hacking at stumps with an axe. *Chuck. Chuck. Chuck.*

"That your landlord?" I ask him.

"Yup. Also my mother."

"Huh." She hasn't stopped her chopping, not even for a moment, to see who's pulling up to the house.

"Thanks for the ride," says Jeff, the door half open. "And hey," he says, placing a hand on my shoulder.

"Yes?"

A gust of wind floats some errant snowflakes into the back seat. Jeff pokes his index finger into the thin veneer of snow on the glass, leaving a small circle of translucence. Whatever he meant to say, he doesn't say. "See you next week," he says instead, and heads into the house.

THE SNOW DID NOT last long. Within two days it melted to blotches of brownish slush along the roadways, and then seeped back into the ground. If you look closely you can still see a little patch of white here or there—under a tree, say, where there is day-long shadow—but your time is probably better spent on other things, things like shooting hoops at BF James's house.

The day is crappy, drizzly and dark, and the ball no better, shedding shreds of faded rubber. Our taciturn host is cleaning the screen of his Game Boy with a small blue cloth. Freesia sits brooding on the half-wall, arms hugged tight around her chest.

"You're quiet today," I say.

"I'm thinking," Freesia says.

"Well, don't let me stop you," I say, kicking the ball against the half-wall.

"Don't you want to know what I'm thinking about?"

"Always."

If you hit the ball just right it will bounce off the wall in perfect time to meet your foot again as it sweeps forward.

"I'm thinking about Jeff."

"Good," I say. "Now I don't have to."

"He seems depressed. He's changed somehow, don't you think?"

This is true: our humble, sweater-wearing yearbookmeister has lost some of the slobbering enthusiasm he had back in September. In Yearbook he just sits at the back of the class, for the most part, doing crossword puzzles and reading birding magazines. And in AP Humanities, we do a lot of silent reading. One can only suppose that it took him this long to assume the appropriate attitude toward his new environment. Unlike Freesia, I take it as good news that Jeff seems to have dropped his Surrealist ambitions, and is ready to toe the line so clearly drawn by Pancake and his forebears.

"It's called regression to the mean," I say. "In this case, of course, the mean being the Template."

"Why do you think he's living with his mom?"

"I don't know, cheap rent?" (King's Island isn't exactly a hotbed of high-priced real estate.)

"I think we need to do something," she says.

"He's a grown man, Freeze," I say. "He can take care of himself."

"I miss the old Jeff. Class was fun. Now it's boring. Why can't he just teach what he wants? It's not like we were reading *Mein Kampf*."

"It's not our war," I say.

It is *her* war, however, it would seem. "It's just not right. I really wanted to read *Beloved*."

"Who's stopping you? I mean—"

"Wichie," utters BF James, rising to his full, wide six foot three.

"Come again?" I say.

"We bring him to Yearbook."

"What the hell are you talking about?" says Freesia.

"Wichie has powers," says BF James. "Let's put them to use."

"No way," I say. "That's a complete non-starter." How can Wichie's well-being be ensured in that adolescent pandemonium? Who will look after his safety?

"I have an idea," says Freesia. "Let's think of something that might actually work, instead of something that is completely idiotic."

These are fighting words.

"Toss me the ball," says BF James. "I'll shoot on it."

I straighten. This is historic. I bounce-pass him the ball. He spins it in his hands.

A Freesian rolling of the eyes. "Don't be ridiculous."

"Backwards shot," I say, seeking an appropriate level of difficulty, "from just inside the free-throw line."

"You're on," he says, striding toward the invisible free-throw line. He arches his back and lowers his head toward the pavement, sizing up his first-ever shot.

"You guys are absurd," says Freesia, nonetheless positioning herself at courtside to take in the attempt. If only she knew how much BF James is offering here. She regards him in a way that suggests she might be getting it. "Take the shot. If you miss—which you will—we'll bring your stupid sandwich maker to class."

"No deal," I say. "It has to be the other way around. You have to be shooting for the thing you're going to do. The status quo is always tied to a miss. A miss means nothing changes. That's foundational."

BF James nods in solemn agreement.

He lines up the shot again, forward and backward, right-side-up and upside-down; he spins the ball in his hands a few more times; he bend his knees; he shoots. Historic.

The shot goes in. The Oracle has spoken.

"Do what you have to do," I say to BF James. "But please—take care of him."

Freesia freezes him with a glance. "You better make it count."

"I will," says BF Jamison, ascending the steps to the front door. "Now y'all got to get out of here. I'm due for a nap."

BF JAMES IS AS COOL as the Yoo-Hoo in his fridge as he comes into class, carrying an extra canvas duffel—a somewhat ratty one, red with white handles—and setting it on the floor with utmost nonchalance. Business as usual, folks. Nothing to see here. Just an extra duffel down here by my feet. Nothing special. Just this extra duffel containing the greatest sandwich-making apparatus the world has ever known. Carry on.

He waits twenty minutes before making his move. By then, Jeff's feet are up on his desk, and he's opened his copy of *Audubon*.

Clunk.

Wichie has landed.

Jeff looks up. Towering over him is BF James.

"What's that?"

"This," says BF James, placing a broad hand on Wichie's curved lid, "is Wichie."

Jeff raises an eyebrow.

"Allow me to demonstrate," says BF James, left-handing Wichie into the air, and wheeling toward the front of the room.

He sets the apparatus on the collapsible table, along with half a baguette still in its crumpled paper sleeve, half a round of camembert, and a Ziploc full of sliced tomatoes (this is one of his staples; he calls it "Primordial Glop").

"Watch and learn," I say, drifting over to Jeff. "The man is a master."

BF James plugs in Wichie and the small orange indicator light comes on. He rubs his fingers together in anticipation, then lays open the jaws of that wonderful machine. Jeff is watching in what looks like mild amusement as BF James lays two slices of baguette on the scuffy teeth of Wichie's grill, then layers in the cheese and tomato with equal care. Then, from the inside pocket of his parka, he draws out a plastic baggie, opens it, and shakes a few green flakes onto the tomatoes and cheese (this is BF James's proprietary herbal mixture—a fine, fine touch). Then he returns the baggie to his jacket and, from the chest pocket of the parka, withdraws a small brown vial. (Is this really happening?) He unstoppers the vial and drops six drops of a brownish liquid onto the herb-dusted tomatoes and cheese. (Yes, my friends, it is! Proprietary herbal mixture *and* proprietary oil, all in one!) He caps the vial and tucks it back into his pocket, then tops the ensemble with another slice of bread and stoops to examine it from table-level. (BF James is known, in certain circles, for his attention to this detail—namely, the proper elevation of the sandwich, in its pre-cooked state.) He nods in satisfaction, then smashes the jaws of Wichie together and latches the latch that latches it closed.

"And there you have it, ladies and gentlemen," says BF James, with a magician's flourish. "Wichie in action."

"Rad," says Cam. "How long does it take?"

"Just three minutes," says BF James, "and three easy payments of $9.99!"

We sit in silence, staring at the small, smudged orange light until it fades to black and BF James lays open Wichie's jaws. A tantalizing aroma fills the room.

"And that," pronounces BF James, "is what we call perfection." He places the sandwich on a small green metal plate, and slices it into quarters with a butter knife.

He brings the plate to me. "Your expert assessment, if you please."

I hold it to the light. It passes visual inspection with flying colors. I take a bite and chew for several seconds, eyes closed. "You've outdone yourself," I say. He really has.

Next is Jeff. "Here," says BF James, holding out the plate for him. "Try it."

"Before I do this," says Jeff, "can I ask what's in the vial?"

A solemn shaking of the head of BF James.

"That's a non-starter," I say. "Believe me, I've tried."

Jeff eyes the sandwich. Cheese is oozing from the seams. A rogue tomato skin protrudes from the crust.

He takes a bite.

"Wow," he says, still chewing. "That's good. That's really good."

"Let me try that," Freesia demands.

"Yeah," says Cam. "You're making us hungry."

"Wichie is abundant," BF James reminds them. He gives a piece to Freesia, and another to Cam, then heads back toward the front of the room. "I'll get started on round two."

Freesia takes a bite, cocking her head as she chews. "Not bad."

"Not bad?" I say. "Not bad?"

She passes the rest to Tina. Tina holds it out at arm's length. The look on her face would suggest that she's been asked to kiss a dragonfly.

"Come on, Tina," Jeff implores. "Just give it a try."

"Yeah," says Cam, who has already polished off his portion. "It tastes like meat."

Tina brings the sandwich slowly to her mouth and nips off a tiny piece. "That's gross," she says, with a pucker. She hands the rest to a willing Cam.

Jeff takes another bite, and then another. And then a smudged orange light in his brain ticks on and glows through the glow in his eyes. "This gives me an idea."

"For a sandwich?" wonders Cam, mouth full.

"No," says Jeff, rubbing his hands together in the way that he does. "For the yearbook!"

"What is this 'yearbook' you speak of?" asks BF James, sprinkling his secret mix of herbs onto sandwich number two.

"Let's do a section on this," says Jeff.

"On what?" asks Tina.

"Sandwiches," he says. "Freesia, do you have your camera with you?"

"Uh, yeah. Why?"

Jeff nods at Wichie. "Let's put it to work."

"Yeah," says Cam. "For the yearbook."

Freesia pulls her Nikon from her backpack. Jeff and Cam and I join BF James at the front of the room as he opens Wichie's jaws. The second sandwich is browned to perfection and redolent of herbs and cheese and—is that truffle oil?

"Perfect," says Jeff. "Now put it on the plate."

BF James shimmies the sandwich onto the plate.

"Okay, Freesia. Let's get some shots of this."

She rises and aims the camera at the sandwich. "It needs a garnish."

"Use this," says Jeff, handing BF James a Boggle cube that happens to be lying, Z-up, on the table.

Freesia snaps a few shots of the sandwich with its Boggle garnish. "Now pose with it," she says.

BF James obliges, holding the sandwich in one hand, giving a thumbs up with the other, and grinning a toothpaste-commercial grin.

"Perfect!"

Tina, who's been watching with her arms crossed, scowling, offers some further instruction: "Take a bite. We need an action shot."

BF James obliges. Freesia snaps away.

"Now a picture of the plate," says Cam.

"Yes!" says Jeff. "The crumbs on the plate. That'll be so French New Wave!"

Freesia gets a shot of the crumbs, and then another of BF James holding the plate like a Frisbee, about to sling it Jeffward.

"Okay," says Jeff, "this is starting to get interesting."

"I have an idea," says Cam.

"I think you're thinking what I'm thinking, Cam."

"I am?"

"It's time to shake things up!"

"What do you mean?" Tina looks worried.

"If the Proctor wants to shut me down, fine." Jeff's pacing now, and stroking the beard he doesn't have. "But I won't take it lying down!"

"What are you talking about?" says Tina.

"I'm mad as hell," says Jeff, with a wolfish grin, "and I'm not gonna take it anymore!"

"Is this about the reader?" says Freesia.

"It's about everything, damnit!" says Jeff, pounding his fist on the collapsible table. "This sandwich maker is only the beginning."

"The beginning of what?" asks Tina, worried.

If only he had a clear answer to this question. All his bottled-up frustration—with the Proctor? and the reader? and the winter?—has come uncorked. But how to channel it, Mr. Traversal? How to act the fact of not taking it anymore?

"Club sandwiches!" says Cam.

"What's that now?" says BF James, wiping Wichie down with a chamois.

"We invite in all the clubs," says Cam. "And give them sandwiches."

"I like it," says Jeff.

"Yeah," says Freesia. "And they can all come up with their own recipe!"

BF James pats Wichie's dented hull. "Time to hit the big time, little guy."

"What do you think, Lester?" says Jeff, turning to me. "Will the Template abide this culinary intrusion?"

I stand and dust the crumbs from my trusty blue flannel, then turn to Jeff.

"Watch this," I say. "I'm about to *engage*."

"Lester," Freesia warns. "Remember our deal?"

I wave her off. What I'm about to say isn't prohibited speech.

"Here's the thing," I say. "Yearbooks aren't Surrealist games. They aren't about just doing whatever you want." I pause to look around the room, then hold my arms out wide. "They're about *us*. A yearbook tells a specific story, in a specific way, about a specific time and place. That's the magic of the Template. And the Template *doesn't* have a Dining section."

"That's why it sucks!" says Freesia.

An invisible line divides the room, with Jeff, Freesia, Cam and BF James on one side, and blessed Tina McTovey and I on the other.

"If it ain't broke," I say, with a gentle pat on Wichie's hull, "don't try to break it."

"We're not trying to break it, Lester!" bristles Freesia.

"In any case," I say, returning my attention to Jeff, "it doesn't really respond to the assignment, now does it?"

"What do you mean?" he says.

"Oh come on, Lester," says Freesia, seizing me by the shoulder. "This is a great idea."

"I give it a B–," I say. "Or maybe a B slash B–." I down the rest of sandwich number two.

"Oh," says Jeff, nodding slowly. "I get it."

"You can't have it both ways, Traversal. You can't be the falcon," I say, lifting the sandwich, "and the falconer," I say, letting the sandwich fall back to the plate.

"What's that mean?" says Cam.

"It's a metaphor," says Jeff.

"Cool."

"Anyway," I say, prying open Wichie's jaws, "how about another sandwich?"

THE RIDE HOME from school has become trying in the days since I relinquished my music-choosing rights. The Subaru is now an ongoing medley of Alanis Morissette and James and U2 and Ani DiFranco. The light-starved skies aren't helping matters much.

When we get to the Subaru on this dark Wednesday afternoon, a familiar figure awaits us, hunched over in a black wool jacket, with a scarf wrapped tight around his neck.

"Jeff," says Freesia. "What are you doing here?"

"We're charging for parking now," he quips. "I'm the meter."

"Here," I say, flipping him a quarter. "Give it a wax while you're at it."

"Hey," he says, "I have something for you in my car. I'll give you a ride home."

I shrug and look to Freesia for counsel. She approves the change of cars. "Pick you up tomorrow?"

"Yes," I say.

She fires up the Subaru, and Jeff and I make for the faculty lot, swimming against the current of bodies that is flowing from the main dodecagon. When we get to Jeff's car—a seafoam green Ford Taurus station wagon, long on wear if not on tear—he tosses the books and papers from the passenger seat onto the books and papers on the back seat, clearing just enough space to accommodate a passenger.

When I get in, he's holding a plastic bag. "I thought you might like this," he says, opening the bag. "You see, I went through a little Ramones phase myself, once upon a time."

"Excuse me? Phase?"

"Well, whatever you want to call it. Anyway, when I was in college, I visited a friend of mine who was living in New York. And that's where I got this." He unfurls the object in question. A black shirt, with the telltale letters in large white block print: CBGB.

"Wait, did you go there?"

"I did indeed."

"Can I see that?"

He hands the shirt to me. "You can have it."

"Really?" I hold it up for inspection. The dye is quite faded, and the letters are pleasingly cracked.

"Yes," he says, rubbing his hands together in the way that he does—this time with a genuine need for warmth. "I've held onto it too long already."

Let's face it: Ramones fandom can be bought very cheaply. Your T-shirt here, your hooded sweatshirt there. But this is the genuine article, the original manuscript.

"Did you see them there?"

"Nah," he says. "They did their last show there in '79. We saw some other band. I couldn't tell you who."

"But you were there."

"I was indeed."

"Are you sure you don't want this? I mean, shirts like this don't just grow on trees."

"I want you to have it. Listen, Lester," he says, downshifting into a sitcom father's tone of voice, "you were right. I can't be the falcon and the falconer. I told you to let 'er rip, and then I shot you down. I'm sorry."

I feel a need to fill the air with words of some kind or another, but the air will have to stay empty for now.

"So do what you want with your make-up essay, okay?"

He fires up the Taurus and coasts toward the throat of the lot. Washburn's beige Datsun is rattling ahead of us. Flough's shiny magenta LeBaron is still in its spot. No sign of the Proctor's off-white Saab.

"Anyway," says Jeff, having arrived at the highway, leaning forward to check for traffic, "tell me something. *Paradise Lost.*"

A large backhoe rumbles by, half on the shoulder and half on the road.

"What about it?"

"I get that it's a great poem. But why does it have such a hold on you?"

"I don't know," I say. I've never thought of it in terms of holding. "It started when I was a kid, I guess. I really liked the cover."

It was bright orange. The Father kept it on his desk.

"Did you see it at the library or something?"

"No," I say. "My dad—he used to read it to us at bedtime."

"You're kidding," says Jeff, easing the Taurus onto the highway.

"I'm not," I say. I'm really not.

"You poor kid."

"I don't know," I say. "Who doesn't want to fall asleep to images of Satan?"

Rain is starting to dot the windshield. We approach and then sweep through the curve where Freesia and I staged our arctic rescue of Jeff earlier this month.

"His novel—he published one novel—it was this weird rewrite of *Paradise Lost.*"

"Oh dear," says Jeff, over the groan of the wiper blades. "Have you read it?"

"No." I haven't. "I started it once when I was a kid. But he took it away. He said I wasn't ready for it yet."

The trees are bare and brown. Jeff's eyes are mostly on the road. "Really?"

"I had this dumb idea," I say. "Back in September? I wrote a letter to the Morgan Library in New York, asking to visit their copy of *Paradise Lost*. Did you know they have the only surviving manuscript?"

"I didn't know that. And that doesn't sound like a dumb idea at all. What did they say?"

The wiper blades are losing their battle against the smearing of the windshield.

"I never sent it."

"Why not?"

"I don't know." I was out of my depth.

"You should."

Now we're passing Haugenbuck Construction, where two large piles of dirt stand guard against a backdrop of ancient trucks and sheds.

"This place is such a wasteland," I say. Especially in December.

"Have you ever been to Florida?" quips Jeff, as Haugenbuck Construction gives way to woods.

"What were you doing there?" I ask. It's time to turn the tables.

"Grad school."

"What was the topic of your dissertation?"

"Well," he says, cocking his head to the side, and sighing, "it was sort of looking at contemporary poetry and conceptual art—poetry *as* conceptual art was sort of the gist of it."

"Sounds like bestseller material."

"Well, yeah. No. Exactly."

"And now you're back at Victory Memorial."

"Indeed."

"Your alma mater."

"And yours too," he says, with a sideways glance, "if you can manage it."

"Let's keep our eye on the ball here," I say. "Tell me something. Why did you come back?"

"Why did I come back?" Now we're pulling into town. "Well," he says, with yet another sigh, "my ship ran aground, and I had to come back into port."

"Care to elaborate?"

"On the day I filed my dissertation, my fiancée left me."

"Fiancée?"

"Vivian. I had picked up an expensive bottle of champagne on the way home from campus. And I was whistling all the way. And then there she was, waiting on the porch, with her bags already packed."

"Oh man."

"It's okay. I should have seen it coming."

We're at the main intersection in town, a four-way stop with a red light blinking in each direction. Jeff stops the car for a breath, looks left, and turns. I don't have the heart to tell him he's going the wrong way.

"And I don't know," he says, "I'm not really cut out for academia."

"So why'd you even do it in the first place?"

"I don't know," he says. "It was that spark, you know? It was the pursuit of that spark. You know what I'm talking about."

"Apt numbers!" I pound my fist on the dashboard for old time's sake.

"Exactly. As long as I could focus on that, I figured I'd be happy."

"But where you fly is hell, yourself are hell," I paraphrase.

"Thanks. It's been, what, days since I've been compared to Satan?"

"You know what I mean."

"Yes, I do. You know he stole that from Marlowe, right?"

"Really?" (Don't tell The Father!)

"But the sentiment is pretty good, I'll give you that. Hell can be anywhere, and heaven too."

"Exactly," I say. "So what's the point of all the fuss?"

"What do you mean?"

"All the struggle, all the strife. I mean, why bother with it, if you're just going to be the same stupid person at the end? Look at you. With all due respect, you've come out the end of the achievement cycle looking basically the same. I mean, you didn't exactly learn ten languages, did you? And last I checked, you weren't at Victory to give a speech."

"Well," says Jeff, then laughs, "I'm not exactly in a position to argue with you, am I? But look at it this way: what if I hadn't done anything? What if I'd just graduated from VMHS, gotten a boring office job, and sat around muttering to myself for years on end?"

"Sounds fine to me." At least I think it does.

"And maybe it is. But I guess the point is, if you have that spark in you—and I know you do; you wouldn't be such a pain in the ass if you didn't—if you have that in you, you're doing yourself a disservice to ignore it." He quiets for a moment. The rain is coming harder now, and the wiper blades are performing heroically, if not adequately. "At least that's what I think," he says, "or what I think I think. But who knows. Most file clerks are probably a lot happier than I am. Hey, can I show you something?"

He swings a sudden U-turn, a little too fast. The tires of the Taurus squeal in protest, and I'm thrust against the door, and half the books and papers on the back seat spill onto the books and papers on the floor.

This latest maneuver completed, Jeff turns down a side road that leads to a gravel parking lot at a small beach.

"The Chadlowe Reach," I say. "It's a good beach. Under-appreciated."

He parks and kills the engine, freezing the wiper blades at a sixty-degree angle. It's fair to say that this isn't beach weather. Gusts of wind, flurries of rain on the windshield.

I came here with The Father, not long before he left, in conditions that were similar to these.

"This," says Jeff, "is the scene of one my stupidest moments on record. I was seventeen years old. How old are you? Seventeen?"

"Eighteen next month."

"So I was seventeen, and it was November, and I was feeling sad—about who knows what. And I came down here, all by myself. It was a crappy day, kind of like this. Windy, a little bit of rain. I got out of my car and went out to the edge of the sand. And I was starting to come back to the car when I saw a boat—a little rowboat, upside down against a log, right over there."

He points in the direction of his memory of that rowboat.

"And I don't know what possessed me, but I decided to take it out for a spin. So I flipped it over and dragged it down to the water and got in and started rowing. With no real destination in mind. And before long I turned to look back, and I was nowhere *near* where I'd started. I was like halfway across. So I decided what the hell, I'll just go all the way."

He stares out at that earlier version of himself, struggling against the waves.

"Did you make it?"

"No." He laughs again. "Not even close. A few different things conspired against that. The wind, for one thing. And the current, it wanted me to go that way," he says, pointing down the shoreline. "Rowing was kind of pointless, so I just kicked back and took in the sights. I was cold, and the waves were pretty big, but I wasn't really thinking about the danger of it. You don't start to worry about dying until later in life—am I right about that?"

I answer only with my eyebrows.

"Anyway, someone saw me out there, stupidly adrift, and hauled me up into their boat. They put a blanket on me and gave me some hot soup. That whole ride home was blurry. I don't remember it that well. But when I got back, my mom—it was the only time I've ever seen her truly distraught. She just broke down. I felt pretty bad about it."

The rain is coming even harder now, and streaming down the wiper-blade water slides.

"But you know what?" he says, returning that leaky metaphor of a rowboat to the shore.

"What?"

"I'm still glad I did it."

He starts the car and puts it in reverse.

THE COAST: MY MOTHER has decided that we should spend the holidays at the coast. Sometimes the Sound isn't water enough, I guess; sometimes you need the full, fat ocean. We've been coming to the coast in the winter for a number of years, but never to pass the Christmas rituals. As usual, she is a tight bundle of preparation for the journey, gathering clothes, snacks, books, bags, reading lights, board games, cards—anything to push away the darkness of a moment's contemplation. Grace stays in her room until the last possible moment.

Most of the drive we spend in silence—a silence which the ladies of the house have prepared for, my mother with her battery of books on tape (*Undaunted Courage* is the apt selection for this ride), and Grace with her Discman, her pouch of CDs, her outsize headphones, and her vacant gaze.

The rental house is small and cold and drab and old. There's a TV but no cable. The kitchen is small and cramped. The family of porcelain dolphins on the back of the toilet looks desperately lost, displaced from their native porcelain ocean, longing for return.

"This place sucks," is Grace's assessment, before leaving said place for a headphoned walk among the dunes.

"She didn't take her jacket," is all that my mother can find to say.

As I coil up to read from a book on the Explorers of the Great Northwest, my mother begins to busy herself about the place. Opening rolls of paper towels, mounting one on the roller, with another in wait on the counter, just in case. Putting Diet Cokes in the fridge. Setting the placemats. Things like that. When all the things like that have been exhausted, for the moment, she goes to the window to look out at the low clouds and the dunes.

"I'm going to the store," she says. "We need candles. We don't have any candles."

The Explorers only hold my interest for so long, so I am forced, in a sense, to turn to the two Traversal tomes, which I shoved, on a whim, into the bottom of my backpack just before we left. I start with Pound's *Literary Essays*, which has a garbled, garbage portrait of the author on the cover, and a little sticky note popping out of the top of it, on which Jeff has scrawled, "You're going to *love* this." The text he marked has been marked for obvious reasons: it's a broadside attack on mine own John Milton.

"Very funny, Jeff," I say, aloud. "Can you hear me laughing all the way from here?" The Explorers of the Great Northwest and I share a laugh, and then I turn to volume two, *The Collected Poems of Wallace Stevens*. The poem that Jeff has bookmarked here bears a dubious title: "Notes Toward a Supreme Fiction."

"Sounds about right," I tell the lack of candles in the room.

I skim through the poem, which is mostly just a bunch of mush. It seems a little transparent, really, the whole gesture: Mr. Traversal, earnest of intention, trying to hook me with this 20th century update of Milton's glorious blank verse. Just as I'm about to return it to my backpack for the duration of the trip, I flip ahead to a passage that's been marked on more than one occasion, by the looks of it. There's a big box of green ink around it, as well as two penciled stars in the margin *and* a line of thick black ink running alongside the text. Clearly, Jeff has returned to these lines more than once, and each time with a different writing implement. I read the lines, then read them again.

> He had to choose, but it was not a choice
> Between excluding things. It was not a choice
>
> Between, but of. He chose to include the things
> That in each other are included, the whole,
> The complicate, the amassing harmony.

I put the book back down on the table and jot down a few notes toward a rebuttal. I try out a few working titles and sketch out the beginning of an outline, plus a few marginal notes. But nothing else comes. And nothing comes. And still nothing comes. At last I put my pen down and head over to the window, where the clouds are amassing a harmony of grays.

ON CHRISTMAS DAY, we sit around the small table of the small rental house in silence, examining the remains of the ham. I still haven't figured out what can be said; and if my mother has, she hasn't found a way to get it across to us; and if Grace has, she isn't letting on. So we sit in silence. A silence to make candles seem noisy.

"So, Lester"—my mother, attempting, perhaps painfully, to pierce through that membrane of silence—"did you get your applications out?"

The question is forced, asked as if she's been tracking the process throughout its failure to unfold.

"Yup," I say, not looking up.

"Well," she exhales briskly. "That's worthy of a toast, don't you think?" She raises her glass. "Here's to the future."

I look at Grace. Grace looks at me. I raise my glass of milk, which forces Grace to raise her metal mug of tea. The glasses come together, somehow, over the center of the table, and then retreat to the safety of their places by our plates. We'll need a little silence now. We get it, thankfully. But then my mother speaks again.

"How is Freesia?"

"Well," I say, "I'll bet she wishes she was here instead of Costa Rica!"

To be truthful, it pains me a little to think of Freesia and her family, who are probably, at this very moment, deep in some extravagant jungle, about to enjoy one of the all-time Christmas repasts, a meal rife with inspired, exotic, non-traditional dishes, while I am forking through the rubble of ham-skin and family tradition.

"I still think she likes you."

"Is that a fact?"

"Why don't you ask her out?"

This from a charter member of the Disastrous Marriage Club.

"Okay," I say, "even if we set aside the assumptions you're making, how am I supposed to ask her out when I see her basically every day?"

"I mean something different."

"Would I be just like, 'Hey, do you want to do something? Oh, wait, we're already doing something. Because we're always doing something.'"

"What about you, Grace? Any boyfriend candidates?"

"No."

A sideways glance at her older brother. Will he break the code of silence?

"What about Flynn?"

A look—a real dagger of a look. A claw-sharp, ice-forged dagger, straight to the heart of the throat of my heart.

"Do tell," says my mother, clearly enjoying this opportunity to wade even shin-deep into the personal lives of her children, aided in the effort by a glass and a half of wine (which has likely doubled her total wine consumption for all of 1996).

"I'm going outside," says Grace. She gets up and makes for the door, leaving a folded-up paper towel on her plate. I follow.

The sky is dark and gray, initially, but then the sun breaks bright through the clouds and shatters the sand with brazen light. Grace trudges head-first toward the water, into the wind, her arms held tight around her midsection. I follow her into the dunes. The wind is bracing and cold, and the walking a chore, up and down the dunes, over the grasses, two steps forward, three steps back.

She stops halfway down the last dune, the sand stretching out before us to the water. Her gaze is fixed on the distant waves, rolling in in endless expanses of themselves, eons of wave-tops extending out in the direction of the open ocean, beyond which lies more of the same, same open, open sea. It's the look she had when I found her in the kitchen on that cold March morning, as she handed me the postcard of a fluffy orange kitten. A gaze fixed nowhere.

"Why does it even happen?" Her voice has flattened out. "I mean, what's the point?"

"The point of what?"

"Of having kids. Of human reproduction. It seems really dumb to me."

"Well, it kind of is, but—"

"Why did you lie to mom?" she says.

"What do you mean?"

"You didn't apply to college."

"What makes you so sure about that?"

"Did you?"

I turn from Grace to the open sea. "No," I say. "I didn't."

"So why did you lie about it?"

"I don't know. Why do *you* lie about what you lie about?"

"I don't," she says, the wind wreaking havoc on her hair. "Why didn't you?" she says.

"Why didn't I what?"

"Apply to college."

"I don't know," I say. "I don't want to be institutionalized."

Grace shakes her head. "You're such a hypocrite."

We stand in silence, braced against the wind. I try to change the subject, to conjure a memory from another, much earlier trip to the coast. "Do you remember when Dad—"

"Fuck Dad."

He had brought a kite—a kite of his own making, for which we, for his having made it, made fun of him the whole ride out. We were certain it couldn't and wouldn't fly. Even my mother got in on the action, razzing him, jabbing him. But he was stout in the defense of its construction. "It will fly," is all that he would say. When we got to the shore he headed straight toward the water, and we all followed. We were still razzing him a little, but we'd lost some confidence. We were starting to think he could do it. It might fly after all. The sun came through the clouds and hit the sand almost blindingly.

That light, it now occurs to me, was the same as the light on the sand out here with Grace, a light to send you back in time to other lights of like kind.

JANUARY

New year, same Jeff: seven minutes late to Yearbook. We don't mind the wait. But the same might not be true of the Proctor, who is standing magisterially at the front of the class, awaiting the belated arrival of our belated arriver. He got here before any of us, and he hasn't said a thing. There's some kind of egg he's sitting on, and he wants to make sure we're all there to see it hatch.

"Good afternoon, everyone," he says, before Jeff can even plap his satchel on his desk. "I will be brief. I'm afraid that I have some things to say which you may not like. The first is that I have been reviewing the school's budget, with the assistance of the Fiduciary Council. As a result of this review, we have determined that funding for Yearbook will have to be reduced."

He seems to take a certain pleasure in having delivered this news, in affecting the solemnity and gravity he's affecting. In pretending he wishes it weren't so.

Jeff looks gut-punched. Freesia is mad. "What do you mean?" she demands.

"The situation is still fluid," dissembles the Proctor. "And I would like to reassure you that there *will* be a yearbook. We just may have to make certain difficult choices, so as to live within our means."

"Can't we just increase the price?" says Tina.

The Proctor shakes his head in majestic negation—as if this were something he'd already thought of.

"What sort of 'choices' are you referring to?" Jeff has found enough wind to ask this question. The tone of his voice is remarkably calm. Not so his expression.

"That remains to be seen," says the Proctor. "You are a resourceful bunch. I'm sure you'll have some good ideas. For example, we might do without so many photographs. Or even none at all. That's just one idea," he adds, with a nervous, churlish laugh.

"What else?" says Jeff.

"What else?" says the Proctor, wiping the lenses of his glasses with his handkerchief.

"You said that was the first thing. What's the second?"

"The second thing," says the Proctor, now sending the handkerchief up to his forehead for some dabbing, "is that the class is being moved."

"What do you mean?"

"Enrollment is down," says the Proctor, "and Mr. Fleniston could use the extra space this period."

"What extra space?"

"This room," says the Proctor.

"My classroom?" Jeff's tone of voice has caught up to his expression.

"Well," says the Proctor, dabbing, "technically, it belongs to the District."

Is Jeff even going to bother to ask why Mr. Fleniston needs his—Jeff's—classroom? Yes: "Why does he need it?"

"For his drama class," the Proctor explains. "This way we can do two plays this year!"

(We wouldn't want just one!)

"And I," continues the Proctor, with a grin that's dripping with smugness, "I will be directing *The School for Scandal*!"

(When do tickets go on sale?)

"So what are we supposed to do?" demands Freesia.

"We have that all worked out," says the Proctor, turning to Jeff, who doesn't seem to know whether to sputter, shout, accede, or merely glare. "New digs, Mr. Traversal!"

OUR NEW HOME IS a cold and musty room—little more than a utility closet—way off in a far corner of the campus, the last of a little string of rooms in a shabby little outbuilding that sits across a small, pothole-pocked parking lot from the Arts building. This part of the campus—which doesn't even seem to have a name—has traditionally yielded little in the way of anything. And still might not, other than to clarify for BF James the purpose of his parka on this earth. It's the last outpost of civilization before you enter the woods where Mr. Knorr teaches Outdoor Survival, a realm that lies beyond the blob of polygons at the heart of the campus; beyond the Vortex, where Pancake plies his humble, noble crafts; beyond the gym; and even beyond the tennis courts and always-covered swimming pool.

In short: we've been banished.

The room has a handful of desks—none of them like any of the others—plus a bunch of boxes at the back. In lieu of a collapsible table, there's a rickety metal shelf, beneath what appears to be the mounting for a chalkboard that's no longer there. I doubt I need to mention just how bad the lighting is.

"It's cold in here," says Tina, eyeing a dust-covered chair, not sitting in it.

"Yes," says Jeff. "It is." He rubs his hands together in an all-too-utilitarian way, gazing out the lone, rain-smeared window of the room at a large fallen tree, with a craze of mossy branches forking out of it.

"It's really cold," says BF James, zipping up his parka.

"Yes," says Jeff. "It is."

Somehow it feels even colder in here than it does outside, even in my combo of flannel *and* sweatshirt.

"What's this all about?" asks Freesia, who has managed to find an inhabitable desk, and is hugging her knees to her chest, her feet perched on a neighboring chair.

"I guess the rent is cheaper out here," says Jeff. "Man, it's freezing." Now he is rubbing his arms.

"So what did you do to deserve this?" I inquire.

"I don't know."

"What does he mean about our funding?" says Tina. Her eyebrows are asking the question, really, and they mean business (when don't they?).

"I don't know," says Jeff.

"This sucks," says Cam.

A vent at the back of the room starts rattling, then stops.

"Yes," says Jeff, running in place. "It does."

AND IT ONLY GETS WORSE. Tina has taken ill. She missed the rest of the first week of class. She's back today, heroically, huddled under an electric blanket, but she's clearly not feeling 100%. She has a box of tissues at her side, and it looks like she plans to get through them pretty quickly.

We're in our hovel, standing, waiting. Waiting for Jeff. Waiting for this next week of what's become an increasingly dismal project. Waiting for the weather to get warmer. Waiting for longer days, and less dreary nights.

"Maybe the Proctor's right," says Freesia, standing at the window, waiting for the clouds to lift.

"Yeah," says Cam, leaning against the cardboard boxes at the back, underdressed as always (do Carhartt pants have hidden heat-packs?).

"How so?" says BF James, sitting in his deskless chair.

"Maybe we should just phone in the yearbook and call it good."

This doesn't sound like Freesia. (Is the Proctor's relocation program working?)

"Phone it in?" I say.

"Yeah," she says. "I mean, why bother?"

Just then, Jeff bursts into the room, like a fighter entering a ring, a heavy underdog with nothing to lose, and everything to gain, by wildly swinging his fists—a fighter who lost his last bout but doesn't care, a fighter who's ready to get pummeled again, and maybe again after that.

"Hey guys," he says. "Sorry I'm late. But," he says, thrusting a finger into the air, "I have a good excuse!"

Uh-oh: we know how this movie goes.

He marches to the front of the room—the wall where the pillaged blackboard used to be—and plaps his satchel on the rickety metal shelf. He looks out the window for a moment, then turns to the deflated faces of his skeleton crew, smiling a smile filled with guile. "I have something to show you."

He unclasps the clasps on the satchel and gets out the something that he wants to show us—a scuffed-up pamphlet, from the looks of it—and holds it to the light. On the cover, in big, bloppy, handwritten letters—later photocopied—read the words *Badger Shmadger.* And under that: *Victory Memorial High School, 1982.*

"I found this in a box over the weekend," he says.

"What is it?" Freesia wants to know.

"It's my senior yearbook," says Jeff.

"Uh, no it's not," I point out. His senior yearbook is a little volume that goes by the name of *Changing Times,* a fine exemplar from the Golden Age.

"Not the official one," he says. "The *unofficial* yearbook."

Unofficial?

"Rad," says Cam.

"Can I see that?" I say.

"Only fifty copies were made," says Jeff, handing me the pamphlet. "And only about a dozen survived the school-wide ban."

"Why was it banned?" asks Tina.

"I think you'll see," says Jeff.

I begin to page through it, with Freesia and Tina and James and Cam looking on over my shoulder. In lieu of a Table of Contents, there is a "Table of Remnants"—a photomontage of carpet scraps. Then we move into the photos—or should I say, the photo. In lieu of the rows of pictures that we usually get—the freshmen, then the sophomores, then the juniors, then the seniors—there's just one big mishmash-hodgepodge, a collage of *all* of the pictures of *all* of the students in the school, cut out and vomited willy-nilly onto the page. At the top of the page are the words, "Photographs of Students Who Go to this School."

It only goes downhill from there. A copycat M.C. Escher spread. A large section toward the middle that is meant to be a flip-book of an astronaut running in a hamster wheel. A photomontage of the lunchroom kitchen. The pages are cut out in places, with text from one page poking through the empty windows of others. The fonts change throughout. It's a good thing I am sitting down.

Then I hit the centerfold, which answers the question of why the book—or should I say, the pamphlet—was banned. Under a heading that reads "A Message from Bernie the Badger," there is a connect-the-dots array, which has, in this, Jeff's copy, been filled in. The resulting image presents a pretty forceful message from Bernie the Badger indeed—a message delivered with two hands in the air, and one finger thrusting upward from each hand.

"Damn!" says BF James.

"Oh wow," says Freesia.

"That should be our logo," says Cam.

I continue paging through the pages. It isn't until we get past this unfortunate turn for Bernie the Badger that the book begins to take itself seriously, beginning with the seniors, who got a pretty impressive section, it turns out, with not just a photo-copied picture and a quote, but a whole half page to work with. This allowed for longer quotes and extra photographs, in some cases, as well as a personalized background decoration. I flip ahead to "Traversal." There it is: our favorite smirk. Under the photo is his quote: *Two roads diverged in a yellow wood, and I—I took the one less traveled by.*

"Really, Jeff?" I say. "You got a *second* senior quote, and you used the same crappy one you used the first time around?"

He shrugs. "It was a phase."

"Sweet use of Dark Side," BF James chimes in. Yes, that too: for his personal background, he chose a hand-drawn reproduction of the cover of *Dark Side of the Moon.*

"Goes well with the Frost," I say. "Didn't they collaborate at some point?"

"Can I see that?" Says Freesia. I hand her the book. She continues where I left off, going into Power Mode.

I turn to Jeff. "Is that what you want us to do? Yearbook as exquisite corpse?"

He shrugs, then dives back into his trademark vagueness: "I just wanted to show you another approach."

Yet another another approach. But what are we approaching?

"Did you make this?" Freesia's on to him.

Jeff eels away from the question with a shrug.

"You did, didn't you?"

"Maybe," he says.

"Really?" says Cam. He's clearly impressed.

"I had some help."

I try to picture a younger version of Jeff, shaggy and nervous, stooping over a massive photocopier on the sly.

"Hey Les," says Freesia, "look at this."

She holds up the inside back cover of the book, where we are greeted by none other than Joey Ramone, soaring over a backdrop of gray squiggles. A dialogue bubble sprouts from his cartoon lips.

Hey! Ho! Let's Go!

She hands it to me. I consider the image, then turn again to Jeff.

"Can I borrow this?" I say.

He smiles and nods. "I was hoping you would ask."

I'm sitting in my bedroom. With no other immediate demands on my time, I've dug *Badger Shmadger* out from under my bookshelf. It won't hurt to flip through it just once more, will it?

I can't help but smile again at the sight of Jeff's half-smiling face, and the mash-up of Frost and Floyd that frames his Senior Profile. I turn to the back, to that portrait of a soaring Joey Ramone. *Hey! Ho! Let's Go!*

The phone rings in the hall. A moment later there's a clacking at my bedroom door: it's Grace, holding out the phone in dead-fish position. It must be The Father. I take the receiver and hold it to my flannel for a moment, watching as Grace returns to her room.

"Hello?"

This time he begins by breathing. Then: "How's school?"

"Good," I say.

More breathing. "Let's talk about your worldview," he says. As if this is something we were just discussing. "As I said before, it's about having a framework, Lester. A framework of ideas. Of principles. Of things you know you know."

Now it's my turn to be silent. (Let the world itself be view of world, I say.)

"You need to make this happen on your own, Lester. Your teachers will not do it for you."

I slide down the wall and onto the floor. The cord of the phone is a fingerless glove on my left hand.

"Some of them are actually pretty good," I say.

A silence. Breathing.

"Like in Yearbook—"

"You're doing Yearbook?" he interrupts.

"Yeah." I start to unwind the cord, a finger at a time. "We might do something a little different this year."

"Different how?"

I steal a glance at *Badger Shmadger*, lying face down on my bed.

"I don't know," I say. "Something experimental, maybe."

"Explain what you mean by 'experimental,'" he says. "Because I doubt you really know what that means."

"I don't know. We might take a new approach."

"No."

"No?"

"That's what I said," he says. "A yearbook is not an experiment, Lester."

His breathing is especially roughened by static tonight. The rest of the house is still and silent.

"Why not?" I say.

He breathes, and then he answers. "We're talking about tradition, Lester."

"Tradition," I say. "We need to make sure we're upholding tradition, do we?"

"That's what I said. Listen, Lester—"

"No," I say, sliding up the wall. "You listen to me." I'm trembling a little. "Yeah." My voice is trembling too. "How about *you* listen to *me* for a change?" I start to talk, and soon the words are coming out beyond my capacity to stop them. You don't know what the hell you're talking about, I say. That's right—I continue with something along these lines—you just up and leave, I tell him, and then you expect us to still care about you, and listen to you, when you obviously don't give a shit about us, I yell—I'm yelling now, I find, and try to quiet myself, and then explode again. You can't just call whenever you want, I say. I'm pacing now, back and forth across my room, the phone cord tightening and slackening and tightening again as it follows me in my pacing—and gesturing somewhat wildly with the hand that isn't holding the phone. You can't just this and you can't just that, and you can't, and you can't, and you can't you can't you can't you can't you can't.

By the time I'm done, my heart is pounding, and I'm panting, and there's a busy signal on the line.

My mother comes into my room. "Lester, are you okay?"

"I don't know."

Grace appears, a hand on the frame of the doorway. Her Hello Kitty slippers: they're so puffy, and pink. So puffy, those slippers, so puffy that I start to laugh. It's funny, to me, the puffiness of those Hello Kitty slippers, their pinkness. I'm laughing uncontrollably now. And then I'm back on the floor, bent forward, and the laughing almost turns to sobbing—but I hold it back. I hold it back.

My mother's hand is resting on my shoulder. "Do you want to talk about it?"

"Not now, mom," I say, with a sigh. I stand back up. "I need to get some air."

I don my sweatshirt and tell my mom I'm fine and head outside. The moon is bright behind the clouds. I start to walk, and as I walk I replay the conversation—the non-conversation—over and over and over again. A cold, soft rain starts falling, a rain I barely notice as I'm replaying, and retracting, and revising, all the things I said to him, over and over and over again, all the way to Freesia's house.

David is there to answer my knock.

"Lester," he says. "What's the matter?"

"Nothing, David," I say. "Is Freesia still up?"

She is. She's sitting on her bed, reading a novella in Spanish.

"Hey Les," she says, bookmarking the book. "What are you doing here?"

"I don't know. I had to get out. And I ended up here."

"What's going on?"

"I just kind of, I don't know, I guess I kind of yelled at my dad."

"Oh man. Come here." She gets up, and comes over and gives me a hug. Her hair smells like a flower in bloom.

"Nice shampoo," I say.

"Thanks. Do you want to sit down?"

I sit in her chair. She sits on the bed.

"I don't really have anything to say," I say.

"You don't have to say anything."

"It's just—I'm just tired of him, you know? All these stupid phone calls." Freesia's screen-saver—an ever-self-destructing rhombus—bounces off the side of the screen and ricochets down to the bottom and then back up toward the top. "It just—it just pisses me off."

Freesia gets up and puts a hand on my shoulder. "I'm glad you're finally talking about this, Les."

"I don't know," I say. "It doesn't really help."

"Yes, it does. I'm serious," she says. "It does, okay? Just have faith that it does."

"Whatever. I should probably go."

"No," she says. "Stay a little longer. I'll make some hot chocolate."

"You know what set me off?" I say into the screen, where that multi-colored rhombus continues on its never-ending path to nowhere.

"What?"

"Yearbook." In the reflection of the screen, I can see that I'm smiling the half-smile made famous by Jeff. "It was Yearbook."

I WAKE AT 3:19 AM and look outside. The moon is up. The sky is dark. It's deathly quiet. I'm eighteen years old.

I turn on my lamp and get my writing table and a sheet of clean white paper. *Pound is right*, I write. *Milton is boring. Let us turn, then, to Badger Shmadger.*

I begin with some speculation about the volume's underground history (pirates, Finland, Tolo, ransom notes). Then I compose a very long paragraph describing the cover. Then I plunge into my analysis of the book itself. *It invites the traditions of the Yearbook Arts into its front parlor*, I write, *only to dump cold Gatorade on their unsuspecting heads. The result*, I write, *is clearly a wrong turning for the genre—just wrong enough, perhaps, to be right.*

And from there it's all a blur of words. The sentences come easily, quickly, running eagerly forward as sled-dogs before the call of the musher. My head stays down until six pages have been filled, feverishly, one running seamlessly into another, and the last paragraph comes showering out of the end of the night.

I venture out into the living room and fire up the family computer. I open WordPerfect and begin a new document. I can't type nearly as fast as BF James, but I do enjoy it, this process of transferring my messy blue writing onto the screen. Within an hour I've typed it all, and the pages of raw handwriting are all on the floor in a catastrophic heap. I read what I've written again on the screen, making a few changes here and there, and then Print.

As the pages are making their laborious way out of the printer, I shower, dress, and grab two fig bars from the pantry and stuff them in my jacket. Then I come back for the finished document and tear off the edges of the pages—leaving the ends of the pages connected, like a foldable scroll—and slide them into my backpack. Then I go to the phone.

A groggy David Price picks up.

"Hi David, it's Lester. Can you tell Freesia I don't need a ride today? Thanks," I say, before he can probe me on particulars.

I layer up for the dark, cold walk to school—a sweater, a vest, a jacket to rival that of BF James; The Father's old wool hat, a pair of mittens, boots—and then head for the door.

Not so fast, old man: your mother has other ideas. She greets me in the hallway, wrapped up in her faded pink terrycloth robe. She is smiling.

"Happy birthday, Lester."

"Thanks."

"What do you want to do?"

"I want a steak," I say, "and a cake. And a rake," I add, for symmetry.

She laughs. "You got it."

I kiss her on the cheek and bolt for the door.

THE DAY STILL ISN'T day just yet. The moon is on the road. There are no cars.

One bus, empty, passes me as I turn, head down, warm enough but cold, into the student lot and make my way toward Room 9. Jeff is, I am somewhat surprised to discover, already there, rubbing his hands together, mouthing something to the shelves of books he would prefer to reject, if only he could.

I knock on the window. He turns and comes to let me in.

"Hey," he says.

"Hey," I breathe.

"What brings you here so early?"

"This," I say, dropping my backpack on his desk. I hand him the essay.

"Oh, hey, cool," he says, folding it out on itself, so that it is the full six pages tall, then struggling to fold it back together. "I was starting to wonder."

"A little lighter on the dictators this time."

"Pound and Milton notwithstanding?"

"Yes," I say. "But no. Not quite."

Freesia bursts into the room, smothered in a down jacket, a white winter hat with a big red fuzzy ball on the top of it, and crimson gloves.

"Hey," she says. "You're here."

"Yes," I say, "I am."

"Happy birthday!"

She hasn't forgotten—of course she hasn't. She hands me my gift. The handles aren't long for this world, and there's a rather perilous hole in one corner, but the letters still burn bright against the midriff of that beautiful woman: *JILT.*

I HAVE TO KEEP COOL as I follow Freesia into Ms. Flough's classroom for the Issue Compilation Meeting. I'm not exactly undercover—more like hidden in plain sight. Nothing to see here, folks. Just a scheming interloper, interloping.

I'm not here on official Issues Initiative business, you see. No, my aim is more direct and clear and simple. There's a very nicely glowing space heater just below the blackboard—the kind of nicely glowing heater that will brighten up our hovel of a Yearbook room considerably, enough to bring wellness to Tina and good cheer to the rest of us. I'm happy to see that Ms. Flough still has it, and I don't intend to leave the room without it.

Ms. Flough's classroom is like a private museum, or zoo. For the most part, she has risen up in arms against the District-sponsored overhead lighting, which shines only in the space above her desk, creating a cold, bluish glow at the front of the room. Throughout the rest of the room, she has installed an intricate network of lamps, chili pepper lights, candles faux and real, and, on a low shelf beneath the interior windows that give onto the library, three lava lamps. On one wall there's a row of posters: Teddy Roosevelt, Hillary Clinton, Madeleine Albright, Bob Ross. And on a little table at the back sits a cage filled with wood shavings and a heat lamp, beneath which her small pet mammal probably sleeps. There's a beanbag chair in one corner, with a Gloria-sized indent ghosting its center. On the blackboard, the motto of the Issues Initiative has been written out in flowing letters: ~ *all ideas are valid* ~.

Freesia and I are sitting in adjacent desks in the middle of the room, that region which is lit partly by the fluorescent lights at the front, and partly by the mellower light at the back. Gathered alongside us in this dim and bright pavilion is a motley collection of students and teachers, who appear to have been selected according to a set of criteria that may only be clear in the mind of Ms. Flough herself. Most of the teachers fall into that large majority of faculty members whose classes I try to avoid. And the students are mostly unfamiliar too. At the back of the room, Jeff is leaning against the wall, side-lit by the lava lamps. As Flough makes her way into the light at the front of the room, he gives Freesia a goofy, jazzy wave. A chubby kid in the library, truant to some class or other, looks in through the window. Jeff waves at him too, a bit less jazzily but jazzily enough. The kid starts, and scampers away.

"Okay everyone." Gloria Flough, standing in the full fluorescent sun at the front of the room, rubbing her knuckles together, going on tip-toes and then coming back down. "Welcome to this subby. Let's settle down. It's time to get started. I have some sheets."

The heading of today's sheet reads, "The Issues Initiative: Where ~ *All Ideas Are Valid* ~." Beneath that, I notice, skipping ahead of Ms. Flough as she begins to read aloud, the first heading reads, "Purpose": *A student-inclusive struggle to define the parameters of the Victory Memorial goal production structure, borne of various meetings and brainstormings.* Then, "Conclusions": *It has been concluded that the following areas are seen to be "in focus" as we "round up" the project:*

   * repave the student lot *
   * new vending machines *
   * weight room *
   * community outreach *
   * wormgarden *

The final item on the sheet—a conclusion, we can only suppose, beyond the reach of mere "Conclusions"—reads "Action steps/action items": *In the final phase of the Initiative, stakeholders will convene to determine the final courses of action to be determined (TBD). And what we can do is we can erect a little platform. In the lunchroom.*

By the time that Flough has finished reading through these points, aloud, and just about verbatim, most of the allotted time has passed.

"Any questions?" she asks, rising again onto tiptoes.

Freesia raises her hand.

"Yes?"

"Where are all the ideas we came up with in November?"

"What do you mean?"

"The brainstorming sessions," says Jeff. "You know, when we met in different classrooms?"

"Well, what I decided," decides Flough, "is I decided to just go ahead with the most workable proposals. The most pressing of issues."

"But isn't the point to explore them all?" asks Jeff.

"Yeah," says Freesia. "Otherwise why did we even bother to have those sessions?"

"Hold on," says Flough, a hand to her brow. "Hold on. Hold on."

"Gloria," says Jeff, detaching himself from the wall, "I have an idea. Why don't you give the brainstorm notes to me, I'll photocopy them, and we can include them in the final packet. How does that sound?"

"I don't know."

"Yeah," says Freesia, "that makes sense."

"Well, I suppose I can staple them all together," says Flough. "Or paper clip them. But they won't have a border. So why don't you let me do it. And I can have my T.A. put a border on them. I have my own T.A."

There are a couple of other questions, having mostly to do with scheduling, and then the meeting is pronounced over. Jeff bolts quickly from the room. I turn to Freesia—"watch this"—then drift up to Ms. Flough's desk and start to examine a large hunk of amethyst she keeps there as a paper weight (or private oracle?).

"Be careful with that," she cautions.

"Ms. Flough," I say, setting down the crystal, "I have an idea. For the Issues Initiative."

"You weren't on the invitation sheet, you know."

"Ah," I say, pointing a playful finger at the opal pendant dangling from her neck, "you caught me!"

"What's your idea?" In her purple glasses, she looks part amethyst herself.

"Let's move the Issues Initiative," I say.

"Move it where?"

"Oh, I don't know," I say. "Let's put it in some horrible classroom, way out in the middle of nowhere. Or maybe a broom closet? A broom closet might be good."

"I don't know," says Flough. "That sounds like too much ammonia."

"I'm just joshing, Ms. Flough. Seriously, though, let's talk about that space heater."

I've come around to the meat (or should I say, "the heat") of the matter. It's lying at the foot of the desk, angled strategically for maximal foot-warming. It's really a quality model. I stoop to hold my hands in front of it.

"It's for my feet," she points out.

The warmth of it is warm, and so is its light.

"I have a proposition for you, Ms. Flough."

"Okay. But I don't have a lot of time. In Fourth Period we're doing Filibusters."

"Let us borrow this heater, and we'll do a section in the yearbook on the Issues Initiative."

Her gaze goes blank. This isn't what she was expecting.

"A full page," I clarify, "with two photos."

"Photos? Why would I need photos?"

"Right," I say. "Let's do wing-dings, and call it good."

The kid at the window is back. There's something in that section of the library—Biography, I think it is—which he just can't bear to leave behind.

"Two pages," she says. "A full spreadsheet."

"You drive a hard bargain," I say, unplugging the heater. It starts to tick a bit as the coils go dark.

"And I get to design it," she says. Now she's getting excited. Her hands are joined at pendantside.

"You're on," I say.

"And I can keep warm with my blanket. I have a blanket in my desk."

As she opens the appropriate drawer, I make for the door. The heater has a quality handle to go with its quality light and its quality coils. It's too soon to wrap the cord around it, so I just let it drag across the carpet.

THE HEATER ISN'T all that heavy, but it's heavy enough to notice by the end of the long walk to our Yearbook shanty. When we get there, Jeff is standing in the doorway—and waiting for me. He holds up my latest production in greeting.

"Lester," he says, "I read this at lunch. It's brilliant!"

"Thanks," I say, hugging the heater to my chest, where there's a sudden inner warmth I haven't felt in many months. "Come on. I want to show you what comes next."

I glide past him and strut to the front of the room and clonk the heater down on the metal shelf that sits beneath the ghost of a blackboard. I plug it in and turn it on. The coils start glowing to life. The warmth of the heater spreads to the expression on Tina's face.

"What's that?" says Cam.

"It's a metaphor," I say, rubbing my hands together in the way that Jeff does.

A smirk from BF James. A scowl from Freeze. "Lester," she says, "what are you talking about?"

I look around some more, then speak.

"Metal covers."

Cam laughs a Cam laugh: his dented dream has been revived.

"What's that supposed to mean?" says Tina, still draped in her blanket but no longer shivering.

"It means," I say, "we're going to make a kick-ass yearbook. Who has the floppy?"

All of our efforts to date—not many, to be sure—are stored on a blue floppy disk, which gets passed from hand to hand—usually from Freesia's hand to Tina's and vice versa—like a sacred goblet that must not be dropped. At the mention of the precious floppy, Freesia and Tina both turn instinctively to their backpacks. Today, Freesia has it. She fishes it out, and holds it to the watery light eddying in through the window.

"May I have that please?" I say.

"Uh, why?"

"I'll tell you in a minute. Just hand it over."

She hands me the floppy.

"Watch this," I say. I grip the disk and make to break it. There's just one problem: it won't break.

"What are you doing?" gasps Tina. "Stop!"

"I'm trying," I grunt, "to break it."

But the disk still won't break. It has merely given way a little in the middle, bending just enough to form a pale white crease. So I turn to Plan B: I grab Freesia's Nalgene bottle and douse the disk with water.

"I don't think that's going to destroy it," BF James informs me.

Still, the metaphor has been dispatched.

I fetch out *Badger Shmadger*. "This," I say. "This is what a year-book can be. All this and more. Let's let *Badger Shmadger* be our guide."

"What about the Proctor?" Tina asks.

"What about him?"

For the moment, I've out-Tina'd Tina. Freesia, for her part, is beaming. If Jeff is startled by my sudden change of mind and mood, he isn't showing it. He's sipping his coffee. He looks relaxed, and a little mischievous. His smirk is in full bloom.

"Deep Blue, baby!" bellows BF James.

"Metal covers!"—Cam.

"Metal covers," I rejoin.

The glow of the heater is full and bright. The room, at last, is warming up.

FEBRUARY

OUR LITTLE TEAM IS hitting its stride. The farmer, the mechanic, the typist, the eye-roller, the muckraker, the scribe. Wichie has been deployed to great effect, as a maker of sandwiches, and as a maker of friends. Cordial, handwritten invites, personally delivered by Messenger Cam, have gone out to all the clubs and teams of the campus. Appointments have been scheduled, photographs taken, hot sandwiches made and shared—"Club Sandwiches," as our fair Cam has dubbed them, with each club inventing its own recipe for Wichie. *Badger Shmadger* has been granted pride of place on the lip of the blackboard that is no more, there to be consulted whenever we need it. Enough of the key traditions of the Yearbook Arts are being preserved that the door can now be opened, at least a crack, to small- to mid-sized dollops of newfangledness.

Better still, Flough's heater has worked wonders on our musty, dusky, mildewy shanty, and on the humor of our blessed, fragile Tina, who likes to sit right next to it. Glowing its glow, heating with its heat, it has earned the nickname given it by BF James: "Bride of Wichie."

Banishment has proven to have its advantages. In our case, the advantage is clear and specific and marvelous: we have our own driveway. Yes, this little atoll at the far end of the Victory Memorial archipelago has its own short access road, which leads straight onto 177th Ave. SW—which, in turn, leads to the highway, and points north, south, east, and west. The upshot is simple: if you're so inclined, you can easily leave this part of the campus without being detected.

It seems that Jeff has noticed this as well. When he gets to the outbuilding on this cold February afternoon, seven minutes late, he's dangling a set of keys, and coughing up canary feathers.

"Okay everyone," he says, standing at the threshold, tossing the keys from hand to hand. "I have a little field trip in mind. I talked to the debate coach, Mr. Durkie. And he says we can use their van. Who wants to milk a cow?"

"Who doesn't?" I say.

"Hell yeah!" says Cam.

"Come on," says Jeff. "Let's go!"

"Wait a minute," says Tina. Her arms aren't just folded—more like clamped to her torso. "Are we going to leave campus?"

"Yeah," says Jeff, "unless you know of any cows around here?" He makes a show of looking around. No cows.

"Don't we need permission?"

Jeff catches the keys and purses his lips. He's been Tina'd.

"Well," he says, "yes, we probably do. But sometimes"—he looks off in the direction of the cows that are hovering just above the tree-tops—"sometimes you have to leap before you look."

"Leap where?" says Cam.

"Come on, Tina," Freesia says. "No one will notice. And a little fresh air will do us good. Lester, race you to the van!"

Her head start is insurmountable, and she easily secures shotgun in the van, a beautiful old beaten-up thing with faded blue paint. The rest of us pile in behind her—except for Tina.

"Come on, Tina," says BF James, descending from the van, and proffering a gentlemanly hand. "I'll keep you out of harm's way."

Whoa: what's this? I'm not quite sure, but it's gotten poor Tina's attention! Is she blushing? Maybe. Is she smiling? Yes, a little. Is she moving toward the outstretched arm of BF James? She is! And then she's in the van, with BF Escort climbing in behind her. This, my friends, is money in the bank.

Our destination, it turns out, is a familiar one. Hambecker Farm looks quite a bit different without a layer of snow. Soppier, browner, riddled with hoofprints. We pull up next to Jeff's mom's huge red Ford and pile out.

"Here it is," says Jeff, taking it in. "The farm!"

Without further notice, he glumps over to an ax that is wedged in a piece of wood and hoists it up and then back down on the stump. No dice: the ax remains buried; the wood doesn't split. He hammers it down a couple more times, without success, then abandons the attempt and starts showing us around. (Cam, I notice, bringing up the rear, one-hands the ax through the wood, then jogs a few steps to catch up.)

Off in a far pasture, a figure is scurrying toward the barn, carrying an animal—a rabbit? dead?—in each of her hands. This must be Arletta, the mother of the man who is her son. She vanishes behind the barn before Jeff or anyone can threaten to get her attention.

After Jeff leads us through a brief tour of the grounds—the outside of the barn, the yard, and the edge of the woods—we are left to our own devices. The others want to look at animals and fences, but I go into the house. I wander down a hallway, through the dining room, and into a cluttered living room. In the corner there's a dresser. Jackpot: photo album, the Hambecker-Traversal family yearbook. I bring it over to the couch and dig in, and am rewarded with a montage of Jeffly delights. Jeff as a kid, climbing a tree. Jeff in a tent he has made in his bedroom. Jeff and a man who looks like his father, playing softball in the yard.

"Sit up straight."

Here she is: Arletta, filling up the doorway with her small but wiry frame. (I'm pretty sure that's blood she's wiping on her smock.) Her gaze is fierce and piercing. And one thing is immediately clear: Jeff didn't get his slumping posture from her. No, she stands straight as a rake. The effect of this is to make her look taller, more imposing, somehow, than Jeff, even though he's got a good eight inches on her.

"You look like a wilted iris." (She has no reciprocal appreciation for my posture, it would seem.)

"Is this Jeff?" I ask, gesturing to a photo that is clearly a photo of Jeff. The question is not a good one.

"Come on," she says. "Get up. Let's go to the fields."

En route to the fields—for some reason—she peppers me with questions. Terse, direct, severely articulated.

"What are your aims?"

"Aims?"

"Don't act like an idiot. You know what I mean. What do you hope to achieve with your little book?"

"The yearbook?"

"No, the book of Job."

"Well," I say, scrambling to keep up, in every sense of the phrase, "I guess we kind of want it to be an infusion. Or a concoction, or an eclection."

"Your sentences trail off at the end. Listen to yourself. You start off fine, and then mumblemumblemumblemumble. Bullshit. Speak like you *mean* it. Mean the whole sentence. *Mean* it, and people will listen. What the hell is an 'eclection'?"

Large puddles mar the surface of the muck, like craters on the moon, the clouds in them like paintings of clouds.

"Well," I say, "we want it to fuse together various things, you know?"

"No," she says, stopping, and staring into me as if I've just murdered her peacock. "I don't know."

"Different things coming together," I manage to get out, looking into and then away from her unwavering gaze. "You know," I continue, staring into the muck, sensing that I'm digging myself into it, "moods, tones, influences, styles."

"You've been spending too much time with Jeff," she says, then surges forward.

She may be right.

"We just want it to be fun," I say, from a few paces behind.

"Come join me for a slaughter some time," she says, turning

to me, and finally smiling just a little bit. "That'll give you something to fuse together." I seize the chance to get on her fenceside, where the footing is slightly less treacherous.

"Got any siblings?" She isn't finished with me yet.

"Yeah," I say.

"Are you an older or a younger?"

"Older."

"Thought so. Sister?"

"Yeah."

You get the sense that if you were to place a carcass half a mile from the farm she would be able to identify the species and sex from the back porch.

"You two get along?"

"Well enough," I say.

"What do you mean, 'well enough'?"

"We're different."

"Who isn't?"

"She's been hanging with a bad crowd."

"What makes her crowd worse than yours?"

She looks upslope, where Cam is flinging a mallet.

"I had a sister once," she says. "You've got to give her some room to roam. Let her out of the stall, and open the gates of the goddamn pasture."

"Is anything not farm to you?"

She hears me or she doesn't. Either way, she's slipping through a metal gate, and expects me to follow her into the mire. "Come here," she commands. She's standing over something at the edge of the grass—what grass there is, a patch that hasn't yet been February'd into muck. Now she is smiling without restraint. "This is the most useful thing you'll see all day," she says.

"This?" I say, looking down at the pile of brown mush she is beholding so reverently.

"You know what that is?"

I don't dare hazard a guess.

"Bullshit," she pronounces. "That right there is a pile of bullshit."

OUR TRIP TO THE FARM—which was, by all accounts, a roaring success, despite Tina's complaints about poop on her loafers—has tripped some wire in Jeff's brain. And the tripping of that wire, along with the fortuitous fact of our back access road, has inspired a flurry of similar journeys. We have taken to the field on numerous occasions since, scattering ourselves outward into the wider world in search of inspiration. We rumble off campus during lunch, and if Jeff drives aggressively enough (as he always does) he can get us on the 1:20 ferry from Bremerton to Seattle, where we avail ourselves of popcorn and Pepsi and plot our course for the day.

So it has gone for the first few weeks of February. One day we spent at the Seattle Art Museum, where I borrowed Freesia's Nikon and took some pictures of the drinking fountains, the benches, and the doors on the restrooms, and where Cam was particularly taken with the Hammering Man ("It's this great big man, hammering"). On another day, we went to local cemeteries and made rubbings of the graves of Bruce Lee, Jimi Hendrix, and other graves with other names on them. We have scavenged the bus tunnels in downtown Seattle, and run laps around the Kingdome (or, in BF James's case, sat on a nearby bench feeding pigeons). We have watched trains come and go at King Street Station. We have elevatored up and down the Smith Tower. We started an extremely short-lived lemonade stand in the International District, and dispensed quite quickly—in one frantic afternoon—with the Ballard Locks, the Pike Place Market, and the Space Needle.

These trips are doing exactly what we want them to: they're distending the yearbook past what might previously have seemed reasonable and right. The things we are seeing and doing, no matter how random-seeming or haphazard, invariably bear fruit in the form of potential additions to the book. In a section, for example, with the working title "Bluey Upon the Boulevards," we have assembled a photo homage to Bluey (as we've dubbed the van): Bluey on the Seattle waterfront; Bluey on the ferry; Bluey bedecked in Doug Fir boughs. For a section to be called "The Sound Garden Sound Garden," Cam proposed that we assemble a sound collage using built-in speakers—"like in a birthday card"—featuring a mix of recordings of the Sound Garden at Magnuson Park made at different times. "Come Join Me for a Slaughter" is to feature a photograph of the specimen of bull feces that Arletta Hambecker so courteously brought to my attention, and "The International Headquarters of Yearbook Corporation, Inc." will feature a series of pseudo-architectural sketches of our crumbling outbuilding, courtesy, mostly, of Tina McTovey, whose skills as a draftsperson are impressive.

We have, in short, adopted a "zero intolerance" policy, which is to say that pretty much anything that anyone comes up with will go into the book. In class—when we're actually there—Jeff bangs out clanging clongs on a large gong (a flea market find from Fremont) whenever someone thinks of something new: a photomontage of the Proctor's various blazers (for instance); a comic-strip rendering of the Issues Initiative; a faculty section that replaces the names of the teachers with phrases from sessions of Exquisite Corpse. With each passing day, the PageMaker file on BF James's father's laptop grows larger and larger, sagging under the weight of our whims, and in defiance of the Proctor's budgetary admonitions. We're doing exactly what we want to do—nothing less, and nothing more—and it feels good.

Freesia is sitting at the Command Center in her bedroom—Toshiba and wooden chair—on this, the evening of the twenty-fifth of February. Her heels are on the chair, such that her knees are at her chin, and the tiny, jagged "K" on her ankle is visible (she razored this tribute upon learning Kurt Cobain was dead—it was a phase).

I'm lying on the bed, tossing a fuzzless tennis ball into the air, trying to get it as close to the ceiling as I can without hitting the ceiling. BF James is submerged in Freesia's purple beanbag chair, playing *Dr. Mario.*

Blingity-ding: a new message has come over the wires (the air? the sea? the stars? Like BF James, Freesia has begun to dabble in e-mail. Me, I'm not a fan of it—too many superfluous characters).

"Oh man," she says, her eyes still on the screen. "Guys, come here. You have to see this."

Often I ignore her when she calls me over to look at the latest message that has *blingity-dinged* onto her screen—a poem by a friend from camp, a political joke that's being passed around from screen to screen—but this *blingity-ding* is different.

> *Subject:* Help!
> *Author:* Jeff Traversal
> *Body Text:* Are you (and Lester? James?—don't have their em addresses) free this evening? I need your help—Proctor R wants to see the yearbook—and is coming to class tomorrow!

"Oh snap," says BF James.

"What should I tell him?"

Response is futile—she's already typing, typing this: *Ha! Yes— we can help u!*

"We can?" I say.

"Shut up." And then the sign-off: *Where/when? —FP.*

It is decided, over further electronic note-passing, that Jeff will come to us, mostly because Freesia's Toshiba houses the last surviving copy of the yearbook as it was at the time I drenched the floppy.

He shows up looking both anxious and enthused, frazzled but fresh, greeting David Price in the entryway with a warm, brisk handshake.

"Mr. Traversal."

"Mr. Price," says Jeff. "Good to see you again."

"And you as well."

(As if teachers stop by all the time.)

"I'm guessing you're in on our little secret?"

"What secret?" says the world-wise David Price.

"What up, Jeff!" I yell down the stairs, preparatory to sliding down the bannister.

"Hey."

I engage him in an improvised secret handshake.

"Come on, you guys," scolds Freesia from the top of the stairs. We go up.

"So what happened?" asks BF James. (Is he still wearing his parka, you wonder? He is.)

"The Proctor called me into his office this afternoon," says Jeff.

"I know the one," I say.

"And after all the usual huffing and puffing, he asked me how we're 'coming along' in Yearbook."

"To which you replied?" says Freesia.

"How would you describe the smell in there?" asks Jeff.

"Like an ointment, maybe," I suggest.

"Answer the question," Freesia demands.

"Well," says Jeff, "he said he wanted to pay us a visit. I told him that would be fine. Then he proposed tomorrow, and I said that would be fine. And here we are."

"You couldn't shine him on a little?" I say.

Jeff shrugs. (I think it's fair to say that a career in the FBI is not in his future.)

"Let's get to work," says All Biz Freeze.

We get to work, with Freesia at the controls.

"Okay," she says. "Here's what we have so far."

"I can't tell you how relieved I am that you have a copy of this," says Jeff.

"We've got the standard-issue photo layout."

"Rows and rows and rows of faces," BF James explains.

"We can just tell him that it's an easy upload into the document," says Freesia.

"Yes," I say, "perfect. The more words like 'upload' you can use, the better."

"We also have a draft Table of Contents," she adds. "You know, all the usual stuff. Clubs, sports, all of that. Plus section title pages."

"Good," says Jeff, as if surprised that anyone had been doing anything on the yearbook during the first four months of school.

"So I think we have a lot to work with," says Freesia. "We just need to add some bells and whistles."

"Yeah," says BF James over the peppy soundtrack of his game, "but it also needs to look cheap."

"Right," says Jeff. "'Within our budget.'"

"Clip Art, Freeze," I say. "Empty the vault."

"What's Clip Art?" queries Jeff.

"Here, I'll show you," says Freesia, doing some more rapid-fire clicking of the mouse. Soon the screen is filled with frilly delights: perky trees, bulging rainbows, smiling clouds, mischievous puppies, debonair starfish.

"Perfect. He'll eat that up."

"Got any wrestlers?" wonders BF James.

"Let me see," says Freesia, with another flurry of clicking and typing. "Looks like just this one."

"Oh," says Jeff, "that's perfect."

It's a little round-edged cartoon of two singleted castrati, grappling expressionlessly in the vacuum of a pure white background.

"Let's use that a lot," says BF James.

"More than a lot," I say.

"Also, we need an 'If' reference," says Jeff.

"If?" says Freesia.

"Kipling," fills in BF James.

"The gold standard for Bloviational Poetics," adds Jeff. "He quotes it every other second."

"Brilliant," I say. "Do you have a poetry anthology, Freeze?"

"Yeah, sure," she says, abstractedly, covering her face with her hands. "Okay. Okay okay okay." Re-emerging into open air. "You guys have to leave now"—turning to us to speak these words, though her hands and head are still on the keyboard, and still typing. "I'm going into Power Mode."

"She means it," I say, standing to leave. "Don't fight her on this one, guys."

Obeying Freesia's orders, we head back downstairs, where the inimitable David Price has settled into his reading chair with a Scotch about as old as I am.

"How goes it?"

"It goes well," I say.

"We made some really good fake progress," says BF James.

"Good to hear." Turning to Jeff: "Can I interest you in a taste of Lagavulin 16?"

"Twist my arm," says Jeff, abandoning his beeline for the door.

"We'll leave you two to catch up," I say, making for the mud room, with BF James in tow.

"So Jeff," I hear David ask as I lace up my Converse, "where do you see yourself in five years?"

As seen from the driveway on this cold clear February evening, the Price residence is like a mock-up of a warm, congenial household in a magazine ad for a car or a security system. I blink slowly and deliberately, uploading the image to my own internal archive, before turning toward the road with BF James.

I WAKE FRESH AS a daisy in a Safeway fridge, humming a Proctorian tune, a breakfast blend of the morning's dream-detritus, as I make my English muffin, blasting *Morning Edition* loud enough to wake Grace up.

"I can't believe you listen to this crap," she mutters, shuffling in her Hello Kitty slippers across the linoleum. "Why are you in such a good mood?" she asks, opening the fridge.

"I don't know," I say. "I guess I just woke up with a Frisbee in my bonnet."

From there the day Frisbees me forward irrevocably toward fifth period. And it's a good thing that I have my wits about me, sharpened and gleaming, when said period comes calling, for I have company on the slog of a walk out to our shanty: none other than King Archie himself, laboring across the Common, toting a pink pastry box. I slow my pace to synchronize with his.

"Mr. Smith."

"Mr. Proctor."

"Are we headed in the same direction?"

"I do believe we are. What's in the box?"

"Oh, this?" (a coy grin; a chortle) "These are lemon squares. I do have a bit of a sweet tooth, I must say."

"May I?"

He hands over the box. "Be careful. They shouldn't be jostled."

"And they won't be."

Off to our left, I spy Pancake under an awning, swaying, a sky-blue baby carrier draped over his belly.

"As you can probably surmise," says the Proctor, "my business goes beyond those lemon squares. I also want to check up on your progress. I expect great things!"

"You shan't be disappointed."

(Shan't!)

"Good."

When we get to our abandoned shipwreck of a classroom, everyone is seated at the ready. This is already a significant change, as the room is typically abuzz with sandwich-making, music, and invented indoor sports (when, that is, we're even there). *Badger Shmadger*, I notice, has been removed from its lectern.

"Proctor!" says Jeff. "Thanks for coming. Have a seat. We don't have much in the way of chairs, I'm afraid. You can have one of ours"—plastic, flimsy, dodgy—"or I also find that those boxes"—scattered all over the back of the room, exuding must and forgottenness—"work well too."

"Awfully drafty out here, isn't it?" says the Proctor, hazarding a seat on one of the boxes. "I'll have to speak with Maintenance."

"Yes," says Jeff, "we've sort of given up on ambience."

"You know what they say," I say. "Coldness is good discipline."

"So everyone," says Jeff, stepping nervously forward, and then back, "the Proctor is here to see how we're coming along." I take it on faith that Jeff has, in some fashion, prepared the others for the day's theatrics. Cam looks as placid and passive as ever, but Tina might prove to be a wildcard. "So what we've done, Proctor," he continues, reverting to his standard offhand manner, "is we've made you a printout of the yearbook as it looks right now. Freesia?"

Freesia gets up, packet in hand, and couriers the document back to the Proctor.

"Here you go," she says, with a wide and charismatic grin. "So, this is the Table of Contents. As you can see, we've only got a basic border right now, but I'm working on uploading some additional fonts."

She goes on for several minutes, ushering the Proctor through the pages of the dummy yearbook she Power-Moded into being just last night (I haven't seen the final product yet myself, but I have no doubt whatever that it is as good as any school's actual yearbook).

At the conclusion of this demonstration, the Proctor flips deliberately back through the pages of the packet, then thumbs the staple holding them together. He takes a drink-like glance around the room—blank his gaze, pursed his lips—and then he starts to nod.

"Mr. Traversal," he says, after a long, nerve-rending pause, "this"—he holds the packet in the air, glancing again around the room, as if only to torment us—"is wonderful. And it appears to be well within budget. Well done, everyone. Let's open up those lemon squares."

THE 28 MONDAYS of February, out here on our lonely peninsula, bring a slurring-together of coldness and slop, broken only by the eyelets of daffodils. It's not a time of year that has a lot to offer.

But not everyone detests the slurpy, muddy end of winter. There are those among us who take the thawing of the ground as a sign that it's time to make for the mud bogs. If you walk nearby the Turlock Pond late of a Friday evening you can hear the engines sputtering, the roaring of young voices, the slish of stuck tires spinning. You can see the floodlights glowing over the treetops. And on Saturday mornings you can see them driving through town: these trucks, nothing less than everlasting, caked in mud, left carefully unwashed, baring themselves in all their battered glory. They honk at each other. They yell and whoop. They leave tire tracks at intersections.

We are wise, we think, to stay away. But Grace, it would appear, possesses no such wisdom. She has been seen in the cab of Flynn's large-tired 4×4, his alternate mount, wheeling through the slickness of the mud, laughing, drinking. This BF James has confirmed by way of Jimmy Tolt, his man on the inside. And I confirm the same myself at BP, where I see her sitting shotgun in Flynn's plein-air, roll-caged, mud-caked 4×4.

He tumbles from the machine, sets the pump, and charges headfirst into the mini mart. I use this opening to approach the vehicle.

"Hey," I hey.

Grace looks at something in her lap. "What do you want?"

The space behind the seats is filled with empty cans of Mountain Dew, a gym bag, a face shield.

"Why do I always have to want something?"

"Because you do," she says.

"Well think of this as Lester *not* wanting something. Think of this as Lester opening the gates of the pasture, and letting all the little lambs run free." (When all else fails, resort to Arletta.)

In the sunlight slanting through the window, I can see that the natural brown of her hair is coming back in at the roots.

"I heard what you said to Dad," she says. "On the phone."

"Oh yeah," I say. "So did I."

"He can't—" She shakes her head. "Whatever."

Flynn returns, thwacking a pack of cigarettes against his palm.

"Nice ride," I say.

"You bog?"

"No. I'm just a fan."

"It's got—" He finishes this sentence with a list of special specifications—specifications which doubtless make his 4×4 quite special indeed—but no sooner has he rattled them off than they vanish from my consciousness, like shooting stars that light up the heavens oh so briefly before the sky goes dark again.

"Anyway," I say, with a tap on the roll cage, "have fun. Be safe. I'll see you at home."

Flynn gasses the engine and cranks up the Pantera. Grace stares straight ahead.

BY THE TIME THAT Jeff gets to our booth at Melky's, Freesia has stopped crying, but her eyes are still red, and her nose is still a little runny. He doesn't notice at first, and approaches us with energy and verve, raising a hand toward each booth-bench to high-five us in greeting. Then he sees that Freesia has entered Panic Mode.

"What's going on?"

She starts to cry again, and buries her face in her hands. He places a hand on her shoulder. "What's wrong?"

I slide him the envelope: a small envelope from Brown University, in which there is a letter informing Freesia that her application couldn't be considered because it was incomplete.

"I forgot to include my essay," she blubbers. "I'm so stupid!" She breaks into a new round of sobs.

"It's okay," says Jeff. He pulls up a chair. "This is just a minor setback."

She raises her head. Her eyes are red, her cheeks flushed. "But what if I did that with all of them?"

"I seriously doubt that," says Jeff.

"I'm so stupid."

"You're not stupid," I say.

"How many other places did you apply to?" asks Jeff.

Here I can't withhold my grin.

"What?" says Freesia.

"Tell him."

"Well?" says Jeff.

She sighs, then spills the beans. "Thirty-seven."

"You applied to thirty-seven colleges?"

"Yeah. What?"

"And this is the first one you've heard back from?"

"I'm off to a flying start."

"That's tough," says Jeff. "Not what you wanted to hear first, is it? But something tells me you're going to be all right."

"I guess so. I just—I just feel so stupid."

"You can't be perfect," he reminds her. It's not necessarily a statement she's prepared to agree with.

"Brown was my first choice. It sounds so cool."

"Eh," says Jeff. "You'll be better off elsewhere. How about a milkshake?"

"She's on a strict regimen of Diet Cokes," I say.

"No," says Freesia. "Today I want a large chocolate shake."

"There's progress!" I say. "I'll take the same."

Jeff gets up to get the shakes, including one for himself, and I help him haul them back to our booth.

"So," he says, removing the lid of his shake to inspect its contents, "you guys actually like this place?"

"Yeah," I say. "We do. It has a certain Wichie-like appeal."

"Like a battered teddy bear, I guess," says Jeff, looking down at the shake as if he expects to find a battered teddy bear at the bottom. "Anyway, here's to you guys," he says, raising his cup. "You saved my ass the other night."

The twenty-something man running the place comes out to turn the sign on the window from OPEN to CLOSED (or from CLOSED to OPEN, as it is to us).

"There's just one thing I'm still a little worried about," says Freesia. The shake is working its magic. Panic Mode has given way to Worry Mode.

"What's that?" says Jeff.

"We made that fake yearbook to placate the Proctor, right? But what's going to happen when he sees the real thing?"

MARCH

The Price family residence is sparkling in the setting sun, which has just emerged below a bank of clouds to brighten the rain on the lawn and the driveway. Spring is getting closer.

"I can't go in there, Les," says Grace.

"Why not? What's the matter?"

"I don't know. It's just too—*perfect*, you know? Like I bet they have cloth napkins, and matching silverware."

As if on cue, Marian Price enters the frame of the picture window, carrying two handfuls of silverware, which she begins to set out on the dining table. She is shortly joined by David, toting a tray of ice-filled glasses.

"Why did I agree to this?"

The front door swings open.

"Hey!" yells Freesia. "You going to come in, or just spy on us all creepy-like?"

I wave scowling Grace ahead. David and Marian are there to greet us at the door.

"Hey, Les," says David. "And you must be Grace."

"Hey," says Grace, with an awkward wave and an overdone smile.

"Come on in."

The house is redolent of roasted meats. A cello suite from an earlier century establishes a background of tastefulness and order. We head over to the island in the kitchen.

"Would you like a pop?" asks David.

"No thanks," says Grace.

"Do you want to hang your sweatshirt up to dry?" asks Marian.

"No," says Grace. "It's fine."

"How about some prosciutto-wrapped melon?" tries David.

"No thanks."

A few more attempts at friendly conversation stall out before we concede the round and sit to dinner. Grace's placemat pushes mine out of its customary place at center table right. As the dishes make their way around the table, David gives it another go.

"So Grace," he says, serving himself some roasted Brussels sprouts, "Lester says you're quite an artist."

"Not really."

A look of mild betrayal from David to me: have I fed him bad intelligence?

"Grace is a *really* talented illustrator," offers Freesia.

No input from Grace, who has weathered this exchange with her head down, forking peas, one per tine.

"Yes," I say, "that's the word: illustrator."

"That's terrific," says David.

"Do you work in pencil or ink?" asks Marian.

"Mostly ink." A murmur—just a breath above a mumble.

"I'd love to see some of your work."

"My mom is on the board of the County Arts Commission," says Freesia.

"Oh," says Grace.

I shrug helplessly at David. His hands go up in understanding, held aloft there by a warm, sly smile from Marian—a look to remind me not to push too hard.

"What exactly does that mean?" says Grace.

"Well," says Marian, "we make decisions about what to do with public funds for art. You know, installations, things like that."

"That sounds cool," says Grace.

I steal a glance at Freesia. Eyebrows go up.

"Yes," says Marian, "it's very interesting work. Right now, for instance, we're reviewing bids for a new sculpture at the county courthouse."

"Really?" says Grace. "My mom works there—our mom, I should say."

"That's right," says David. "How's she doing?"

Grace looks at me. I look at her.

"I think she's doing okay," says Grace. "All things considered."

Where have all these words been hiding?

"One of the proposals," says Marian, "my personal favorite, is a sculpture of a man being lifted off the end of a diving board by a dozen balloons. The balloons would be cast in bronze, but the man would be made out of wire. It's a fun little play on the scales of justice."

"Wow," says Grace. "That sounds really cool."

"I'm glad you think so," says Marian. "If only I could get my colleagues to agree!"

She sips her wine. David pours her more, then turns to other topics. By the end of the meal, Grace has exceeded her speech quota for all of 1997, and her plate is miraculously clear.

"This was delicious," she says to David.

He turns to me. "You told her to say that, didn't you?" Then back to Grace. "You have your brother's knack for flattery."

Grace laughs. "I guess we have something in common after all, huh Les?"

"I guess so," I say.

She looks outside. "I'm sorry, but I have to go. Flynn's here."

So he is. The Brat is idling on the road. He greets us with a mid-range rev.

She gets up. I follow her into the entryway. She opens the door.

"Thanks," I say.

She turns back. "See you later."

I watch from the doorway as she heads out to the road and gets into the Brat.

Back at the table, everyone is beaming.

"She's delightful," says Marian.

"She is, isn't she?" I say.

"I told you my cooking would do it," says David, clearing his plate.

"Freesia," says Marian, "tell Lester your good news."

Freesia hops over to the sideboard and retrieves a large white envelope. She hands it to me. It's addressed to "Freesia Price '01," from Dartmouth College.

"No way!"

David throws an arm around Marian.

"I'm speechless, Freeze."

"How about congratulations?"

"I'm—congratulations. Seriously."

"Now come over here and give me a hug."

THIS DAY HAS BEEN going to come for quite some time, and now it has. My mother rose early and went to the store for garbage bags and packing tape. After resuscitating some boxes that have been lying dormant in the attic, she kneels in the hall outside The Father's study in old jeans and a gray T-shirt that probably used to be his, her hair held back by a faded green bandana, drawing out long, loud *hwaeaealps* of the tape, which she uses to assemble the boxes. Her arms are surprisingly wiry. I haven't ever thought of her in terms of physical strength, but it is indeed the case that she possesses an almost Linda Hamilton–like arm-strength, a strength, you might say, that is almost proportionate to the silence of her suffering.

"I figure it's about time," she says, seeing that I have emerged from my room, and leaning back into an upright kneel to address me, knees on the hardwood, hands on her thighs. Grace is still asleep.

"Here," I say. "I'll assemble, you apply the tape."

Armed with garbage bags and boxes, we enter the unenterable study. The room is cold and still and radically silent. There isn't much adorning the walls—a poster for an arts festival in Oregon from 1974, a photo of T.S. Eliot leaning against a mantel. We pack up the papers on the desk and the books on the shelf and then turn to the closet. The closet: it goes without saying (and isn't said) that the closet is where the rubber of our ridding will hit the road.

"Look at all this, Lester," she says, beholding the shelves and shelves of his stuff. "All this crap. Promise me you'll know when to get rid of things."

"Are you calling this crap?" I say, pulling out a broken plastic ukulele.

She laughs, which seems to be a good sign, a sign that it is indeed about time to be doing what we're doing.

"The things he held on to," she says, shaking her head, whipping another garbage bag open. "I guess I'll start on the left. You take the right. No need to be cautious. Just empty the shelves."

And so begins the process of ridding. The objects in isolation—an old word processor, a Bible from his college days, endless notebooks filled with notes written out in his microscopic hand—seem almost, but not quite, to make sense of his life. It is only in their aggregation—bag after bag, box upon box—and in the fact of their having sat there, untouched, for so many years, that they begin to approach a larger significance. Until, that is, I come upon a box marked "AOW." It opens to three stacks of yellowing, hardcover editions of *All Our Woe*, by Edwin Nash Smith. I lift one to the light and examine the cover, which is remarkably similar to that bright orange cover of his old paperback copy of *Paradise Lost*, except that in the place of a falling angel, there's a falling man. On the back cover, a much younger version of The Father stares out with a world-weary expression, his beard still without a trace of gray.

"Look, Lester," says my mother, coming up for air. "Remember this god-awful outfit?" She's holding up a kilt and sporran.

Yes, I do not need to say, I do remember it, with something like an icicle to the heart. He bought that "bagpiping getup," as my mother used to call it, along with some actual bagpipes, shortly before my fifth birthday, and I loved them so much right away that I insisted that he wear the outfit at my party. But none of the other kids understood the importance of his bagpipes, I felt, the sheer thrill of their nasal wailing and the exotic bravado of the outfit that went with them. But Grace and I—we got it. We knew. And for weeks thereafter we pestered him to wear the kilt and play for us. And sometimes he did. He would parade us through the yard, through the unmowed grass, under the neglected apple trees, and along the wall of blackberries. We followed piping our own imaginary pipes, hopping and skipping in the unreal sunlight, the perpetual sunlight of a moment that is fixed, as it was or has become, in time.

I fall into my mother's arms, clutching the book, holding tight to the memory of those sun-filled days, and sobbing. Something has burst, is flowing out, like air. And something else, perhaps, is flowing in, like air.

When I gather myself again, a tad ashamed and very silent, not sure where to stand or what to start to do, I see that Grace is standing in the doorframe, still half shrouded in the fog of sleep.

"What—?"

And then she's gone. Her door slams down the hall.

We finish the packing in sober silence—I stash one copy of his book for my private collection—and lug the bags and boxes out to our station wagon. Then I head inside for one more item.

I lift my mattress and slide it out. The cover—a puffy fake leather, maroon with an embossed gold border—is dusty but otherwise pristine. *Southwest High School, 1967.* I turn to the inside back cover. There's a note in it from him to her in the lower right corner: *I'd love to spend some time with you this summer. ~Eddie.*

I bring the book out to my mom.

"Where'd you find that?"

"Let's add it to the pile," I suggest.

"No," she says. "I want to keep it."

"Really?"

"Yes," she says, running a finger over the faded ink of The Father's note, "I do."

She takes it inside, and I continue loading up the car. Just as I am hoisting in the last, half-full bag, Grace comes out, squinting in the sunlight.

"Take these too," she says.

She hands me two postcards. One is a shot of the Metrodome taken from a great height, the other has a Twins logo on it. One is headed "Postcard 2 of 3," the other "Postcard 3 of 3." Both are dated 24 September, 1996, and both begin, "Dear Lester." But on each the text has been crossed out with a thick black pen.

I look at Grace, who has pulled her hoodie over her head. Saying nothing further, she starts to backpedal, then turns around and goes inside.

I hold the postcards to the cloudlight, trying for a moment to read what is written beneath that thick black ink, then slide them into the garbage bag.

After my mother has left with his stuff, I go out behind the house, the only house I've ever known, out to our small back yard, where the grass still isn't mowed, and the trees are still in disarray, and the blackberries have extended their reach over time.

Ms. FLOUGH IS STANDING on her fruit-crate dais, waiting, triumphant and proud, as we come filtering into our hexagonal lunchroom. Standing behind her, and off to the left, is the Proctor. Today is most decidedly a bow-tie day for our fair Proctor—sky-blue, with a certain sheen to it. The jacket is beige. The pants are also beige. The loafers reddish-brown.

This is it, folks: the culmination of Ms. Flough's vaunted Issues Initiative (the "Issue-stravaganza," as the flyers call it).

"I am so delighted," Flough delights in telling us, once some—if not quite most—of the noise has died down, "so *delighted* by the civic engagement that this Initiative has allowed us to comprise. And I'm so excited about Phase II of it," she says, rocking back and forth from heel to heel, pushing her oversized glasses up her nose, then checking to see that they're still there. "Phase II of The Issues Initiative. Which this is the last and final phase. So let's all be excited. Let's all get involved. All ideas are valid!"

The Proctor applauds limply, then folds his hands again at his belt.

"Phase II" of the Floughian brain-child, so she informs us, involves breaking into groups, yet again, and revisiting the Issues we discussed in the fall—and then discussed again, in Flough's zoo-like classroom, in January—and discussing them (again), and debating them (again), and honing them down to pinpoints of perfect proposal. "You're now dispersed," she finally concludes, "to do exactly that."

In the earlier part of the day, as we gather in the various wings of the campus for our Phase II Break-Out Sessions, I decide it's time to dredge Cam Drinker, Jr.'s fledgling proposal—that the VMHS Expansion Funds be used to adorn the 1997 VMHS yearbook with metal covers—from out of the back pages of the Final Pamphlet. Gently, but persistently, I remind my colleagues to consider it. To my slight surprise and slight delight, they do. And quickly the idea gains traction among certain segments of the student body—the skaters, the debaters, and Cam's home crowd, the Pancake Bloc.

By late afternoon, as we come chittering back into the lunchroom—after everyone's been forced to have lunch in places other than the lunchroom—the final list of discussion items has been written out on a flip chart in Flough's bubbly script: *Final Issues/ Proposals.* "Metal Covers" is the first item on the list (presumably, I suspect, from my outpost at the edge of the room, so that it can be that much more quickly shot down).

As Flough makes her final introduction to the conclusion of the project, I scan the room. The crowd is restless. The light quite bad. Freesia's sitting in the middle, looking bored. BF James is buried in a book. On the far side of the lunchroom, I spot Jeff, trying to escape through a little-used side door. It's locked. Too bad, Jeff: you're stuck here with the rest of us.

"Okay," says Flough, "metal covers. What is that?" She looks around the room. The room is silent. So I speak.

"Ms. Flough," I say, more loudly than I'm usually apt to talk. "May I say a few words?"

"What?"

I start walking toward the little makeshift stage. Then I'm on it, next to her.

"What are you doing?" She says this as much with her hands—one devouring the other—as with her milk-pop of a voice.

"This will only take a moment," I assure her. I grab the mic and face the crowd. This is a new way of looking at things. Everyone gathered there, all at once. Everyone looking at you.

"Hey," I begin. "How's it goin'?"

In the back of the room, someone shouts something.

"Good lookin' crowd," I continue. "Listen, I'm not going to waste your time up here. I'm not here to bloviate. I just want to say a few things in support of this here proposal that's been proposed by one of Victory's finest, our own Cam Drinker, Jr."

Another shout: this time a whoop of approval from the Pancake Bloc.

"Throughout history," I say, in a voice that suggests I'm reading from a World Book, "metal has been a symbol of man's capacity to make things metallic. Think of all of the wonderful things that are made out of metal. Your spoons, your cars, your decorative plaques."

I clear my throat. I've lost some of them, but gained some others.

"It is my firm belief," I say, "my *firm belief*," I repeat, "that our yearbook should be added to this list."

The silence of a crowd is its own kind of silence. I catch the smiling eye of Freesia, and smile back.

"Okay Lester"—Gloria Flough, advancing to reclaim her stage. "You've had your fun. It's time to be moving on with the remaining agenda. We have some really good ideas here. Some really serious things."

A few of the students seated at the front are nodding their heads in agreement. Your Stan Harveys. Your Charity Carrington Moores. No sign of the Proctor.

I turn to Ms. Flough. "Ms. Flough," I say, "it was my understanding that every idea would be discussed."

"Lester," she says, clenching her fists, then flexing her fingers. "I think that enough has been said about your metal yearbook."

"What happened to all ideas being valid?" Blessed, storied Tina McTovey has stood to ask this question. She is boring into Flough with her gaze.

"Excuse me?" says Flough. This shot across her bow has come from what she took to be a friendly ship.

"Yeah," says Cam, standing, hands clenched at his sides. "What happened to that?"

Flough pierces him with a flustered glare. But before she can concoct a response, a low voice at the back of the crowd—is that Jimmy Blatt?—starts chanting: "me-TAL, me-TAL, me-TAL." The chant spreads to a few more students, and then a few more, and then catches like wildfire, engulfing the room. *me-TAL, me-TAL, me-TAL.* It's a highly pleasing sound. Forceful, iambic.

I can picture what happens next—Flough tries to silence the crowd, but the chanting continues, unbidden, unstoppable, louder and louder and louder—but by then I am safely out of the room and through the foyer and into the glistening air of almost-spring.

AFTER SCHOOL, SOME PEOPLE come up in allegiance. Others are angry. (Most, of course, don't care at all.)

Word even gets back to my mother, who raises the subject of the afternoon's farandole over a delicious supper of roasted chicken, mashed potatoes, green beans, biscuits, and thick, delicious gravy, her specialty. Even Grace, in her thinness and silence, is eating with gusto.

"I hear you're causing quite a stir, Lester," says my mother.

"From whom?"

"I have my sources." (Most likely Ms. Knapford, the VMHS librarian—they knit together, here and there.)

"It's nothing, Mom," I say, tearing another half-biscuit from the clobber. "Business as usual. Capulets and Montagues."

"You know, your father used to be like that."

"Like what?" says Grace.

"He used to have a real take-no-bullshit attitude." She holds the butter knife in the air, mid-spread. Glistening with a mix of butter and jam. "He just couldn't stand to take things."

"Like what?" I ask.

"I don't know. Things he didn't like. One time we were on a trip to California—this was before you guys were born. We were on the pier in Santa Monica. It was a gorgeous day. This guy came running by and bumped into me. I almost fell over. But the guy just kept going, and ran into a little girl. And she *did* fall. And her ice cream too. But the guy just kept on going." She shakes her head, spreading the jam in little figure eights. "Your dad was *pissed.* He ran after the guy."

This is the hardest part to imagine: The Father moving at anything faster than a halfhearted shuffle.

"Turned out the guy was just trying to catch up to his girl-friend, or something stupid like that. Your dad got in his face. I thought he was going to throw a punch."

"And?" I demand. "Don't leave me hanging, Mom!"

"You know, I don't remember!"

"What do you mean, you don't remember? Your husband fought for your honor in a foreign land, and you don't remember what happened?"

"I don't. I just remember him running after the guy, and con-fronting him. And the anger in his eyes. But no, it wasn't really anger. It was *energy.* Just not being willing to take it, you know?"

It takes some effort, but I can picture it (in my version, he's holding the guy up by the collar of his shirt).

"Well," says my mother, getting up, dinner dish in hand, "who knows where *that* man went."

The problem, perhaps, is that we *do* know where he went—and that the Metrodome of 1997 is a long way away from the Santa Monica Pier of 1976.

Our mother has left the room. Which leaves Grace and me in a rather strange situation, doesn't it? Sitting at the table, alone, facing each other, and seemingly about to talk in a way that's almost comfortable.

"Lester," says Grace.

"Graciela."

"I wasn't there today, but I heard it was pretty cool."

"I do what I can."

"I mean, Flough and all those people—they're so dumb. I mean, isn't it pointless to ask kids who are leaving in like two years to decide the school's priorities?"

"Precisely!"

"I don't know. Seems really dumb to me."

"Because it is."

"So," she says, examining her fingernails, "what did you think of that story about Dad?"

"What about it?"

"Do you think it was true?"

"I do," I say. "But that was a long time ago."

"Yeah, I know, but isn't that kind of the point? Dad would never defend anyone now. When people get older, they just— they stop caring."

"Not necessarily."

"I don't know. Look at all our teachers. Do they really give a crap?"

"Yeah," I say, "I think they do. Most of them are just trying to do their jobs."

"Even the Proctor?"

"Well, yeah, since you mention him. Even the Proctor, I guess."

"I don't know. Whatever. But anyway, thanks. I owe you a thank you, I guess. So here it is: Thanks."

"For what?"

"Don't be an idiot, Lester," she says, getting up, leaving her plate on the table.

There are still three biscuits left, and plenty of butter, and plenty of jam. These will fuel me as I write. I take the somewhat-wrinkled postcard—a shot of King's Island taken from a plane or blimp—from my pocket. My message is brief:

Heavenly Father Who Art in the Metrodome:

I am coming to visit for Spring Break. My train arrives on
April 23rd.

~ L. E. S.

I walk to the highway through a cold drizzle and drop the
postcard into a mailbox on the side of the road.

THE LAST DAY of the trimester is always a downer. You're looking
ahead to the next ride at the fair, but you're still strapped into
this one. You're neither here nor there.

Jeff seems to think otherwise (rookie mistake), and announces
at the beginning of Yearbook that he wants to do something special to cap off the term: "I want to do something special," he says.
"To cap off the term." He's dangling the keys to Bluey. "What do
you say?"

We board Bluey and escape down our back driveway, off-
peninsula, and onto the freeway heading north. Jeff's special,
term-capping something, it turns out, is a down-on-its-luck pizza-
and-game parlor called Fredzilla's.

As kids, Grace and I had a particular fondness for Fredzilla's—
the pizza, the Skee-Ball, and, above all else, the giant pit of multi-
colored plastic balls. We'd submerge ourselves in them, hiding
from our parents, perched in utter stillness, peeking up at the
ceiling through the gaps between the balls.

The Fredzilla's of today is more than a little rough around the
edges. The plastic sign over the door is cracked, and the electric
door-chime, low on juice and self-respect, emits little more than
a low, slow moan.

We have the run of the place: the maze of arcade and carnival
games; the vaguely smelly dining area; and, at the center of it
all, that giant pit of multi-colored balls (have they been there all
this time?). The popcorn machine looks like it hasn't been used

since Jeff was in high school, and the mop and bucket in the center of the room probably weren't part of the original design. There's only one person on duty, from the looks of it, a guy around twenty who must be wondering how his life has come to this. Still, he takes our order cordially enough, and we make for a table that runs along the northern border of the ball-pit.

"My dad got kicked out of here once," says Cam.

"Dare I ask why?" asks Jeff, pouring himself a tall cup of root beer.

"He knocked Excitebike over," Cam explains.

"That," says BF James, "is worthy of a trophy."

"Dare *I* ask," says Freesia, "why you brought us here?"

"I don't know," says Jeff, taking in the dusty stuffed animals drooping from the walls, "it just seemed fitting."

In the empty arcade, a few of the machines are plinging and jingling away.

"It's part of our apprenticeship," I say.

"Our Dagobah," adds BF James.

"It can only feed our efforts," says Jeff.

"How?" says Cam.

"Well—" says Jeff. He isn't exactly sure.

"Here's how," offers Freesia, snatching the keys to Bluey from the table, and tossing them into the ball-pit.

"You're getting those," says Jeff. The tip of the key-fob is visible at the surface of the balls, just ten or twelve feet distant, floating precariously, like a lost kite on the surface of a half-frozen pond.

"Nope," says Freesia, leaning back, arms crossed. "You are."

"I'll get them," says Cam.

"No you won't," says Freesia. "Jeff will."

"Okay," says Jeff, standing to size up the ball-pit. Its depth, its width, the diameter of the balls. The likelihood that he will, within a few minutes, be escorted out of the establishment by that hapless 20-year-old counter-man.

"Cam," says Jeff, "if you go get those keys, I will guarantee you an A for the term, and for next tri too."

"Hold your ground," I say to Cam. "I bet he'll throw in some air and some lint to boot."

"Come on, Cam," pleads Jeff. "Help me out here."

Cam's grin widens. "What are *you* offering, Lester?"

What am *I* offering? "I'm offering two things," I say. "First, you get to watch Jeff scramble around in the ball-pit for his keys. Second, you get to watch Jeff scramble around in the ball-pit for his keys."

"I'll put ten bucks towards that," says BF James.

"Make it twenty," says Jeff, "if you do it."

"Come on, Jeff," I prod. "Think of it as a metaphor."

"Okay," he sighs. "I see how it is."

He rolls up the sleeves of his sweater, steps gingerly over the padded wall enclosing the pit, and wades out into the balls. Slow is his approach, deliberate the dragging of his legs through all those multi-colored spheres, until he finds himself on the precipice of triumph. He begins to bend down, slowly, arm extending, slowly, toward the keys, drawing ever closer to the object of his—

"Kamikaze!!!"—Cam, bellyflopping into the balls, and surfacing from his dive with a look of sheer exuberance, then diving back into the pit, where he does a turtle-like breast-stroke to nowhere. Hard on his scissor-kicking heels is Freesia, hugging her knees with one arm and plugging her nose with the other as she cannonballs into the pit. Jeff begins frantically dragging his hand through the balls and along the sticky, rubbery bottom of the enclosure. In the meantime, Freesia and Cam, who have been pelting one another with the balls, turn their attention to me. I ward off their attack, swan-dive into the pit, return their fire, then—as our bewildered server arrives with the saggy, cheese-greasy pizza—I crawl like a monitor lizard over the padded wall to the popcorn machine. There I grab an empty paper bucket and put it on my head, then seize the mop and scale the padded wall of the ball-pit.

"Don Traversal," I intone, brandishing the mop, "I am the Knight of the White Moon, here to unseat you from your seat. I challenge you to a duel, in heavenly arms, for the title of Ruler of Fredzillastan."

Jeff rises from the balls, still keyless. Will he join me on this wall that stands beyond the bounds of *guidelines* and *core principles*? He will: "I accept your challenge, Vuestra Merced," he says, after a pause, in a tone of absolute solemnity. "Squire," he says, addressing himself to Cam, "my lance and helmet."

"Huh?" says Cam.

"Give him this," says BF James, tossing Cam a party hat.

"And this," says Freesia, handing Cam her umbrella.

Jeff dons the party hat, holds the umbrella aloft, and begins to walk a slow, sideways circle. I jump into the ball-pit and join him in this circuit. The employee is nowhere to be found.

"Here you shall fall, Don Traversal," I taunt, sloshing through the balls.

"You are mistaken, O Knight of the Crap Haircut," counters Jeff, "for it is you who shall fall."

"Your lance is no match for the strength of my right arm," I hypothesize.

"Your region will be forgotten for generations to come," he warns, sloshing.

Then he charges, lurching through the balls, umbrella-first. He makes it almost all the way across before he falls. And by the time he emerges, I'm holding the umbrella—lately his lance—over my head.

"Spread the word far and wide," I declaim, "all ye who have witnessed this victory, that the Knight of the White Moon has vanquished Don Traversal, for now and forever. Or a little while, anyway. Like a few days, maybe."

Jeff bows in mock defeat to the soundtrack of plinging and jingling from the arcade.

"Got 'em!" says Cam. He's holding the keys. Somehow, it seems, Cam is always holding the keys.

WE BLUEY HOME in silence. As we turn onto 177th Ave. SW, the clock on the dash reads 8:57. In the dark of night, the campus looks like an abandoned mental hospital.

Jeff eases Bluey into our driveway and we tumble out into the cold, damp air. Freesia stretches her arms to the sky, and then stops, arms frozen in an upright position. "Uh oh."

I turn—we all turn—to where she's looking. And where she is looking is the doorway of our classroom. And standing in the doorway of that classroom is the Proctor. His hands are folded at the front of his blazer. His scowl is deep and deep with shadow.

"Mr. Traversal," he pronounces, "you are to be suspended, effective immediately."

APRIL

THE STORY HAS SPREAD like a virus all over the school. No particular story, that is, has spread like a virus all over the school, finding its hosts in bathrooms and classrooms and Hondas and Chevys. Mr. Traversal has been suspended. He made inappropriate advances at a student. He got caught smoking pot in the faculty bathroom. He punched the Proctor in the gut. He put glue on the driver's seat of Flough's LeBaron. The truth is lying somewhere else—under a mossy rock, perhaps, just north of campus.

As for the rest of us: we got off with a slap on the wrist, in the form of individual meetings with the Proctor, coupled with stern warnings regarding the milking of cows and the jousting of jousts in ball-pits. The word "probation" has been severally deployed. I think it's fair to say that Yours Truly has been downgraded from "keen and kindred" to something more like "daft and disappointing." We all have a cross to bear.

You might think we'd fold our little Yearbook table, close up shop, and move on to something else. But no: We have double the reason now, in fact, to keep on going—if not triple, or quadruple. In the first place, there's a certain pride at stake—a *Badger Pride* ('81), you might say, a sense of investment. Much of our time and youthful energy has been given to the effort, and there isn't any sense in throwing all that over all at once. More pointedly, however: Ms. Flough. Glorious glorified Gloria Flough, the person named to take on Yearbook in the wake of Jeff's suspension. This is a show not to be missed.

My opening strategy is simple: to delay, dilate, digress, and distract. In short: to take her on a pleasant stroll through the labyrinth of rooms inside her head and inside mine. My goal is to carry out the task in the manner—if I may mix my metaphors—of a pickpocket hired for a private event, who takes everything away from his mark, only to make a show of giving it back at the end.

The lighting in Ms. Flough's classroom gets most of the attention—and for good reason. But a lesser-known reason to avoid it is the smell. It isn't just the smell of that rodent. It's the smell of that rodent coupled with some awful herbal concoction gone awry, as if a hippie shaman got lost in the medicine aisle of Shop Rite. So we have to contend with those smells, to be sure, but also with a clutch of yearbook upstarts—a little gaggle of Floughites who see Jeff's demerit as a chance to glom on to the new show in town. Four are they, and four are we, with Tina McTovey perched somewhere in the middle (ready, most likely, to shuttle messages between enemy camps). We—Freesia, Cam, BF James, and I—bivouac in the back right corner of the room. They—let's call them Bloop, Blop, Blap, and Blorf—sit at the front, diagonally opposed to us. And there, as the pivot, sits Tina M.—more like the Bloop-Blop-Blap-Blorf consortium in temperament, perhaps, but sharing a certain wonderful history with us.

The bell rings, and Flough stands to greet this diagonal roster. Bride of Wichie is beaming her orange glow at Flough's heels. It's good to see she's doing well.

"Okay," says Flough. "Yearbook. This is Yearbook. The class."

I join in the earnest nodding of the Blorfsortium.

"So the situation is a little frazzled, really," says Flough, shaking one fist back and forth really fast to demonstrate its frazzlement. "As some of you know, we had to change teachers. I wasn't the one doing it before, but now I am. I'm the one doing it now. Which this was going to be my planning period, but now my planning period is during period three. And Ms. Ortega is teaching U.S. Presidents this term, so that's really exciting for her. Any questions so far?"

I raise my hand.

"Yes?"

"I love that blouse."

"Thank you," she says, touching her blouse. "It has a special coating, for your glands."

Freesia gives me a wise little kick—I'm peaking too early.

"So as I was saying," says Flough, "we have to start over. Which is great in some ways, but in other ways not—not great. I have some sheets."

She passes out some sheets, sending ours over McTovey Pass.

Flough's sheets are always bordered with wingdings, but these have a *double* wingding border. I can't help myself.

"Marvelous."

A look of suspicion from Gloria F. (her wariness: warranted, I suppose I should concede).

"What is it now, Lester? Did you find a typo?"

"No. The border."

"He digs the double ding," says BF James.

"The what?"

"It's really quite an achievement," I say. "I just didn't want it to go unnoticed."

"Okay, Lester, that's enough," choughs Flough. "Now everyone, look at the sheet. Because what the sheet is is the sheet is important, because it tells you about my policies and procedures. Regarding the assignments. The yearbook."

"Could you please read some of it out loud?" says BF James. "My glasses are foggy."

"Well that's what I was about to do, if you could just hang on for just one minute."

As she reads she taps her feet, first the left, and then the right, first the toe, and then the heel. When she finishes reading, I raise my hand. Blorf sighs.

"What now, Lester?"

"One more quick questch. It says here that the yearbook is quote 'going to be based on some really interesting Issues Initiative doctrines' unquote."

"Yes. That's what I just said. When I was reading it."

"Can you explain exactly what that means?"

"It means," she flusters forth, "that we're shifting foci. So if you want to do your metalworks, forget about it. And no more joyriding out and about all over town. Which you shouldn't've been doing that, you guys."

"But we love Bluey."

"It's pronounced Floo-y."

"Bluey."

"Flough."

Blap: "Can you give it a rest, Lester?"

"Fair enough," I say, hands raised in submission. "I'm just making sure I've got it all down."

"Any other questions?"

"What computer program do we use?" asks blessed, careful Tina McTovey.

"Well," says Flough, "the beauty of it is that I can do most of it on my computer at home. It's a Tandy. And what we'll be using is we'll be using the cross-supplied input from the Issues Initiative. To input the data. And I can do columns. And I can use the computer lab for graphic designs. All under budget, of course."

Columns? Data? Now my hand shoots up unbidden.

"Can we stop with all the questions?"

"No," I say. "We can't."

"Well what then?"

"What, exactly, do you mean by inputting data in columns?"

"Well, if you were listening—"

"I *was* listening," I say. "But I don't know what you're *saying*."

"Here's what's going to happen," she manages to say. "I'll come in every day and give you all a progress report on how I'm doing. How it's going with the book I'm making."

The book *she's* making? I don't know what to say. I exchange a frightful glance with Freesia. Tina's hand goes up.

"Yes? Tina?"

"What about us? What are *we* supposed to do?"

This stops Flough in her tracks. It clearly isn't something she's considered.

"Yeah," says Freesia. "Where do *we* figure into this book that *you're* making?"

"Well," floughs Flough, "if you would just look at the sheet—"

Cam raises his hand.

"Yes? What? Can we stop with all these questions? What's your name?"

"Cam."

"Yes Cam?"

"With Jeff we were talking about metal covers. Can we still do that?"

"No," says Flough, re-scrunching her face, "I don't like that. Too expensive. And too heavy."

The Bloof-Blorfs agree, noddingly.

"See? That's where all that stuff went off the tracks," zoughs Flough. "That stuff you all were doing over there? You got way too pranky. With sandwiches and fieldwork. That's not what it's about. It's not about just putting everything in metal, and going off on junkets."

"Then what *is* it about?" asks BF James.

"Well," quoughs Flough, holding up her copy of the sheet, "that's why I made this. Okay? Just look at the sheet. It's all on the sheet."

It's all on the sheet. She's taking the yearbook, that crucial record of our collective affairs, and wrapping it up in a sheet. A wingding winding sheet. And there is nothing we can do to stop her.

JEFF IS BACK—contrite and refreshed, no doubt—and BF James and I are there to greet him, in one of his more promising new offerings: Study Hall. If you think about it, it's the perfect class for Jeff to teach. It has everything for the failed scholar: silence, stillness, lack of plan. It will require nothing more of him—of any of us, really—than bodily presence. That much we can manage.

He's sitting at his desk when we come in, feet up on a box, arms crossed behind his head. He's wearing pretty much the same thing he always wears—a slightly wrinkled button-up shirt and jeans—but he's let his beard grow in.

"Hey guys," he says.

"Nice beard," I say.

"Thanks."

"You look like a young Rick Wright," says BF James.

"How's your trimester going?" (Apparently this model of beard comes with small-talk pre-installed.)

"Yearbook with Flough sucks," says BF James.

"Yeah," says Cam, who has also answered the call of Study Hall, and joined us at deskside. "It does."

It really does. There are only so many sheets you can process.

"What are you teaching this trimester?" I ask him.

"This," he says, "and a session apiece of Freshman, Sophomore, and Junior English."

Ah: Freshman, Sophomore, and Junior English—each comes with a stable of unwilling pupils, and each has a syllabus long chiseled into stone by Mr. Fleniston.

"Has the Proctor talked to you?" says Cam.

"I met with him first thing this morning," says Jeff. "He told me to toe the line, then he issued some vague threats, and here we are."

"Threats?" I say.

"*Mr. Traversal,*" he says—and again, his impersonation is impressive—"*let's finish out the year without further incident.* And the rest," he says, gesturing to the half-full room, "is Study Hall."

Which is pretty much the opposite of incident.

"Anyway," he says.

If there was something he intended to say after this, it doesn't come out. We find some desks and sit in them, without further incident.

SPRING BREAK HAS BROKEN upon us with a whimper. Freesia is off to New England to visit Dartmouth before she visits Dartmouth again over the summer. BF James is off to New York to see his mom and visit Deep Blue's childhood home (I told him to drop into the Morgan on my behalf; he won't). And I: I chose the road less traveled by, a road that isn't actually a road, because it's train tracks. I'm taking the train to Minnesota. This is a trip that The Father and I used to take every summer to visit my uncle. We'd get a roomette and, when we weren't staring blankly out the window, we'd read or play chess or backgammon or cribbage. On one of those trips, we invented a game of baseball using playing cards (if you drew a nine you drew a walk). I'd sleep (or fail to sleep) on the top bunk, with The Father snoring away below. At the station in La Havre, Montana there was an old vending machine that dispensed ice cream sandwiches. A highlight of the trip, to be sure.

Most of the ride to the station is ridden in silence. This is a scene we've seen before, a scene called "Lester and his Mother, Going Somewhere Together." But then, as she exits the freeway, my mother breaks character.

"So Lester," she says, "when do you expect to hear back on your applications?"

"Pretty soon, I think," I say, speaking to the shadow of the Kingdome.

"Lester," she says. "You didn't apply to any schools, did you?"

The cat, which I made no real effort to hide, has sprung from the bag.

"No," I say. "I didn't."

She drives, thinkingly, then speaks.

"It's okay," she says. "I mean, I'm okay with that if you are."

Am I? Maybe, maybe not.

"I don't know," I say. "I guess I should start doing something about it."

"There's always community college." She's trying to be helpful. And maybe she is.

"Yes," I say. "Or vocational school. I could live at home. Save a little money, you know?"

She pulls the Corolla up to the curb at King Street Station and turns on the hazards. She joins me on the sidewalk, wishing there were something she could help me carry. But I've only got my backpack.

"Are you sure you want to do this, Les?" she says, sliding her hands into the back pockets of her jeans.

"Yes," I say, looking up at the hands on the clock tower. A brisk wind kicks up.

"Here," she says. "Take this." She hands me an envelope. I open it. It's filled with cash, which can only have come from her rainy-day fund.

"Thanks," I say, and hug her goodbye.

She kisses me on the forehead. "Be safe."

I make for the door of the station.

"Lester," she says. I turn. She's standing on the street side of the car, her hand on the door. "You're not responsible for us, okay?"

I give her a look, backpedaling, then duck into the wind.

THE TRAIN CRAWLS ALONG the Sound at sunset, then turns inland. There is snow in the Cascades, and clearer skies beyond them. And then night falls over the expanse of eastern Washington. The coach cabin is teeming with listlessness. You wonder who these people are, where they've come from, where they're going. You sleep however much you can (not much).

On the morning of the second day, as we haul across Montana, I make my way down to the snack car. I buy a Danish in a plastic wrapper and a carton of half-frozen orange juice and sit at a booth facing backwards. I dive into the Danish and open *All Our Woe*.

The first chapter—"Book I: Disobedience"—introduces Nathan Stanley, the former CFO of a San Francisco banking firm. Nathan places an ad in the paper, "A Call to Disgruntled Employees of DeityCorp." The response is improbably strong, and within days he finds himself leading a motley, all-male band of disenchanted middlemen into the redwoods. By the end of the chapter, they have built themselves a compound, and Nathan has called for a council to plot his revenge against DeityCorp. The writing is hard to follow, at times, but striking at others. The references to *Paradise Lost* are suitably many and obvious.

Nathan Stanley: The Father must have taken great pleasure in inventing a name that echoes "Satan" not just once, but twice. And it seems fitting to me, as I skim through the rest of the book, in which Nathan becomes increasingly frustrated in his attempts to topple DeityCorp., that he would identify so closely with the one who was cast out of heaven.

I stash the book in my backpack and look out the window at the endless fields of endless grasses. *You're not responsible for us,* my mother said.

I scrape the frosting from the wrapper of the Danish and buy another one and eat it. The chunk of orangeish ice at the bottom of the juice is holding firm. But I can wait it out.

I STEP ONTO THE platform in St. Paul early in the morning and get to the stadium two hours before game time. I begin on the 100 level, going from section to section, examining the wall-length photos of Twins past, Twins present, and promotions yet to come. The booths selling ice cream in upside-down helmets. The building is starting to fill, the hum becoming buzz or proto-buzz. It seems clear now why he came here, to a place so conspicuous, a place nigh recognizable from space. He wants to be found. His presence lurks darkly somewhere beneath this sagging, off-white roof. (The roof of the Metrodome: it's a source of intrigue and difficulty. Riding on air, taking on snow. We went to a game here when I was a kid. The event has since lodged apocryphally in The Father's brain as my first baseball game.)

After a full lap around the 100 level concourse, I purchase a root beer, readying myself for the climb up to the heights of the 300 level. That improbable edifice, so empty and gray. The roof that relies on the pressure of air to keep it aloft. You can't help but look at it in a kind of mood that might pass for reverence or wonder.

The shiny concrete floor extends before me, as broad and barren as an open plain. I walk what must be close to a complete circle before I find him, stooped over a bucket. He stands with the look of an animal caught off guard, unsure whether to flee, pursue, or pretend he hasn't noticed he's been seen. I stand at an unadmiring distance. A woman with a pink skirt walks by. I get closer. Without saying anything, he places the mop back in the bucket and gestures with his head toward the tunnel that leads out to the seats.

I follow him out to the edge of that world, which is covered in Teflon and ringed with fixed blue chairs and lighted displays. We climb the stairs, Icarus and Daedalus, prevented early in our journey to the sun by the presence of a large Teflon roof, he to the very top row, me to the row in front of him. He continues along to the middle of the row and sits.

"Sit," he says.

I sit.

The field below is an unreal green, with little men in uniform running around and throwing baseballs back and forth. A bank of seats has been folded upright, standing on end in lieu of a right field wall, partially draped in a large blue baggie. I can hear his breathing, long and slow.

"You came to find your father," he begins. "You are not the prodigal son returning, but rather the bereaved son setting out in search of meaning and order by way of the father. I commend you. What you are attempting goes beyond the range of most of our fellow men. You are seeking your own manhood, and in the process you are forging it. For manhood is *made*, Lester. Manhood is not given or inherited. It isn't even earned. It is forged in the smithy of your will like a hammer. Will, Lester: will. The will is the thing. You understand?"

I take this pause as leave to turn around and look at him. The yellowing bristles of his mustache, the wrinkles of his face a caricature of toil and struggle. His finger at his temple, gesturing toward Will.

"You feel you must be disappointed in me, in this which you think I have become. But you must resist this, this impulse to assess the world in terms of surface facts."

The PA announcer comes on to provide some important information about our visit to the Metrodome.

"I will not stoop to melodrama," he says. "I will not tell you that I tried and failed," he says. "And I will not attempt to justify myself. But I will say this," he says, pausing to retrieve a pouch of tobacco from his overalls. "I have refused, willfully have I refused, to stray from the path of what is true. I have not strayed, Lester; I have continued, iron-clad in my resolve. I will not be institutionalized."

With unforeseen meticulousness he molds a pinch of the tobacco into something resembling a rotten pear, which he then inserts, tenderly, into a pre-formed, pre-blackened groove in the southeast quadrant of his jaw.

I will not be institutionalized: this phrase shuttles me back in time, to a swing, in a park, in the summer, by a beach. I had asked him why he didn't finish grad school. He didn't want to be *institutionalized*, he said. He didn't want to sell his soul for others. He didn't know, he probably couldn't know, that his soul was only there in others.

"You have to slim down, Lester," he says, then spits. "You have to get the grit out of your life. You have to be ready at a moment's notice to cast off what isn't essential."

"Like us?"

His eyes scan the distant tarpaulined horizons of the right field bleachers.

"You must miss us," I say. "You must miss all of it."

A kind of deep freeze comes over him, a statuing. He seems to have stopped breathing. He is a postcard of a man.

"I have not strayed, Lester," he says through the bulge of melting tobacco-pear. "No, I have not strayed. I have not abandoned my worldview. Nor will I."

And then he rises, slowly, and goes back down the steps to the concourse.

The game begins, and then ends, and then the crowd flows out. If you could know the sensation of leaving that stadium, the unexpected *whoosh* of it. You walk toward the door among a smattering of chattering people, reveling in victory; you begin to sense a sense of transition from inside air to outside air; and as you make your way back out into the cloud-driven night you are swept up in a sudden blast of air that is expressed from deep within the stadium. It pushes you forward, propels you, releasing you back into the open.

THE STATION IN St. Paul is quiet as midnight approaches. The vending machines glow dimly in the dimness of the depot. I approach the counter and ask how much it will cost to go New York.

"Do you want to buy a ticket?" asks the woman behind the counter.

I look up at the clock, then count what is left of my money. There is just enough to get there. I peer backward through my fancy at the lobby of the Morgan, at the sign above the door at CBGB. Then I shake my head. "No thanks," I say. Not yet. I'm going to go back home.

The half-empty train pulls out of the station more slowly than seems possible, but soon it gathers steam, and soon we are rolling out toward the American west in the fullness of night. You can't see them, but you know they're there: the decrepit barns, the spit-shined tractors, sitting dormant, and field after field after field after field after field.

We reach the depot in Minot, North Dakota early in the morning. I step onto the platform. The air is cold, and my breath makes clouds to match the ones gathering in the sky. No wind. I lay *All Our Woe* on a bench under an awning and place a small stone on top of it. Someone will find it there. Someone might read it and pass it along.

Back on the train, I get out my notebook and turn to the first blank page.

I GET TO FREESIA's house at dusk. The air is ripe with cooling grasses, and the jasmine bush beside the porch is exploding into blossom, infusing the air with its dizzying nectars. David greets me cordially and summons Freesia to the entryway.

"Lester!" she says. "You're back."

"Yes," I say. I am.

We proceed to the swing on the porch, where we can drink in the fragrance of that bountiful jasmine, with Hiram standing sentinel. I gaze out over the driveway and the yard and the road and the trees beyond. The light has changed even in the short time since I left. It's a lighter light, a brighter one, and longer.

"How was Dartmouth?"

"Oh my god, Lester. It's so awesome! I talked to an Art History professor, and he was really cool. And then I met a Women's Studies professor, and she was even cooler! And she's *young*. She's like someone you could actually *hang out* with. She gave me her email address and told me to get in touch when I go back. And the dorms are actually pretty nice. I'll probably have to have a roommate, and who knows who it'll be, but that's kind of the fun part, right? I'm super excited."

When she gushes like this, when she taps a vein of sheer excitement, it's like her whole face is the center of a star.

"That's great," I say. And it is. And yet.

We swing in silence for a moment. She's still in her New Hampshire reverie. And I am picturing her on the plane that will take her away.

"How was Minnesota?"

"Good," I say. "Really good, actually. I started writing an essay. For college."

"Really?" (Just when you thought she couldn't get happier . . .)

"Yeah," I say. "It's actually pretty good, I think. I'm going to look into Evergreen."

"You are? Oh my god, Lester, that would be *perfect* for you. I can't believe I didn't think of that before!"

"Yeah. Why didn't you?"

"And Les," she says. "I think they have rolling admissions. You could start this fall! You and James could be roommates!"

"Settle down," I say. "First things first. I do have to graduate."

"Lester," she says, placing her hand on my arm. "It's so good to hear you say that."

"That's not all," I say. (The train trip home was quite fruitful, in terms of new ideas and how to harvest them.)

"I don't know if I like the look on your face," she says.

"I think you do," I say.

"Well? What is it?"

I spill the rest of the beans, and these are they: that we, Lester Smith and Freesia Price, are to go ahead with *our* yearbook, the Proctor be damned; that we, Lester Smith and Freesia Price, are to recruit our friends and allies for the cause; that we, Lester Smith and Freesia Price, should start tomorrow, rain or shine.

Now it's Freesia's turn to gaze ahead, brow furrowed. The porch is swinging slowly. Hiram has assumed a prostrate position.

"But what about Dartmouth?" she says, still staring straight ahead. Eyes on the horizon.

"What about it?"

"I'd kind of like to go," she says.

"And?"

"And if I get suspended or something, I'm screwed."

"First of all," I counter, "the Proctor can't suspend you. What rule would you be breaking?"

"He'll find something. He makes the rules, right? And we're all on 'probation,' remember?"

"That may be true," I say, "but in this case, it's we who have the upper hand. We're swifter afoot. Less tied to institutional controls."

"You've lost your mind."

"And I mean, come on," I say—now I'm playing my trump card, if in fact I have one—"if we don't do this, do you realize what we're going to be left with for a senior yearbook?"

I can see the wingdings racing in and out of Freesia's thoughts.

"We have a moral imperative to act, Freeze. So come on. Let's let the bastards have it!" I leap into the air as I say this, fist to palm.

"The 'bastards,' Les?" she says, skeptical but smiling. She really is quite beautiful when she lets down that facade of serious seriousness.

"What do you say?" I say.

"Something's come over you, Les."

"Something," I say. Something will come of something.

"It's good to have you back," she says.

"It's good to be back." It strikes me, as I say this, just how true it is.

MAY

I'M ON A MISSION now, a mission that is deeply post-Minnesota. I'm on multiple missions now, in fact, all wrapped up in one torpedoing body. The first item on the agenda is a visit to a particular friend, a sage intellect out of whose orbital pull I've drifted far too far of late.

The lights in Rasmo's classroom are, as they often are, turned off. I press my face to the window. She's facing away from the door, the chopsticks in her hair pointing up like antennae. I enter as quietly as I can, but not quite quietly enough to keep from breaking the silence of her stillness.

"Lester."

"Is my scent that obvious?"

"No one else is ever so intent on going unnoticed. Sit down. It's been too long. What's on your mind?"

She turns to me, the milky grayish blue of her eyes fixed perfectly upon my own.

"I want to graduate," I say.

"I'm glad to hear it. How can I help?"

Next on the agenda is Washburn. I find him at break at his spot at the edge of the lunchroom, chewing on his customary clove. I tell him what I came to tell him. That I want to graduate. That I'm ready to make good on making good. He looks me up and down.

"It's about goddamn time," he says.

"Yes," I say. "It is."

Then it's Pancake time. I get to Woodcraft early so that I can have him to myself.

"How was break?" he asks, fingering open a box of Donettes.

"Fine. Yours?"

"Good. Went fishing."

"Catch anything?"

"Only a cold from my brother. What about you? Where'd you go?"

"The Metrodome."

"The what?"

"The Metrodome."

(Grunt; Donette)

"You going to start doing some work out there?" (Pointing to the shop)

"You know," I say, "I am. I've had a block."

"A block?"

"Carpenter's block. It's an inherited condition. But you know what, Pancake?"

(A slight raising of one eyebrow; Donette)

"The block has passed. I want to make a vase."

NOW THAT PHASE ONE of my mission—Graduation—has been initiated, it's time to fire up Phase Two: Renegade Yearbook. First on this agenda is BF James. I find him at the edge of the student lot after school and spill the beans I spilled to Freesia last night.

"We're reviving the Golden Age of the '97 yearbook," I say.

"The Golden Age?" he asks.

"The February of your soul," I say.

His smile is slow to make itself known—as often it is—but it does, at last, arrive on the scene, and then it spreads, and keeps on spreading. He curls the fingers of his right hand into a loose fist, and presents it for bumping.

"I'm in," he says. "On one condition."

I raise an eyebrow. BF Cheshire has arrived on the scene.

"A wager," he says.

"Go ahead."

"Deep Blue/Kasparov."

The rematch is next week. We all know which side he's taking.

"I got Kasparov," he says. (Or maybe not!)

"Wait a minute—"

But he won't let me interject: "If Kasparov wins," he says, "you ask Freesia to prom."

Prom? With Freesia? Where's this coming from?

"And if Deep Blue wins?" I say.

"I'll ask Tina."

I see what he's done. And so does he: that grin says it all. But I relent, and BF James is in.

Next is Cam. We find him after school in the place where you find Cam: behind the wheel of his massive Chevy Silverado. Freesia takes to the driver's side window. BF James hangs back, crafting plans for prom. I adopt a more direct approach.

"Hey," I say, sliding into the cab.

"Hey," says Cam. "What's up?" His hands are nervous in his lap.

"Why do you get to be in there, while I'm out here in the rain?" Freesia: incredulous, imperious, wronged.

"Come on in," I say, reopening the passenger door. "I'll ride Guapo."

I squeeze myself between the seats and onto the little bench in the back of the truck, then shove the front seat forward so that Freesia can join me. BF James gets in behind her and closes the door. (At last, he's found a passenger seat that can accommodate him!)

"What's going on?" asks Cam.

"We're going ahead with the yearbook," says Freesia.

"I know," says Cam. "I'm in that class."

"Not the Flough thing," says BF James.

"*Our* yearbook," Freesia adds. "The one we started with Jeff."

"The exhibit corpse?" says Cam.

"Yes," I say. "Precisely."

"And we need you," says Freeze.

"You do?"

(You get the sense that these are words he hasn't heard before. But who has, friends—who has?)

"Yes."

"Um, okay. What about Tina?"

"She's next."

Freesia directs Cam to The Crestview, a two-story apartment building just west of town. The building is still and silent and tired of winter, its siding gray and dark with mildew. Freesia makes a beeline for the stairs of the building. We follow. By the time we get to the top of the stairs, she's already knocking on a door at the end of the walkway. (If we *did* go to prom, and somehow danced, who'd be leading whom?)

"Hi," she says to the open doorway, "is Tina home?"

Tina and the rest of us arrive on scene simultaneously, she with folded arms (her default setting).

"What do you want?" says Tina. "I'm making dinner."

"We're going ahead with the yearbook," says Freesia. "The one we started with Mr. Traversal."

"Exhibit corpse," says Cam.

"We need your help," says BF James.

"No thanks," says Tina.

She starts to close the door.

"Wait," says Freesia. "Come on. It'll be fun!"

"I'm sorry," says Tina, looking down, and downcast, "but I can't."

For once in her life, Freesia is at a loss for words.

"Anyway," says Tina, "I have to get back to the noodles."

The door closes softly behind her. We stand there in silence for the space of a sigh, then head back down the stairs, with Freesia bringing up the rear. Her brow is still furrowed as she climbs back into the idling Silverado.

"There's something more to what she said," she says, glancing up at the building.

"You know," I say, "just because someone doesn't do what you want them to doesn't mean there's 'something more' going on."

"That's not what I mean."

"Let's look at the bigger picture here," I say, trying to dislodge her from this last and relatively minor failure. "We've got a pretty solid crew, even without Tina."

"But she's so quick. So *smart*."

"And what are we, chopped liver?" chimes in BF James.

"No, you're teenage boys."

"What's that supposed to mean?" I say.

"It means you're slow. You'd rather shoot baskets than get something done."

"Is there a difference?"

"You know what I mean. Come on," she sighs. "Let's go."

Cam backs out of the too-small parking spot, then coasts to the edge of the lot.

"Hold up," says BF James.

Cam brakes. BF James opens the door and gets out and starts walking back toward the building—and Tina, who is running down the sidewalk.

"Park," says Freesia.

Cam parks, and Freesia flings herself out of the truck. "Tina," says Freesia, walking toward Tina.

Tina drifts a little closer, arms crossed, eyes cast down.

"Change your mind?" says BF James.

Tina shakes her head. (Is she about to cry?) "I just wanted to apologize," she says, softly, into the pavement.

"What are you talking about?" says Freesia.

Tina stares into the concrete. "I told the Proctor what we were doing," she says. "With Bluey, and the field trips, and the yearbook. He called me in. He said—" She looks up, barely holding back the tears. "I mean, I really want to be class president next year." She falls, sobbing, into Freesia's arms.

Freesia lets her let it out for a moment, then pushes her gently away, keeping her hands on Tina's shoulders. "Listen, Tina. You didn't do anything wrong."

Tina nods slowly, wiping her nose on her sleeve. "I'm so sorry."

"It's okay," I say, "okay?"

"Okay," murmurs Tina.

"That bastard," Freesia fumes. "This is blackmail. You can't"—she's pacing now, and shaking her head, and pushing her hair behind her ears, then pushing it back again. "This is unacceptable."

"Settle down, Moloch," I say. "Let's keep our eye on the ball."

"You'd make a dope class president," says BF James. But the headline here is not what he has said, but how he's looking at Tina. (He should just ask her to the dance right now!)

"Thanks," says Tina, blushing, smiling sheepishly. She looks around at all of us, then back at the ground. "Anyway," she murmurs, "if you'll still take me back—"

"Of course we will," I say.

Tina sighs, then nods, then sets her jaw. Tina McTovey, reporting for duty.

"Now," I say, rubbing my hands together in the way that Jeff does, "we're only missing one last piece."

"Let's get Jeff," says Cam.

HAMBECKER FARM HAS UNDERGONE a major wardrobe change since our last visit. The blossoms in the orchard are blossoming. The grass is lush and green again. Arletta is up to her usual tricks, driving cows from one pasture to another. Upslope, at the end of the driveway, Jeff appears to be practicing some kind of wrestling move on an overloaded rucksack. The rucksack is winning.

"Get low!" I low, emerging from the Silverado.

He straightens and laughs and shoulders the sweat from his temple.

"Where you off to?" I ask him.

"France," he says, flopping the rucksack onto the ground.

We thought we were the ones with renegade designs, but Jeff's designs, it seems, are still more renegade than ours. At the end of the year, he explains, he is setting off to get the girl. Vivian, his ex-fiancée. "What do you think of that?"

Silence. What *do* we think of that?

"Dope," says BF James, brandishing his fist to fist-bump Jeff.

"Wow," says Tina.

Freesia is speechless (twice in one day!).

"What airline are you taking?" Cam inquires.

"None," says Jeff. "I'm going by sea."

This is a tantalizing image: Jeff in a sailor's cap, swabbing the deck.

"Anyway," he says, "what brings you all out to the farm?"

We tell him.

"What do you say?" says Freesia. "We could use your help."

"If I help you," says Jeff, palming his beard, "I'll get fired." He grins that trademark grin, the half-grin of his yearbook photos. "Which will save me the trouble of quitting!"

Beautiful: the band is back together, a fact that is confirmed as our honorary tour manager—Arletta Hambecker herself—slams shut a metal gate, then shrieks a shriek of sheer exuberance.

By the time I get home, most of the lights in the house are off. I deliver my backpack to my bedroom and trundle down the hall to Grace's door and knock three times.

"What do you want?"

She is sitting cross-legged on the floor, with a textbook on her lap. She's wearing a black silk kimono over a sweatsuit, a big pink clip in her hair.

"You still haven't asked me about my trip."

She responds by staring into the carpet.

"Don't you want to hear about it?"

"I have homework."

"It can wait."

Further staring at the carpet. There's something very small she's looking for.

"Come on," I say. "Just five minutes."

She sighs, closes the textbook over a sheet of notebook paper, and slides on her Hello Kitty slippers. We head out to the back porch, which hasn't felt the force of human steps in many months. The boards are mostly bare, with hints of white paint here and there. The light of the overhead light is weak and sickly yellow. We sit in the ragged white wicker chairs that overlook the darkness of the lawn below.

"I still don't know why you bothered," she says.

"I don't know," I say. "I just felt like I should."

"What does he look like now?"

"The same. His mustache is a little longer, a little grayer. He looks a little older in general."

"What did you talk about?"

Grace is picking at a fraying strand of wicker that is trying to escape the arm of her chair.

"You mean what did *he* talk about?"

This gets a smile.

"Well, he talked about himself. And then a little more about himself. And then me. And then him. Then him, and more him, and that's about it."

"So let me ask you again—why did you go?"

"I think it's like this," I say. "I had to go out there so that I could come back."

"Spare me the Lesterisms."

"Plus the train trip is pretty fantastic."

"I wouldn't know," she says.

Grace never came with us on our trips to Minnesota. It hasn't occurred to me until now that that wasn't because she'd chosen not to.

"Why didn't you tell me about those postcards?" I ask her.

"I don't know," she says. "I didn't want you to get upset, I guess."

"Was it good?"

"Was what good?"

"What he wrote."

"I don't know." She looks out on the yard. "Yeah. No. Not really. You know how he writes. It's like eating cotton candy made of caviar."

I pause to consider this rather surprising, but accurate, metaphor.

"Let me ask you something else," I say. "We're doing this thing."

"Who's 'we'?"

"Freesia and James and me, and Tina McTovey, and Cam Drinker—do you know him?"

"Nope."

"Anyway, it's a long story, but what it boils down to is that we want to do our own version of the yearbook—you know, something a little different. Something fun."

"Since when do the words 'yearbook' and 'fun' go together?"

"We could use your help," I say, watching as she ties a little wicker knot. "What do you say?"

"Freesia has them," she says, without looking up.

"Has what?"

"My drawings."

"She already asked you?"

"You get your perceptiveness from Dad, don't you?" She gets up. "Are we done now?"

"Yes," I say. "You're excused. I'm going to stay out here a little longer."

IN OFFICIALLY-SANCTIONED Yearbook—or as I like to call it, "The Yearbook Initiative"—Flough has us filing things and licking envelopes—tasks that appear to have nothing to do with her yearbook; tasks at which, I'm not too shy to say, I simply excel. So our tongues are a little bit sticky and gross as we gather after school for the first official meeting of the newly reconstructed Yearbook Commission. We have transferred operations to BF James's house, a swath of friendly territory that lies well outside the Proctor's jurisdiction. We'll miss our little hovel, to be sure, but we like our basketball court, and the scent of the cottonwoods that travels there on warmish breezes—and we need to keep our doings under wraps.

BF James emerges from the house and hands me an envelope. Inside, there's a newspaper clipping: *Deep Blue beats Kasparov.*

I'm off the hook. So why do I feel so dejected?

"What's that?" says Freesia.

"Nothing," I say, shoving the envelope into my pocket, and wondering how I'll hold her off. But she's already on to other things.

"Okay guys," says Freesia, pacing back and forth across the court, "I've been doing a little research."

"Research?" says BF James.

"Yeah," says Freesia, picking up the ball. (Will she go with someone else?) "I've been looking through a bunch of old VMHS yearbooks."

"You have?" I say. (Since when does Freesia pay visits to my satellite office? And since when is she allowed to do something like that without telling me first?)

"Yes, Professor Yearbook Arts," she scoffs. "You're not the only one with access to them."

I raise my eyebrows in approval. (Has someone else already asked her?)

"Anyway," she says, dribbling the ball. "I got to thinking. There's a reason it's done the way it's done, you know?"

"But Freeze," I say, "what happened to no more boring art? And all the other stuff we did? Are you going to turn your back on Baldessari, just like that?"

"Freesia's right," says Tina, detaching herself from the half-wall that abuts the court. "We have a responsibility. To everyone at school."

"I mean," says Freesia, spinning the ball in her hands, "who really gives a crap about our field trips in Bluey, and all that other self-indulgent nonsense?"

It occurs to me, strangely, and suddenly, that, for the first time I can ever remember, I have taken up a position deep within Freesian territory, while she has, at the same time, moved into a position that I myself have long held. Our yearbook-bearing ships have somehow passed each other in the night. It's a little terrifying.

"What do you think, James?" she asks. (Would she wear the dress from Tolo, or get a new one?)

"I think," he says to her, "you're going to start quoting from *Paradise Lost* if you're not careful."

Throughout this discussion, Jeff has sat off to the side on the half-wall, arms crossed casually, watching, waiting. Now he speaks: "you know," he says, "it doesn't have to be an either/or decision."

"Let's do both"—Cam dunk!

Yes: both: you can win and still lose and, in losing, still have won.

"It's not a choice between," I say, yoinking the ball from Freesia's hands, "but of."

"And now *he's* quoting Jeff," says BF James, shaking his head into his Game Boy.

"Old and new," I say, flinging the ball high into the air, "kershmendricked together in a zesty textual goulash."

"Rad," says Cam.

"It could work, I guess," says Freesia, surveying the horizons of her genius for a sense of what the thing, as abstractly proposed, might actually look like. (I kind of hope she wears the Tolo dress.)

"Can we keep the metal covers?" says Cam.

"Metal covers!"—Jeff approves.

"How would we do that?" says Freesia.

"My dad," says Cam.

"Your dad?" asks Tina. As if not everyone has one.

"Yeah," says Cam. "He has a factory."

"This calls for a shot," I say, chasing down the ball, then tossing it to Cam. "Heave something up. The hoop will answer. It's our oracle."

"What's the question?" wonders Cam.

"Should you, Cam, ask your dad to make our metal covers?" That's the spoken question. The unspoken one is this: Should I, Lester, ask Freesia to prom?

Now, I'm not going to sit here and tell you that I have the best shooting form around. I do all right: I make enough shots to pass for a passable shooter. Freesia, for her part, shoots a basketball in the same way she does everything: efficiently, effectively, with just enough panache. BF James has no form to speak of (to have a form you must shoot more than once). But Cam is in a category of his own. What happens is this. He bends deep to the ground, knees at a 90 degree angle. The ball dips even further, drawn down and to the right, his right arm cocked behind it. Then he bends *even deeper*, his body coiled tight like a spring, his lips pursed, cheeks puffed out, eyes almost shut. When, at last, he heaves the ball, his eyes open wide, a high-pitched grunt is emitted, and legs and ball both go flying in directions that can't be predicted.

In this case, Cam goes pirouetting backwards, landing on his backside, hands out behind him for support—resulting in a tripod of Cam—and the ball sails up into the sky and then down through the net.

"Yesssssss," says Freesia, pumping her fist in the way that she does.

Yes indeed: Cam's shot seems to have opened a shaft in the sky, through which the sun pours with sudden generosity.

As JOHNNY MILTON likes to say, a rolling Cam gathers no moss. He has approached his dad about our plan, and now it falls to us to do the same.

Cam swings a sweeping Silverado left into the parking lot of CDMF Industries, an industrial park on the mainland that is flanked by mowed berms and a couple rows of inoffensive trees. A sign announces the presence of the company, while making no attempt to explain what it is or what it does. And then, farther up the paved driveway, there's a second sign, with arrows pointing in two directions: "Nerds" to the left, "Turds" to the right. Cam chooses "Turds."

Jeff's Taurus is already there, its bearded driver leaning against the hood. We pile out of Cam's truck and greet him and head for the walkway that leads to the complex.

Awaiting us at the edge of the lot is a squat, middle-aged man wearing a yellow hardhat and holding a six-pack of additional hardhats, one tucked under each arm, and two hanging from each hand.

"Hey Stubb," says Cam.

Without speaking, the man—Stubb, as he appears to be known—hands us the hardhats and starts waddling in the direction of a large building with metal siding. This is the Production Warehouse. So, at least, says the sign on the side of it, which reads PRODUCTION WAREHOUSE, with the sub-heading, DEAL WITH IT.

The noise inside is deafening, a cacophony of machines grinding metal against metal, sparks flying, plates clanging, and, over and above and somehow *behind* it all, the loud wail of an '80s guitar. I pause to gaze out over the flurry of hardhatted workers working. The idea of a hardhat; the idea of a head.

Our stump-like, wordless escort leads us up a set of metal stairs and along a catwalk to a door marked OFFICE (subtitled, again, DEAL WITH IT). The door flings open without warning, and out lunges a man in his late forties with close-cropped, salt-and-pepper hair. He's dressed in jeans and white sneakers and a red sweatshirt with white letters that read, DEPENDS WHO'S ASK-ING. Ladies and Gentlemen, I present to you: Cam Drinker, Sr. He jerks his cairn-like head toward the interior of the office, then goes back in. We follow.

The office is bare except for a beaten-up metal desk. A long window gives onto the killing floor. (This is, apparently, the preferred term for whatever it is that's taking place below, where a sign on one of the walls reads KILLING FLOOR.) Running along the top of the walls of the small, square room is a model train track, with one dusty derailed locomotive. Tacked to the wall behind the desk is a hastily penned sign: BUSINESS AND PLEA-SURE. Drinker the First sits in a tattered vinyl chair behind the desk, pointing at a little stool in the corner.

"One of you can sit there," he says. His voice sounds like rusty metal looks. "I wasn't expecting an entourage," he says to Cam.

Cam says nothing.

"Hey," I say, advancing toward the desk of Cam Senior, where a plastic plaque stares back at all comers, etched with the words AND IF I DON'T? "I'm Lester. Lester Smith. I'm a friend of Cam's."

"Ah, Lester," says Cam Senior. "Cam talks about you all the time."

"Really?"

"No. He doesn't talk about anything, ever. Except your goddamn yearbook."

I laugh. I like this man. "This," I say, "is Freesia Price. She's the brains behind the operation."

"Hi," says Freesia, shaking the hand of Drinker the First.

"Don't worry," he says. "I only bite on weekends."

She rolls her eyes. He laughs his coarse-grained laugh.

"That's a damn fine handshake," he growls. Then he turns to BF James. "And this must be your bodyguard."

"James," says BF James, advancing for his turn at the woodchipper that is Cam Sr.'s handshake. "James Taylor."

"James Taylor?" Cam Senior is tickled.

"No relation," I say, with a laugh that sounds (and is) more nervous than I'd like.

"You play basketball?" asks Cam the First.

"Chess," says BF James.

Check!

"I'm Tina," says Tina, extending her hand. "Tina McTovey."

"Nice to meet you, Tina," says Cam Sr., taking Tina in. It's possible he's met his match, in terms of gravity and lack of flair.

"What exactly are you making here?" says Jeff, who has stationed himself at the window.

"Things," says Cam Drinker, Sr., elbows on his desk. "Objects." He soaks Jeff in his glare. "You must be the ringmaster."

"Well," says Jeff, with a sheepish grin, "not really. At this point, I'm just along for the ride."

"Listen," I say, dragging a bucket from the corner of the room and sitting across the desk from our boisterous, belligerent host. "We're not here to waste your time."

"Is that right?" he says. "You had *me* fooled."

"I think you know why we're here," says Freesia.

"Yeah, I know why you're here. This kid," he says, glancing over at Cam, whose fists are in position at his sides, "doesn't say shit unless he's hungry, then wants metal covers for the high school goddamn yearbook." As he speaks, it's hard not to get lost in the perfect symmetry of his flat-top. His hair has been chiseled by a clipper into a square of clean, sharp edges to match the sharp, square edges of his speech. "Seems like a waste of money and metal, if you ask me."

"Hard to argue that point," I say. "If I'm being perfectly frank."

"Do it anyway," he says.

"Excuse me?"

"Argue the point," he commands. "Why *do* you need metal covers?"

I look around the room. Cam is silent. BF James is silent. Tina has her pen and notebook at the ready. Freesia leans against the wall, as if to say: *your move.*

"Well," I say, "it's art, I guess."

"Art?" he roars. "I'm supposed to shell out ten grand for art?"

He coughs a loud cough, then clears his throat. I look at his plaque. *And if I don't?*

"Yes," says Jeff. "And you're getting a hell of a deal."

"I don't think I follow," growls Cam the Elder. "Spell it out for me. And remember," he says, lifting a log-like arm to point at Cam, "I'm like him. Not the sharpest ax in town. So dumb it down."

"Deep Blue," I say, and steal a glance at BF James. He answers with a nod. Drinker Senior answers with a blank stare, then a muffled belch.

On I advance. "Are you familiar with the work of John Baldessari?" I glance at Jeff. He's got an eyebrow up.

Cam One clenches his jaw, and clenches his glare.

"Okay, how about the Beatles?" I try.

"Yes," he says, "I know the goddamn Beatles. I'm dumb, not dead."

"Well, it's sort of like that."

"Your yearbook is like the Beatles?"

"Okay, that's a stretch," I allow. "But that's the basic idea."

"I still don't follow. Dumb it down some more."

"Okay. Do you watch football?"

"*Now* you're talking." And now, at last, I've disinterred a smile.

"The yearbook as everyone knows it—as it's always been—is football before the forward pass. We're the West Coast Offense."

Cam the Elder leans back, crossing his considerable forearms over his considerable midsection. He looks at me, and then at Cam (fists still clenched), and then at Freesia (*your move*), and then at BF James (no relation).

"I still think you're full of shit," he finally says. "But that's the whole point, isn't it? You know how to bullshit. Half the world is money, and the other half is knowing how to bullshit." These last words are directed at Cam Junior. A side-session of fatherly advice.

"Half is teaching, half delight," I paraphrase.

"You're world class in the bullshit department, you know that?"

The poet, he nothing affirmeth, and therefore never lieth.

"When's the last time you saw bullshit?" I ask him.

"Other than right now?"

"No, I mean in the wild."

"I deal in metal, not feces."

"It's kind of a thrill," I inform him.

"Where the hell did you find this kid?" he wants Cam to tell him.

"We saw some at Jeff's mom's house," Cam responds.

"The peanut gallery speaks! How is it that I can't get you interested in a porterhouse, but shit—a steaming pile of shit—is magic to you?"

The phone rings.

"Crap. Is it four already? I have to take this." He picks up the phone and barks into it: "What."

While Cam the Elder is on the phone, the rest of us go over to the window overlooking the Killing Floor.

"That went really well," says Cam.

"It did?" says Jeff.

"Yeah," says Cam. "He usually kicks people out."

"So what, exactly," I wonder aloud, "*is* being produced here in the Production Warehouse?"

"Metal panels," said Cam.

"For what?" says Tina.

"Business. And industry."

"Industry?" says Freesia.

"We don't make the final product. We make materials. Other people make the final product."

Down on the Killing Floor, I see someone I know. "Hey, is that Flynn Ross?"

"Yeah," says Cam. "He works here after school."

He's decked out in full welding garb: a long, heavy, rubber-looking gown, big gloves, and a face shield, which is, at the moment, turned up as he turns to say something to a coworker.

"I'm kind of his boss," says Cam.

Cam Drinker, Jr. is "kind of" Flynn's boss. Flynn Ross must "kind of" answer to Cam Drinker, Jr.

Flynn closes the face shield, and it bursts into a flash of molten light.

"He's going to help us make the covers," says Cam. As if this is just another thing you say.

Over at the desk, the phone goes down with a forceful clack. Cam Drinker, Sr.'s elbows are back on the desk. He's staring straight ahead and down, his knuckles pressed whitely together at his chin.

"Let me tell you something, Lester." He raises his head, his hands, his eyes. "I don't give a shit about your bullshit theories. It doesn't make a rat-nut of difference to me what the hell you think you're doing."

I like this man a lot.

"But this shit with the yearbook?" he continues, looking around the room. "Cam is *into* that. He *talks* about it. This kid doesn't talk about jack shit. He could see an elephant crap out a rhino and he wouldn't mention it." This gets a laugh from Freesia. "For all I know he has a Nobel Prize—do they have one for video games?" He directs this question at BF James, who can't withhold a smirk. Cam One is on a roll. "But your club," he says, turning back to me, "he *likes* that. Or liked it. Then you got crapped on."

"Well, it wasn't really a *club*—" I try to clarify.

"So I'm going to give you the money."

"You are?" says Jeff.

"Yeah. I'm going to give you a shitload of money, no strings attached. And as long as Cam likes doing it, the money will keep coming."

"Yes sir," I say, with a little salute. "You won't regret it." (He won't?)

"But promise me one thing, will you?" There's always one more thing.

He leans back in his chair, and smiles the smile of a special kind of cat (a cat that's bred for square hair and straight talk). Then he leans forward just a little bit further, his large arms folded on the table. His eyes are wide. His eyebrows are up. "Put a dick joke in it."

THE SUN IS OUT, and the birds are saying things to one another. Freesia's lost in thought. The Subaru is a true dream of gleaming blue as it glides along the open highway.

I've thought of many ways to do this, but most of them wouldn't suffice. No, this is something that has to be done in the way that it has to be done.

"Are you free on Saturday?" I ask.

"I don't know," she says. "Why?"

I slide in *Festspielkonzertmusik*. I find the song and fast-forward to the 0:23 mark.

> Do you, do you, do you, do you wanna dance?
> Do you, do you, do you, do you wanna dance?
> Do you, do you, do you, do you wanna dance?

I pause it there and look at Freesia. "Well?"

"Did you just ask me to Prom?"

"I guess so."

She rolls her eyes. "You're such a dork."

"Is that a yes?"

"Uh, you know it's in three days, right?"

"Yup."

(How much prep time do we really need?)

"You're so annoying!"

"Come on," I say. "Just throw on your Tolo dress, and leave the rest to me."

It's a sleepy evening at the Smith residence. Grace isn't out, oddly enough, and neither am I. So it's going to be an evening full of cereal-eating and catching up on all the work I haven't been doing for months.

When I get down to the kitchen for my first big bowl of Rice Krispies, I'm in for a bit of a shock: my mother, sitting at the kitchen table. She's often sitting there, but usually she's wearing her faded pink terrycloth robe (I think you know the one). But not tonight. Tonight she is wearing a blouse, and a skirt, and heels, and earrings, and a necklace—and makeup! Makeup of a kind you haven't seen in these parts for years, if not decades. And to top off the ensemble: a smile. A wide and genuine smile.

"Why are you so gussied up?"

She lets the question hover on the air.

"I have a date," she says, at last.

(A date?!)

"No way!" I blurt.

"What, you think I'm going to rot away in this house forever?"

"No no no," I say. "I just—" (I just what?) "Who's the lucky gentleman?"

"He's a banker," she says, with an extra dollop of relish.

"Who's a banker?"—Grace has entered the scene, in sweats and Hello Kitty slippers.

"Mom's *date*," I say.

"What date?"

"I have a date tonight." She leans back in her chair as she says this.

"With who?" says Grace.

"A banker," I inform her.

Grace is standing still in her slippers, allowing the information to become part of her world. This won't necessarily be a rapid process.

"Speaking of dates," says my mother, "have you asked Freesia to the Prom yet?"

"Did you just make this about me?" I say.

"Seriously, Lester," she says. "I know you think those things are dumb. But they're very important to girls. Right Grace?"

Grace gives her a look that suggests otherwise.

"I mean it, Lester. It's more important to Freesia than you think."

I'm holding the trump card—a receipt from The Tux Shop—but I don't intend to play it yet.

A horn honks twice in the driveway. A polite honking, friendly but efficient. My mother pops out of her chair. "That must be Bob."

Bob: yes. Bob. That is a name for a banker to have.

"Can we meet him?" says Grace.

A pause. My mother clutches her clutch. "Let's see how tonight goes first."

"Come on, mom," says Grace.

"Grace," I say. "Just—let her have her fun."

"Thanks, Les," says my mother, with a kiss on my head.

"Be back by midnight," I admonish.

She goes outside. We follow to the living room, and watch her through the window. She's looking good. She walks impressively in heels, it turns out. (Will Freesia be wearing heels?)

Bob emerges from his car, a black Mercedes. He's nothing like The Father, from the looks of it.

"He's so short!" says Grace.

And bald. But there's a gentleness in his expression. And a non-The Father *presence*. He gives our mom a hug, then scoots around the front of the car to open her door.

BF JAMES HAS EVERYTHING figured out. The tuxes: primo. The corsages: refrigerated. The limo: long, and black. The driver: Izak D. The hair of Izak D.: slicked back.

Our first stop is The Crestview. The limo squeezes into the lot and we head up to get Tina. She is looking fetching in a fuchsia dress, with her hair up, glasses off, and makeup on. She greets BF James with a kiss on the cheek and he kisses her hand and gets to work on the corsage. It will take more than one night, I think, to recalibrate to the gravitational pull of this new binary star (the McTovey-Taylor System).

Freesia's on the porch swing when we get to her house, swinging slowly, with a parent on each elbow. She's wearing the Tolo dress—which is long and pearl-colored and even more striking in daylight—with a sheer white scarf around her neck. Her nails are painted, and her hair is up. (Definition of Prom: the day the hair goes up.) Her makeup is subtle, but brings out the light in her eyes. Her shoes are shiny, off-white flats.

David greets me with a smile and a handshake. "Look at you!"

"You look beautiful," I say to Freesia.

I apply the still-chilled gardenia to her wrist, she kisses her parents goodbye and goodnight, and we settle back into the limo for the ride to Melky's. (This was Freesia's idea.)

After a dinner that Melky himself would be proud of, Izak D. pilots us fearlessly off-peninsula and then north to the Prom-barge. Yes: Someone decided that the VMHS Senior Prom is to take place on a faux barge under a freeway—a barge which has, it turns out, been gussied up to look like an Egyptian tomb or palace.

Kids we know and don't know—mostly kids we know—are hanging off the edge of the barge, taking pictures of the parking lot and the mini mall that lies across an empty field. We cross the gangplank—which spans a concrete ditch—and arrive at the Arrival Table, manned by Gloria Flough. Her dress is pink but obscured by the same brown sweater that she often wears. In a nod to the theme, a small gold King Tut effigy has been pinned to the sweater.

"Hello Ms. Flough," I say. "Don't you look lovely this evening?"

"Hello Lester," she says.

"Four, please," I say.

"Okay," she says. "Let me just check here." She checks a list of names, and then another list.

"We didn't prepay," I clarify.

"Okay," she says, "yes. But there's a problem."

"A problem, Ms. Flough?"

"Yes. You're on the Proctor's list."

"The Proctor's list?" I say.

"Yes," she says. "The probation list."

"What's that supposed to mean?" Freesia demands.

"It means you can't be here."

"But we are," I say.

"But you can't be."

"But we are."

Flough is flustered. Her hands go up. "You can't get tickets. You can't go in. You're not allowed at Prom."

"Since when?" says Freesia.

"It's—it's the rule. It's in the rules. It's on this sheet."

Flough holds up the sheet, on which a list of names has been printed. At the top of the sheet is the word, "Probation."

"Is the Proctor here?" I ask.

"Yes," she says. "No. I don't know. He gave me this sheet."

"Can't you just let us in?" says BF James. Affable his grin, soothing his voice, sharp-as-hell his sharp-as-hell lapels.

Flough shakes her head rapidly. Freesia's hands are on her hips. Tina looks worried.

I can feel my cheeks going red, and the small electric eels that shimmy up my legs when I find that I'm about to erupt. "No way," I say. "We're going in there." I start to storm past the table, but am caught at the elbow by a hand with a gardenia'd wrist.

"Lester," says Freesia. "Why bother?"

I look up at the barge—the welcome banner has come loose at one corner, and has folded over onto itself—and then into Freesia's eyes. The brown in them: the rivulets of brown, set off against that deep green background. The brown in them.

Izak D. is a little surprised to see that his cargo has returned so soon. He hasn't even had time to finish his HandiSnack. Nonetheless, he fires up the limo cheerfully.

"This sucks," says Tina, staring out the window at the non-Probation kids who are boarding the barge. Above deck, the Proctor is leaning meaningfully against the railing, gazing off into the traffic on the freeway.

"Let's go to Brogdon," I say.

"No," says Freesia. "Let's go finish what we started."

WE HAVE BEEN PLYING our yearbookly craft deep into the night for the better part of bright and boastful May. We've had cameos from Grace, for graphic design work, and from David Price, with Scotch for Jeff and words of businessy encouragement for us, and even from Flynn, who stopped by with Cam to demonstrate the prototypes from CDMFI. Freesia has put in long hours on her Toshiba; BF James has set up camp in the Deep Blue Memorial Command Center (DBMCC); and the Smith Family computer and I have become intimate companions. Tina has edited everything, and Freesia and I have edited her editing. We have, in short, been getting really low. But this is the first time we've been at it all night. Typing feverishly. Adding wingdings. Making pages in Pagemaker. Summoning Jeff from zestful slumber. Summoning Cam from the bogs.

The morning is cool and still. The maples on the bank are in full, view-blocking bloom. We might be done. But before we can look at the final final draft, we have some unfinished business to settle. I lead my cohorts out to the driveway.

"You still haven't taken a shot," I remind Tina, skipping her the ball.

"Seriously, Lester?" Freesia says. She's still wearing the Tolo dress, but has replaced the flats with Keds.

"Ask a question," I tell Tina, "then heave something up. A make is a yes."

Tina is visibly tired but manages to catch the ball and square her shoulders for a shot from just inside the invisible free-throw line.

"Will I be class president next year?" she asks the hoop, then banks it in. Then she nods, gathers her rebound, and reads my mind by flipping the ball to Jeff. "Your turn," she says to him.

"Yes," I say. "Ask a question, and the hoop will give you its answer."

"Okay, here goes," says Jeff, sizing up a shot from the edge of the yard. "Will Vivian take me back?"

Wow: he came in guns blazing, didn't he? With no thought of pausing to reconsider the question, he heaves an underhanded one-hander. The ball sails upward and then downward and then sticks, with a *thunk*, between the rim and the backboard.

"Whoa," says Freesia. "That's a first."

"What does it mean?" says Cam.

"Here's what it means," says BF James, shuffling over to the hoop, where he dislodges the ball with his fist, then carries it to the edge of the maple-stand and dropkicks it into the trees. It lands down-bank, out of sight, with a soft crunch. This feels like the end of an era.

"All right," says Jeff, "let's go in and see this thing."

BF JAMES RIGS UP a projector on a table in the DBMCC, as Tina tacks up a sheet on the opposite wall. This, friends, is a moment to savor: our final review of the book as a group, our last chance to see it in its not-yet-shining glory, before we send it off to the printer, and then to the Drinker Forge for final assembly.

"The covers are ready," Cam announces. "Now we just need pages."

"I brought a soundtrack," I say. I'm holding an old friend, here to join us for a rare public appearance: *Ramones*. The one and only record that I own.

"Oh no," says Freesia.

"Oh yes," says BF James. "Hand it over."

The projector flickers to life to the opening bars of "Blitzkrieg Bop." BF James begins the show.

The first page reads, *METAL COVERS!*—a mere placeholder, a glorious reminder of what the genuine article is going to be. And then a graphic of the etching that will grace the cover, which is to read, in the ornate Bavarian script recommended by Tina: *The 1997 Victory Memorial High School Yearbook*. Cool, classic, direct. Tell them what it is—with style—and let the metal do the rest.

For the frontispiece we've splurged on a dizzying array of Clip Art wrestlers—those same dough-faced, wide-eyed, round-kneed lads which Freesia found in February, reproduced in various colors and sizes, over and over and over again. And over this the word "FRONTISPIECE" will be printed in large, bold, Hollywood-sign-like letters.

We haven't gotten anywhere yet, and yet I can already see this volume taking its place on the library shelves. People are going to like this book. History is unfolding before our very eyes.

The first section, entitled "Photographs of Students Who Go to This School"—in a nod to *Badger Shmadger*—presents the standard rows of names and faces of the freshmen, the sophomores, and the juniors, the important historical record of the individuals who graced the brazen walkways of our school this year. But we've embellished these pages with all sorts of graphic interjections—borders, robots, insects. Photographs of photographs. We've also sprinkled in a few obvious historical anomalies. (Abraham Lincoln, for instance, has been added to the Freshmen; Ezra Pound has taken his place among the Sophomores; and Emily Dickinson, by way of her lone daguerreotype, is now a VMHS Junior.)

For the senior section, headed "People Who Almost Don't Go to This School Anymore," we have adopted an extremely sound set of organizing principles—those first seen on Freesia's Milton poster from the fall. Each of the outgoing students has been given a quarter page profile, complete with photos, senior quote, a timeline, and other vital statistics. Taken together, these luminous details paint a compound picture of our illustrious careers at Vehemence.

A cheer goes up when Freesia's picture graces the screen. It's a picture that her father took in Costa Rica, a long shot of a waterfall, with a blissful, shrieking Freesia swinging out over it on a long rope, about to release herself into the pool below. For her quote she has taken a line from e.e. cummings: *damn everything but the circus.* (This is a quote that will age well.)

I look at Freesia, looking at that leapsome version of herself. There is a particular kind of glow which you can only get by projecting the projection of a projector off the opalescence of a Tolo dress.

I look to Jeff when my profile comes up. For my senior quote, I've chosen a line that will be more than familiar to him: *He chose to include the things that in each other are included.*

"Wow," he says, "not the Ramones?"

"It really came down to the wire," I confess. "But in the end, Stevens scored the upset." (What can I say? Call it a phase.)

For my photomontage, I have presented myself by way of a mini-collage of four separate photos, each of them taken by Freesia at a different beach on King's Island. Each features Yours Truly in a different pose: standing on a log in one, doing an improvised karate move; handstanding in another; faking *The Thinker* in another; and lying on the sand in the fourth. My quadrupled body, as linked together across all four images, forms an *L.*

BF James, alphabetically the third of the three seniors on our crew, has chosen to represent himself by way of a picture of the screen of his Game Boy, in which, if you look closely, you can make out his faint and faintly smiling reflection. For his quote, as promised, he has taken a passage from William Gibson: *Cyberspace. A consensual hallucination experienced daily by billions of legitimate operators.*

For the final entry in this senior section for the ages, we've fulfilled our obligation to Cam Drinker the First—in letter, if not in spirit. Cam the Second has furnished the pictures—corporate headshots of his father, smiling his close-cropped smile at the camera. For his quote we have chosen BUSINESS AND PLEASURE. And the name of this previously unknown VMHS graduate-to-be? Richard Killingfloor Joke.

There's a gentle progress to the book, you will find, when you find it, wherever you are when you find it, a sort of evolution that takes place in its pages, in that, the further you get into it, the more liberties it takes with the Template. So after BF James clicks through "Faculty," "Club Sandwiches," and "Sports," he arrives at a section headed "The Consulting Firm of Baldessari & Kipling," which will feature little cutout finger puppets of John Baldessari and Rudyard Kipling, as well as an expandable cutout boxing ring, wherein the two might engage in grappling maneuvers.

As you hack your way further and further into the jungle that is this '97 yearbook, the graphics begin to multiply too. An aerial view of the Victory Memorial campus is re-imagined as a massive spacecraft, just beginning to thruster up into the air; in a cartoon rendering by BF James, at a level of mastery that's surprising even to me, we get our battered Bluey being driven by Samuel Beckett; and our very own Grace Smith has contributed a pen-and-ink rendering of Bride of Wichie as a giant monster devouring the school. For the centerfold, we have revised the central image of *Badger Shmadger*, such that Bernie the Badger is giving you a double thumbs-up, Coach Cialuzzi style. After a short montage on the Japanese Club's annual trip to Japan, there's a little one-page aside entitled "Donettes!", a catalogue raisonné of the three known kinds—Chocolate, Powdered, and Crumb—with color photos of the specimens in question, and of a cheerful, Baby Bjorn-bedecked Pancake waving from the margins. In a section entitled "Life Goals," we have left a space for students to write out their life goals—*five to seven of them, say*—with a sentence at the bottom urging them to return to this page repeatedly later in life. In one corner of the section dedicated to the school's art classes, there's a little insert with the heading, "Hammering Cam!" beneath which readers of the yearbook will be grateful to encounter a photo of Cam Two, posing as the Hammering Man outside the main entrance to VMHS. Toward the end of the book, you'll find a full-page tribute to *Guernica*, but in Clip Art, as well as a two-page spread that offers translations of all the senior quotes into wingdings. This segues nicely into a genuinely tasteful spread on the Issues Initiative, with no mention of the infamous Showdown at Metal Covers Junction. Just re-pave, re-pave, re-pave. (Re-pave is what they decided to do with the money, by the way, when no one was looking.) On a page headed "Half the World is Money"—one of many subtler tributes to our square-jawed benefactor—a dollar bill will be stapled into every copy of the book.

I'm pinpricked with pinpricks of sorrow as BF James clicks us ahead—all too soon, it seems to me—to the final paginated section of the book. This may be our best work yet. It's a section we call "Build Your Own Apocrypha," and it's nothing more than 26 blank pages.

Then comes the final flourish, the spread for the inside back cover of the book: a picture of Joey Ramone, soaring across a backdrop of vibrant yellow squiggles, with a little cardstock tab that reveals a dialogue bubble: *Hey! Ho! Let's Go!*

The lights come on. The show is over. One hundred twenty-seven glorious, Proctor-less pages.

"That's all, folks," says BF James.

"So," says Jeff. "What do we think?"

"Mass rad," says Cam.

"I don't know," says Freesia. "It's still missing something. Something more personal, you know? Something *interactive*."

"Can we add a compartment?" I wonder aloud.

Cam shakes his head. "The order's in."

"How about the binding, what's that made of?"

"Spirals."

"Can we tuck something into it?" asks Freesia.

"Oooh, I like where you're going," says Jeff.

"Like a Sharpie?" wonders Cam.

"No," says Tina. "A piece of chalk."

"Yes!" says Freesia. "That's it! With specific instructions, written by hand."

"Yeah!" says Cam.

"Let's see it again," says BF James.

We watch it again, and then again. The book, it seems, is in the books.

JUNE

THE FLOUGH YEARBOOK—the "official" yearbook, *Let's See I to I* (subtitle: "A Year of Issues")—has been released to widespread indifference. It's a rather sad and floppy, really a floppily sad little pamphlet. Poor Gloria: she tried, she really did. The borders are intense; the colors—the ones you imagine through the grayscale of the actual object—are subtle and pointed. And the photocopying alone must have taken quite some time. But the photo-less volume has failed, alas, to capture the collective imagination of our school, and even at a price of "Free!" it seems that product is moving rather slowly. Still, you have to applaud her for trying so very and merrily hard to instill in us a thorough appreciation for Issues, comma splices, and Clip Art—Clip Art like it's going out of style.

More than anything, I think, we're grateful for her timing: she's opened the yearbookly breach into which our version will flood. Timing: yes, timing is everything, and no one knows that better than Cam Drinker, Jr. He has kept us waiting for more than an hour. So that when, at last, the now-familiar rumble of his Chevy fills the air, we all converge to greet it, and are greeted, in turn, by a bigger truck: a flatbed, driven by Flynn, with Grace riding shotgun.

Cam hops out and guides the flatbed into port. Flynn noses it up to the Taylor Family hoop and kills the engine. And there, on the bed of the truck, wrapped in placid plastic on pallets, is our yearbook.

"I got you all something," says Cam. "Limited Editions, with tinted metal covers."

Flynn—who hasn't yet spoken, and might not speak at all—gets down from the truck and hands a box to Cam. Cam passes them around, announcing the colors as he makes the rounds. "Orange for Lester; green for Freesia; red for Tina; blue for James; and brown for Jeff. And yellow for me; and purple for Grace; and black for Flynn."

The next stretch of time is consumed by silence—the silence of our inspection of the genuine article. It's better than I ever thought it could be, a heavy thing, well made. There are murmurs, laughs, the occasional gasp.

"So," says Tina, "what now?"

WE DESCEND ON CAMPUS long after midnight, all dressed all in black. I have chosen this momentous occasion to debut Jeff's old CBGB T-shirt. I have told the others they can find me by those letters. I also proposed a system of hand signals, which Freesia rejected, but I employ a few of them anyway as we make our incursion. Each of us has self-assigned a zone of distribution. And so, like insects active only in the night, we swarm about, pushing CDMF hand trucks, populating the exterior of the school with *The 1997 Victory Memorial High School Yearbook*. In trees and bushes do we place them; atop trashcans, on benches, under the ends of gutter pipes. Tina assembles a hopscotch court out of them, BF James a little pyramid. My *JILT* bag, now one-handled, can only manage one delivery of one book—which, I decide, will be the one I prop against the Proctor's office door.

Within an hour all of them—five hundred copies strong—have been dispersed, such that dawn will break upon a shimmering sea of metal covers.

We stand there, admiring our work, for several thrumming minutes. Then BF James and Tina leave with Cam, and Grace with Flynn, and I am left with Freesia, alone. The moon is big and white and blue.

"Isn't this amazing, Les?"

I kiss her on the forehead. She looks up at me, her eyes like deep, dark moons, and then kisses me back, on the lips, which remain wet on the wind for several long and quaking pulses of the night.

I WAKE EARLY and head out to the driveway. The June sun is already well established in the sky as Freesia's Subaru sweeps around the corner.

We get to school in time to stand and wait. From our customary spot at the edge of the student lot, we watch as the students and faculty arrive and begin to discover the booty. Some who have gotten there early are acting as ambassadors, greeting the others with news of the thing, some of them with extra copies for their friends. A bee-loud hum is buzzing about the campus. And before long the urging in the book begins to be heeded, as a handful of students march fearlessly, chalk in hand, to the middle of the Common. We have asked them, in little handwritten notes that are wrapped around the chalk that is tucked into the binding, to scrawl out a phrase—any phrase of their choosing—beginning with the words "I will."

We keep as low a profile as possible, but there are certain cognoscenti—seemingly everyone, really—who know who we are and what we've done.

"This thing is mass cool," says a kid I've never seen, sidling up to me confidentially.

"No comment. But thanks."

It is all that anyone can do to think about the day's scholastic regimen. And there isn't much of an opportunity to do so. Midway through First Period, the voice of Gloria Flough comes over the airwaves: "Attention students." (Cough) "And faculty. Please come to the lunchroom at eight-fifteen. I.e., immediately." (Some muffled talking in the background, with the intercom still on.) "For a school-wide assembly. It's mandatory. Thank you."

Moments later, we are flushed from our classrooms into the lunchroom. We sprinkle ourselves throughout the room, trying not to draw attention to ourselves (but are we drawing attention to ourselves by not drawing attention to ourselves? Will someone notice that I'm *not* with Freesia or BF James?). Cam is off with the Pancake Bloc, hands clenched at his sides. Tina has found a table toward the front, her pen and notepad at the ready. Freesia is near me, a handful of freshmen distant, but is careful not to look my way. Her arms are folded coolly across her chest. BF James is leaning against a pillar, playing his Game Boy.

Everything's in order. Our cover is holding—so far—but my heart is still aflutter as the Proctor makes his way onto a makeshift stage at the front of the room. He stands there in silence, scowling more deeply than ever, waiting for his audience to finish arriving and settling down.

As the audience finishes arriving, and finishes settling down, Jeff comes in, by way of a side door. Trying not to be seen, but being seen. At his side, I see, he's clutching his brown-tinted edition of the book. (Bold move, Jeff!) He finds Gerald Washburn, and joins him in his casual-seeming lean against a bank of lockers.

The room is unusually quiet and attentive, and into this quiet attentiveness the Proctor wades with more than standard self-importance.

"Students of Victory Memorial," he begins, "it is with no small measure of dismay that I address you today. As many of you already know," he laments, "the campus was vandalized last night. Indeed, it was veritably poisoned by the dissemination of a truly distasteful book, or object, or—I frankly don't know what. Please know," he bellows, "that this bastard yearbook has in no way been officially sanctioned. I am here, then, in the first place, to announce its prohibition. If you have a copy in your possession, I urge you to bring it into the main office immediately. Any student caught with the metal yearbook after the end of school today will be suspended."

He pauses to let this threat sink in. There are a few murmurs of protest, some nodding. I steal a glance at Freesia. She's keeping her cool. I do my best to follow suit.

"What is more," the Proctor continues, "I would like you all to know that those responsible for this travesty will be held strictly accountable. You have violated everything we stand for." Now he is looking directly at Jeff. The room looks with him.

"Wait a minute," I hear myself say, more loudly than I usually say anything. "Our yearbook isn't a travesty. And it isn't a bastard. And you can't take it away from us." I look at Freesia. Her eyes are exclamation points. A few stray cheers erupt.

"Yeah," says Freesia, rising to join me in my stand, "Lester's right. Our yearbook isn't vandalism. It's a *celebration*."

A few more cheers erupt, then Cam erupts: "Metal covers!"

The cheers get louder—loud enough to buoy Tina as she rises. "Here we stand," she says, "loud and proud!"

The cheers get louder still, and many of our fellow students rise in solidarity. The Proctor holds his palms in the air, trying to re-gain the room.

Enter BF James, to seal it with a chant.

"Year-BOOK," he yells—he can do that, apparently—"year-BOOK, year-BOOK." He's pumping his fist in the air as he says this, and soon the room is engulfed in the chant. *Year-BOOK, year-BOOK, year-BOOK, year-BOOK.* It feels good to shout it out. It feels like many months of things kept in go out with it. *Year-BOOK, year-BOOK, year-BOOK.*

The Proctor doesn't know where to look, or even how to stand. But he still has the mic, and uses it: "Silence!" he yells, and the microphone shrieks with feedback. The chanting stops, and a tentative, vibrating silence grips the room. And into this silence steps Jeff, launching a sneak attack from the Proctor's left flank, shouldering through the crowd like a wild animal prowling through tall grass. By the time the Proctor sees him coming, it's too late, for Jeff is up there, on his little platform, yanking the mic away from him.

Someone gasps. Someone yells, "Hell yes!"

"This," Jeff says into the mic, leveling his metal yearbook at the Proctor, "is a work of blood and sweat and tears. My students—my smart, creative, compassionate students—poured their hearts into this book. And you have absolutely no right to censor it."

The Proctor is speechless. And Jeff isn't done. "All you do is bring them down," he says. "You're just"—it's his turn to sputter—"you're just a self-absorbed, Kipling-obsessed tyrant!"

Throughout this improvised speech, he has gotten closer and closer to the Proctor, such that they are now standing close enough to floss each other's teeth.

"Give me that!" bellows the Proctor, attempting to wrest the microphone from Jeff. The two vie for control of it for several strained seconds, as children might fight over a toy or a piece of candy, staggering back and forth, winding themselves in the cord. And then they're toppling, and thud to the stage, with the microphone rolling off to one side, and Jeff's brown-tinted yearbook thwapping down on the other.

For a moment, they seem paralyzed, tangled in the cord of the mic and fighting a losing battle against each other's limbs. "You," says the Proctor, rising to a kneeling position. His white-yellow hair is swirling around his head, as in a stiff wind, and his face is red and reddish-yellow.

"You," he quavers, pointing a quivering finger at Jeff. And then he swoops, nabs Jeff's copy of the yearbook, and runs—runs!—with the yearbook tucked under his arm like a flattened metal football. Jeff jogs after him, out of the lunchroom, down a hallway, and into the faculty lounge.

A swell of the crowd rises and goes to the window to watch. I'm at the back, and here is what I see: the Proctor stands in the corner of the room, brandishing Jeff's yearbook. Finding himself weaponless, Jeff scrambles over to a counter and picks up a suitable lance: an abandoned copy of *Let's See I to I*. (The Flough yearbook has its uses after all, you see.) "Get low!" someone shouts. Jeff rolls up the Flough yearbook, and gets low.

And thus begins a kind of duel, Jeff with the Proctor's yearbook, the Proctor with Jeff's, both men breathing heavily. Jeff advances here and there to strike the Proctor softly on the leg with a broadside *thwap* or lateral *fwap*. He is, I notice, smiling wide. And so am I. *This is really happening!* You just can't help but smile.

After a couple of half-hearted passes, Jeff drops his lance and seizes the Proctor's, and the two of them, each clutching one metal cover, go whirling around the room like a two-headed cyclone, breathing loudly, grunting, planless. At last the Proctor loses his grasp on the book and goes tumbling backwards. Jeff falls too, then scrambles to his knees. And then he's up again, and getting low, and scooping up the Proctor like a child. He spins around, cradling this infant-like administrative stand-in, taking in the crowd of us that's taking him in from the window. Then he dumps the Proctor into a stack of paper cups, which go cascading to the floor, along with Jeff.

There is a notable absence of outside intervention, at first, as if no one there—no teacher, no student—wants or knows how to intervene. We are all too taken aback, perhaps, too immersed in the heated pitch of battle. And they: they are in some separate dimension, projected holographically before us, outside the range of other human influence. It has all happened so quickly, and yet so slowly, so loudly but so silently, chaotically, to be sure, but also as if driven forward by some higher plan or motivating hand. And it isn't until they're there in the lounge, amid that flurry of paper cups, that other people join the scene: BF James, holding Cam back; Gloria Flough, speaking softly to her little rodent; and then Washburn, flanking Jeff, leading him out of the lounge; and Freesia going in to the Proctor, and I behind her, following unconsciously.

He is utterly disheveled. There are bags under his eyes, and his face is pale and damp. Pancake and Cialuzzi help him to a chair, and Ms. Flough brings him water in a paper cup, which he drinks calmly and silently, in the way that a child might drink after a fight with a sibling.

"Proctor," I say. He looks at me, then off into the vagueness of the air. There's a question in his eyes. It might be: *Is this really what you want?* It might be something else.

I leave him there, suspended in the silence of that question.

BACK IN THE LUNCHROOM, Jeff and Washburn are sitting at the end of a long table. Jeff is holding an ice pack to his mouth, with a GET LOW T-shirt for an improvised sling. The room hums with the quiet murmuring that follows a crisis.

"Is he all right?" asks Jeff, moving the ice pack to speak.

"Yeah," I say. "He'll be fine. How about you?"

"Never been better."

The chairs that he and the Proctor left scattered in their wake are only now being picked back up and slid under tables. "You sure know how to make an exit, don't you?"

"Let's go to the bar," says Washburn.

"No, let's go to France," says Jeff, getting up and turning toward the door that leads to the faculty lot—and from there, to a port, and a boat, and to France, or some other far-off place where boring art has been banished forever, and tattered sweaters are always in vogue, and every corpse is utterly exquisite.

I HEAD BACK through the bustle of the lunchroom and out to the Common, where a scene of uncommon harmony is unfolding. The sun is high above, already bright the day. An old recording of an old French song is playing on a boombox on a bench. And gathered throughout the Common, there as if drawn by the same unknowable forces that cause birds to soar across the globe, are my fellow students, bending to the pavement to scrawl a field of phrases beginning with the words "I will." The cumulative effect is a verbal collage in a rainbow of colors. *I will do better next year. I will graduate. I will go where none has gone before.*

I will fight no more forever. I will eat a burger. I will sing a joyous song. I will scratch my shoulder. I will always love you. I will grieve alone. I will be good.

Each is utterly its own, in form and in content alike. Some are small and compact and neat, others large and flowing and all out of proportion. They run into and through and overlap and intertwine with one another, such that the end of one marks the beginning or the middle of another. They form, in this way, a continuum of sorts, you might say, an infinite loop of intersecting words. And something about this has put a charge in the air. Something about the public act of writing on the ground, and the fact of doing it in unexpected unison, has galvanized the student body in a way that nothing ever has before.

The crowd of mostly quiet students grows slowly in size as more and more people come outside to add their signature to the text that is blossoming on the concrete. Some teachers are there, but they don't try to intervene. Cam is there, and Flynn. *I will build. I will XLR8.* And Grace is there, with her gaggle of freshman friends, each of them stooping to the pavement to chalk a different phrase. *I will flourish.* And Stan Harvey is there, and all of the Blorfsortium. *I will meet you half way there.* And BF James, deliberate his manner. *I will move the earth.* Rasmo stands off to the side, gazing out over the field beyond the pavement. Gloria Flough stands at the edges, petting her rodent, then bending to write her contribution. *I will see I to I.*

The doors of the foyer creak open and out comes the Proctor, flanked by Pancake and Cialuzzi. He stops and stands there, waiting stoically, saying nothing, calm his bearing, quiet his body. Someone hands him a piece of chalk, which he holds at his side as he looks out at the students bustling all over the Common, adding new flourishes and phrases, and then kneels gingerly to write his own.

Freesia sees me, bounds over, and hands me a piece of chalk.

"Come on, Lester, let's do ours. I've been waiting for you!"

We bend to the pavement, chalk in hand. Hers bursts forth in a circle of flowing cursive script. *I will see you on the other side of now.* Mine is a line of large, square capital letters, a kind of debt paid late. *I will not make any more boring art.*

Then she takes my hand in hers and leads me toward the student lot.

"I've decided something, Les," she says, as we approach the Subaru.

"What have you decided?"

"You're coming east with me. In the fall."

She may be right. I may yet make it east of Minnesota. But first, I have decided, I am going to stay right here, right where I am, where the days and weeks ahead unfurl like a large plush red rug. Biology and Calculus and World History in July. Then the warm, intrepid air of August, when the beaches of King's Island rise to meet you with open arms. And then we'll see, my friends, what is to come when fall arrives again.

EPILOGUE

THERE'S A QUIET BUZZ in here, broken only by the intermittent clacking of a staff member's keyboard. If you look up you can see, through a gauzy hanging and a network of adjustable light-panels, the blue of the sky.

The manuscript lies open in a plain manila folder, perched in the red, velvety V of its holder. The pages are a dull beige, darker at the edges. The ink is river-brown. A blot mars the *P* in *Paradise*.

As I turn the page, I think of Jeff—as from time to time I do, as I've reached and then passed the age he was when we first collided, and as I have gone about piecing together the foregoing account. He left with the coming of fall, leaving green King's Island for another part of the world. He has since gotten married—the Internet tells me—and is working as an instructor at a small college in Iowa. Still, I can't help but feel that part of him is here with me, peering over my shoulder at Milton's 1667 yearbook, his eyes lighting up as he leans in to take a closer look.

ACKNOWLEDGMENTS

This book would not be what it is without the insightful feedback of its earliest readers. These include Jim Gerlich, Dan Kirkpatrick, Julia Sippel, Isaac Patterson, David Downing, Tammy Greenwood, Scott Driscoll, Stephen Manes, Tavi Black, Casey Muratori, Naomi Loo, Mark Vanderpool, and Alejandro Polo. Many thanks to all of you! Thanks also to Kate Spelman, Sarah Bunch, Peter Mountford, Paula Marantz Cohen, John Baldessari, and the Morgan Library & Museum. And extra special thanks to my parents, to my extended family, to Elicia—the best editor a writer could hope to have—and to Ruby and Quinn.

Jesse Edward Johnson is a writer and artist based in the Pacific Northwest. He has taught literature at UCLA and also taught writing at Richard Hugo House in Seattle and to inmates at San Quentin State Prison.

Jesse grew up on an island in the Puget Sound that is remarkably similar to King's Island, the fictional peninsula where *Yearbook* takes place. He graduated in 1997 from a high school, since razed, that looked suspiciously like the one depicted in the novel—right down to the drafty, dodecagonal library.

When he isn't working, Jesse enjoys traveling with his wife and children, playing guitar, and going to baseball games. For more information about Jesse's work, please visit JesseEdwardJohnson.com.